核心素養
108課綱

Aesop's Fables
Reading & Listening Training Book

英文閱讀聽力素養訓練課

伊|索|寓|言|故|事

•原著 Aesop •英譯 V.S. Vernon Jones •改寫 Richard Luhrs

108課綱閱讀聽力素養培植書 | 以名著閱讀法及聽重點的聽力訓練策略 用英文故事打造聽讀的素養力！

MP3

寂天雲 APP

如何下載 MP3 音檔

❶ 寂天雲 APP 聆聽： 掃描書上 QR Code 下載「寂天雲－英日語學習隨身聽」APP。加入會員後，用 APP 內建掃描器再次掃描書上 QR Code，即可使用 APP 聆聽音檔。

❷ 官網下載音檔：請上「寂天閱讀網」（www.icosmos.com.tw），註冊會員／登入後，搜尋本書，進入本書頁面，點選「MP3 下載」下載音檔，存於電腦等其他播放器聆聽使用。

108課綱閱讀聽力素養培植書！以名著閱讀法及聽重點的聽力訓練策略 用英文故事打造聽讀的素養力！

閱讀英文故事能培養108課綱強調的閱讀理解能力，在讀故事書時，會反覆演練「理解內容、統整前後文推理、反思評價提出概念」的過程。讀懂故事能**深化閱讀素養力**，也可以**培養更寬廣的思辨分析力與想像力**，更能鍛鍊學習腦！

透過本書精心設計閱讀訓練法中最有效的「**名著閱讀法**」學習策略，循序漸進地掌握閱讀故事的重點，幫助讀者培養閱讀原文書的實力，體驗不用頻查字典就能品味原文小說的感動，實戰練習累積閱讀素養。**「聽重點」的聽力策略**，幫助讀者體驗不用字字聽懂，就能輕鬆聆聽寓言名著的樂趣。

《伊索寓言》是伊索（Aesop）所創作的寓言故事，篇末的道德教訓則是由G.K. Chesterton加註，並譯成多種語言廣為出版，至今仍為寓言故事的代表。本書版本，為維儂・瓊斯（V.S. Vernon Jones）於1912年完成的英譯作品。由於完成年代距今已久，部分用法及用字較艱難，本書特以**全民英檢中級程度字彙**加以改寫故事，並列出其中**使用頻率較高的字彙**，不僅幫助讀者學習經典名著，沉浸於閱讀的樂趣，更能藉由搭配精心設計的練習，同步加深字彙記憶，培養閱讀與聽力的能力。

1. 本書精選 **84 篇伊索寓言**，如〈狐狸與葡萄〉、〈下金蛋的鵝〉、〈龜兔賽跑〉等耳熟能詳的經典故事，帶你品味饒富深意的故事情節，扎根人文素養；搭配彩繪插圖，逗趣生動，增添學習樂趣。

2. 本書以每篇寓言所**使用的字數**區分難易度，共分Step 1以及Step 2兩個學習階段，帶領讀者由淺入深漸進學習。

3 本書共有兩大部分，精心設計各種實用學習幫手，讓你更有效率、更輕鬆地學會閱讀原文書：

課本 **Main Book** 全英語呈現，藉由學習彩圖字彙、單字英英註釋、課文英文釋義及文法解析等設計，不需字典也能讀懂。

聽力訓練書 **Training Book** 重點字彙複習，以**聽重點**的聽力策略，引導你無礙聽懂文學名著。

4 讀完一段課文後，隨即有Stop & Think**測驗**掌握推論及細節的能力，以及有Check Up練習各種常見的閱讀測驗題型，如字彙選填、是非題及配合題等6種題型變化，不僅驗收閱讀理解成效，也為日後參加英語檢定作準備。

強力推薦給這些人！

- 準備大考學測的學生。
- 想在多益、托福等各種英文考試中得高分。
- 想上全英語教學或雙語教學課程。
- 想把英語根基扎得又深又牢。
- 想順暢閱讀《時代》雜誌推薦小說原著。
- 正準備出國留學的人。

關於伊索的寓言世界

伊索（620 BC–560 BC）是希臘最偉大的寓言家，亦是古希臘時期著名的說書人。他出身為奴隸，但是因機智與豐富才學，得以被釋放成為自由民。

《伊索寓言》（Aesop's Fables），是在西元前六世紀完成，其中部分由伊索本人創作，其他則為當地流傳已久的民間故事，並由伊索加之彙整演說。伊索創作的寓言多以擬人動物為主角，成為傳達人生道理這類寓言故事的代名詞，亦是今日教育兒童，讓他們學習道德教訓最受歡迎的方式，例如〈狐狸與葡萄〉道出「吃不到說葡萄酸」的道理，而〈放羊的孩子〉的故事更是人人知曉。

《伊索寓言》之後不斷被翻譯為各個語言版本，許多譯者並在篇末加註寓言要傳達的道德涵義，讓人們更容易明白故事背後的教訓。

本書分兩大部分，第一部分為全英文的課本，第二部分為訓練書，訓練書是為培養「聽重點、解全文」的聽力能力而編寫的。

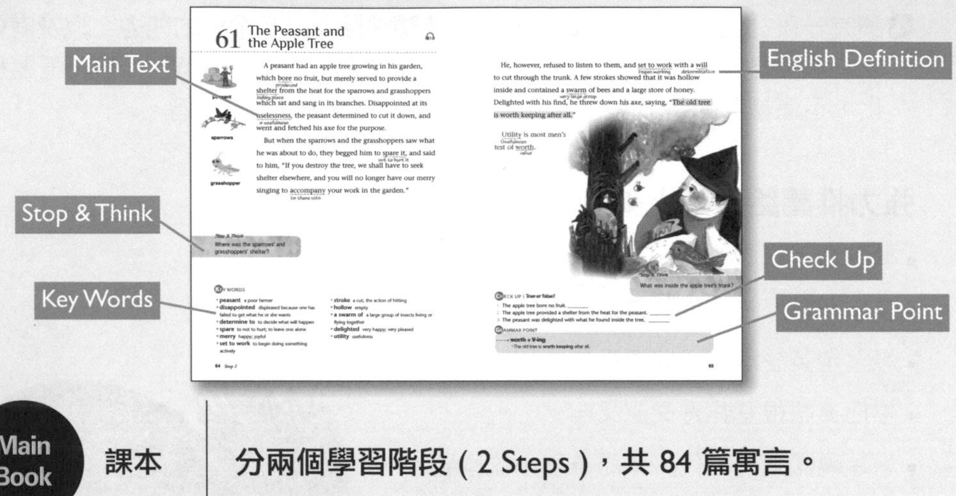

Main Book 課本 | **分兩個學習階段（2 Steps），共 84 篇寓言。**

1 讀課文（Main Text）

首先，只看全英文的課文，不懂的單字、片語或用語，可以透過以下精心設計的學習幫手了解字義，因此不需字典也能讀懂課文：

- **字彙搭配彩圖呈現**，圖像學習超easy。
- 簡明易解的**英英重要單字注釋**（Key Words），快速擴充字彙量。
- **課文中附註英文釋義**（English Definition）、同義字或反義字，搭配上下文，熟練字彙運用。
- **文法解析**（Grammar Point）學習常見句型。

2 試做練習題（Stop & Think / Check Up）

讀完課文後，立即透過綜合測驗題型，檢核文章理解程度及字彙能力。

Stop & Think 引導式問題，**訓練你抓出文章細節**（details）、**推論文章含意**（make inference），以及**培養獨立思考的能力**。

Check Up 6 種英語檢定常見題型，包含**選擇題、字彙選填、是非題及配合題**等，為參加考試作準備。

訓練書

訓練書以配合題（Vocabulary Practice: Match.）複習字彙，再以聽力填空題（Listen and Fill in the Blanks）引導學生聽關鍵字或片語，聽解原文，同時強化記憶單字發音，提升整體聽力能力。書末附有課本練習的正確答案和故事翻譯。

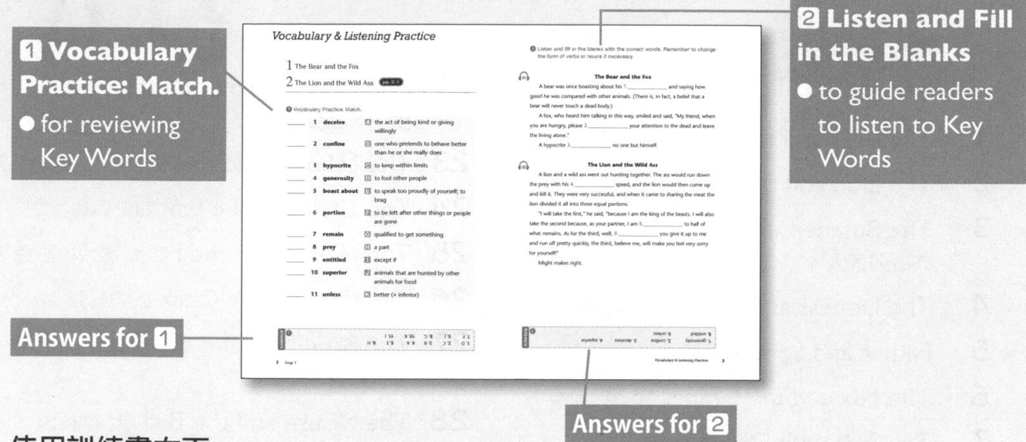

3 使用訓練書左頁

首先做**字彙配合題**（Vocabulary Practice: Match.），替字彙選出正確的英英解釋，複習寓言故事中的關鍵字，奠定聽解原文的基礎。

4 聽MP3使用訓練書右頁

播放MP3，先不要看原文，輕鬆聆聽，遇填空處，再仔細聽，寫下聽到的字彙或片語，不確定時可以反覆播放，再閱讀上下文確定答案。

5 再次聽MP3朗讀並複誦

一面看一面讀出聲音，可以記得更牢。本書課文皆由英語母語人士以正確、清晰的發音朗讀。聽課文時，要注意聽母語人士的發音、語調及連音等。最好自己在課文上把語調和連音標示出來，然後大聲地跟著MP3朗誦，盡量跟上英語母語人士的速度。

6 不聽MP3，自己朗讀課文

接著，不聽MP3，自己唸課文，並盡量唸得與母語人士一樣。若有發音或語調不順的地方，就再聽一次MP3，反覆練習。

7 重新閱讀英文課文

現在再回來看課本，再讀一次英文課文，如果讀得很順，練習題也都答對，訓練就成功了。

★ **正確答案請見訓練書書末的〈Answers〉。**

Step 1

Step 2

MAIN
BOOK

Step
1

1 The Bear and the Fox

01

A bear was once boasting about his generosity and saying how good he was compared with other animals. (There is, in fact, a belief that a bear will never touch a dead body.)

bragging about how kind he was

A fox, who heard him talking in this way, smiled and said, "My friend, when you are hungry, please confine your attention to the dead and leave the living alone."

focus only on / *dead people and animals* / *people and animals that are alive*

A hypocrite deceives no one but himself.

only; except

Stop & Think
According to the fable, will a bear eat a dead body?

boast

KEY WORDS

- **boast about** to speak too proudly of yourself; to brag
- **generosity** the act of being kind or giving willingly
- **confine** to keep within limits
- **hypocrite** one who pretends to behave better than he or she really does
- **deceive** to fool other people

- **prey** animals that are hunted by other animals for food
- **superior** better (≠ inferior)
- **portion** a part
- **entitled** qualified to get something
- **remain** to be left after other things or people are gone
- **unless** except if

2 The Lion and the Wild Ass

02

A lion and a wild ass went out hunting together. The ass would run down the prey with his superior speed, and the lion would then come up and kill it. They were very successful, and when it came to sharing the meat, the lion divided it
when the time came for them to share the meat
all into three equal portions.

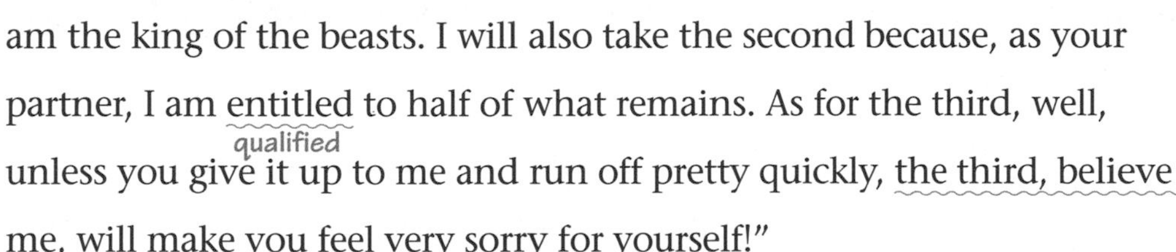

"I will take the first," he said, "because I am the king of the beasts. I will also take the second because, as your partner, I am entitled to half of what remains. As for the third, well,
qualified
unless you give it up to me and run off pretty quickly, the third, believe me, will make you feel very sorry for yourself!"
(the lion warned that he would hurt the ass if the ass took the third portion)

Might makes right.
Power

ass

prey

Stop & Think
What did the wild ass get to eat after he went out hunting with the lion?

CHECK UP | True or false?

1 A bear will touch a dead body. ________
2 The bear was a hypocrite. ________
3 The lion would run down the prey with his superior speed. ________

GRAMMAR POINT

when it comes to + V-ing
- They were very successful, and **when it came to sharing** the meat, the lion divided it all into three equal portions.

3 The Butcher and His Customers

03

Two men were buying meat at a butcher's stall in the market and, while the butcher's back was turned for a moment, one of them picked up a joint (piece of meat) and quickly put it inside the other's coat, where it could not be seen.

When the butcher turned around, he noticed the missing meat at once, and accused the men of having stolen it. But the one who had taken it said he didn't have it, and the one who had it said he hadn't taken it.

The butcher felt sure they were deceiving (lying to) him, but he only said, "You may cheat me with your lying, but you can't cheat the gods, and they won't let you go so easily." (the gods will punish you for what you did)

Avoiding the truth is often the same as lying.

Stop & Think
Where did the man put the joint after he stole it?

butcher

stall

KEY WORDS

- **butcher** someone who cuts and sells meat
- **stall** a stand or counter at which things are displayed for sale
- **accuse someone of** to say that someone has done something wrong
- **avoid** to stay away from; to try not to do something

- **litter** a group of baby animals that are born at the same time
- **cub** a young bear, lion, fox, wolf, or other wild animal
- **nastily** unkindly (≠kindly)
- **grimly** seriously

4 The Lioness and the Vixen

A lioness (female lion) and a vixen (female fox) were talking together about their children, as mothers will, and saying how healthy and well-grown they were, what beautiful coats (fur or hair that covers animals) they had, and how they looked just like their parents.

"My litter of cubs is a joy to see," said the fox. Then she added rather nastily (≠ kindly), "But I notice you never have more than one."

"No," said the lioness grimly (seriously), "but that one is a lion."

Quality beats quantity.

coats

litter

Stop & Think
What do "quality" and "quantity" refer to in this fable?

CHECK UP | **Choose the right words.**

1 The butcher ___________ the men of having stolen the meat. (avoided | accused)
2 "My litter of ___________ is a joy to see," said the fox. (stalls | cubs)
3 "But that one is a lion," said the lioness ___________. (grimly | nastily)

GRAMMAR POINT

V-ing . . . (gerund) (the subject of a sentence)
- **Avoiding** the truth is often the same as lying.

5 Father and Sons

05

A certain man had several sons who were always quarreling with one another, and though he tried very hard, he could not get them to live together in harmony (peace). So, he decided to convince them of their error (make them realize that they were wrong) by the following means (way).

Telling them to fetch (get and bring back) a bundle of sticks, he asked each in turn to break it across his knee. All tried and all failed. Then he undid (untied; undo–undid–undone) the bundle and handed them the sticks one by one, so that they had no difficulty at all in breaking them.

"There, my boys," he said. "United you will be more than a match for your enemies (If you are united, you will beat your enemies), but if you quarrel and separate, you will be weaker than those who attack you."

Unity is strength.

quarrel

match

Stop & Think

What does this fable teach people?

KEY WORDS

- **quarrel** to argue with others
- **in harmony** in peace
- **convince** to make others think that something is true
- **undo** to open something that is tied; to untie
  *undo–undid–undone
- **united** joined together as a group (≠ separate)
- **unity** the situation when people are united

- **in vain** no use (≠ successful)
- **out of one's reach** unable to be touched (≠ within reach)
- **attitude** one's opinions and behavior
- **dignity** pride
- **ripe** (fruits) ready to eat or use
- **criticize** to say that something or someone is bad or wrong

6 The Fox and the Grapes

06

A hungry fox saw some fine (*of good quality*) bunches of grapes hanging from a vine that ran along a high wall, and did his best to reach them by jumping as high as he could into the air.

But it was all in vain (*≠ successful*), for (*because*) they were just out of his reach, so he gave up and walked away with an attitude of dignity and unconcern (*proudly and not seeming to care*), saying, "I thought those grapes were ripe, but I see now they are quite sour."

It is easy to criticize what you cannot get.

vine   out of reach

Stop & Think

Why did the fox say the grapes were sour?

CHECK UP | Finish the sentences.

1 The man tried hard to
2 The man asked each son to
3 The fox did his best to

a. break the sticks across his knee.
b. reach the grapes.
c. get his sons to live together in harmony.

GRAMMAR POINT

so that . . .

- Then the man undid the bundle and handed them the sticks one by one, **so that** his sons had no difficulty at all in breaking them.

7 The Stag with One Eye

A stag, blind in one eye, was grazing [eating grass] close to the seashore and kept his good eye turned towards the land so that he would be able to see the approach [coming] of any hounds, while the blind eye he turned towards the sea, never suspecting [thinking] that any danger would threaten him from that side.

As it happened, however, some sailors who were sailing along the shore saw him and shot an arrow at him, by which he was killed. As he lay dying, he said to himself, "What a fool I am! I thought only of the dangers of the land, from where none attacked me, but I feared no danger from the sea, and my ruin has come from there [the damage has come from the sea]."

Misfortune often attacks us from an unexpected direction.

Where did the stag keep his good eye turned?

stag

hounds

KEY WORDS

- **graze** to eat grass
- **approach** coming closer to something or someone
- **suspect** to think something may be true, especially bad things
- **threaten** to put one in danger; to endanger
- **misfortune** a terrible event
- **unexpected** surprising; not planned

- **charge someone with** to accuse someone of
- **theft** the act of stealing
- **evidence** a fact or object that helps prove something
- **in spite of** even though; despite
- **denial** a statement that something that has been said is not true
- **credit** belief; respect

8 The Wolf, the Fox, and the Ape

A wolf charged a fox with theft,
accused of
which the fox denied, and the
case was brought before an ape to
judged
be tried.

When he had heard the evidence
from both sides, the ape gave this
judgment: "I do not think," he
said, "that you, wolf, ever lost
(the ape thought that the wolf was
what you claim, but I still believe
lying about the theft)
that you, fox, are guilty of the
theft, in spite of all your denials."
despite

The dishonest get no credit, even
Dishonest people
if they act honestly.

ape

give a judgment

Stop & Think

Did the ape believe the fox's denials?

CHECK UP | **Fill in the blanks with the correct words.**

charged denials evidence suspected

1 The stag never ______________ that any danger would threaten him from the sea.
2 A wolf ______________ a fox with theft.
3 The ape had heard the ______________ from both sides.
4 The ape still believed that the fox was guilty of the theft, in spite of all his ______________.

GRAMMAR POINT

the + adjective = Noun (people who have a certain quality)

- **The dishonest** get no credit, even if they act honestly.
  (= **Dishonest people** get no credit, even if they act honestly.)

9 The Three Tradesmen

The citizens of a certain city were debating about the best material to use for the walls which were about to be built for the
would be built very soon
greater security of the town.
safety

A carpenter got up and advised the use of wood, which he said was easy to get and easy to work with. A stonemason objected to wood
disagreed with
because it could burn so easily, and recommended stones instead. Then
suggested
a tanner got up and said, "In my opinion, there's nothing like leather."
leather is the best material to use to build the walls

Every man for himself.

Stop & Think
Why did the stonemason object to wood?

carpenter

stonemason

tanner

KEY WORDS

- **security** safety from harm
- **carpenter** someone whose job is to make and repair wooden objects
- **object to** to disagree with
- **recommend** to say that someone or something is good; to suggest
- **leather** the skin of an animal prepared for making clothes or luggage

- **companion** a person or animal one spends a lot of time with
- **journey** a long trip
- **strength** power
- **statue** a human or animal image that is made of a material such as stone, metal or wood
- **strangle** to kill a person or an animal by squeezing his, her, or its throat
- **situation** the condition that exists at a particular time

10 The Man and the Lion

A man and a lion were companions on a journey, and while talking they both began to boast about their abilities, and each claimed to be superior to the other in strength and courage. They were still arguing angrily when they came to a crossroad where there was a statue of a man strangling a lion.

better than

killing by squeezing the throat

"There!" said the man proudly. "Look at that! Doesn't that prove to you that we are stronger than you?"

"Not so fast, my friend," said the lion. "That is only your view of the situation. If we lions could make statues, you may be sure that in most of them you would see the man losing."

what you see from human beings' point of view

There are two sides to every story.

statue

crossroad

Stop & Think

Did the lion believe that men were superior to lions?

CHECK UP | Answer the questions.

1 What were the citizens of the city debating about?
a. The tanner's work. b. Burning wood. c. Which material to use for the walls.

2 What were the man and the lion doing on their journey?
a. Making a statue. b. Boasting about their abilities. c. Strangling each other.

GRAMMAR POINT

superior to
- Each claimed to be **superior to** the other in strength and courage.

11 The Farmer and the Stork

11

A farmer set some traps in a field which he had recently sown [sow-sowed-sown] with corn, in order to catch the cranes which came to eat the seeds [planted]. When he returned to look at his traps, he found several cranes caught, and among them a stork, which begged to be let go and said, "You shouldn't kill me; I am not a crane, but a stork, as [because] you can easily see by my feathers, and I am the most honest and harmless [≠ harmful] of birds."

But the farmer replied, "I don't care what you are; I find you among these cranes, who ruin my crops, and like them you shall suffer [I will kill you]."

If you choose bad companions [people you spend a lot of time with], no one will believe that you are not bad yourself.

trap

feathers

stork

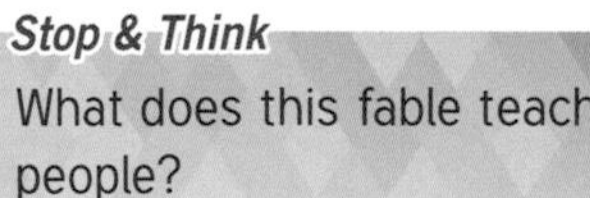

Stop & Think

What does this fable teach people?

KEY WORDS

- **sow** to plant seeds in the ground
  *sow–sowed–sown
- **beg** to ask strongly for something
- **feathers** the things that cover a bird's body
- **harmless** doing no harm (≠ harmful)
- **crop** a plant grown for food
- **suffer** to feel pain in one's body or mind

- **bathe** to swim; to wash one's body
- **drown** to die under water
- **scold** to talk angrily about someone's behavior
- **make (an) attempt** to make an effort to do something
- **assistance** help
- **crisis** a difficult or dangerous situation

12 The Boy Bathing

A boy was bathing in a river and got into deep water, and was in great danger of drowning. A man who was passing along the road heard his cries for help. He went to the riverside and began to scold him for (because of) being so careless as to get into deep water, but made no attempt (didn't make any effort) to help him.

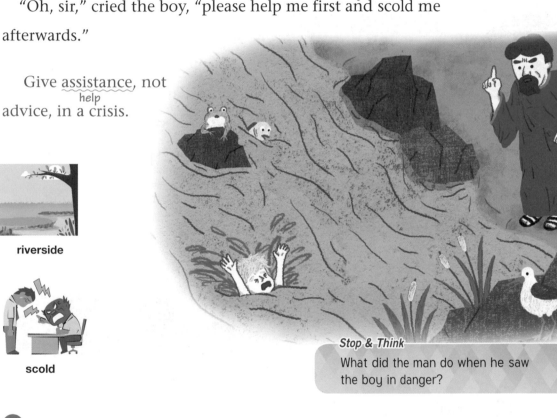

"Oh, sir," cried the boy, "please help me first and scold me afterwards."

Give assistance (help), not advice, in a crisis.

riverside

scold

Stop & Think

What did the man do when he saw the boy in danger?

CHECK UP | **True or false?**

1 The farmer will kill the stork. ________

2 A boy was drowning in a river. ________

3 The man gave the boy assistance in his crisis. ________

GRAMMAR POINT

as (reason) . . .

- I am not a crane, but a stork, **as** you can easily see by my feathers.

13 The Eagle and the Cocks

13

There were two cocks in the same farmyard, and they fought to decide who should be the master. When the fight was over, the beaten one (the cock who had lost the fight) went and hid himself in a dark corner, while the winner flew up onto the roof of the stable and crowed happily (loudly showed how proud he was).

But an eagle noticed him from high up in the sky, and flew down and carried him off (took him back as food). Immediately, the other cock came out of his corner and ruled the roost (a place where birds rest and sleep) without a rival.

Pride comes before a fall (failure).

Stop & Think
What happened to the proud cock?

farmyard

roost

KEY WORDS

- **cock** an adult male chicken; a rooster
- **stable** a place where horses are kept
- **crow** (a cock) to make a loud high noise
- **immediately** without delay; at once
- **rival** a person or thing that competes with another
- **pride** a feeling that you are better than other people

- **thoroughly** completely; carefully
- **creature** a living thing
- **terrified** extremely afraid; frightened
- **do . . . harm to** to hurt
- **destroy** to kill or ruin completely
- **slight** small in degree, size, or amount

14 The Flea and the Man

14

A flea bit a man, and bit him again, and again, till the man could stand it no longer and searched thoroughly for the flea until at last he succeeded in catching it.

tolerate / no more / carefully

Holding it between his finger and thumb, he said—or rather shouted, so angry was he—"Who are you, you horrible little creature, that you attack me so freely?"

bite anywhere on my body

The flea, terrified, replied in a weak little voice, "Oh, sir, please let me go; don't kill me! I am such a little thing that I can't do you much harm."

But the man laughed and said, "I am going to kill you right now. Whatever is bad has got to be destroyed, no matter how slight the harm it does."

small

flea

troublemaker

Stop & Think

According to this fable, what should we do when we find a small problem?

Do not waste your pity on a troublemaker.

one who causes trouble

CHECK UP | **Finish the sentences.**

1 The two cocks	a. bit the man again and again.
2 The flea	b. hid himself in a dark corner.
3 The beaten cock	c. fought in the farmyard.

GRAMMAR POINT

to + V (purpose)

- The two cocks fought **to decide** who should be the master.

15 The Gnat and the Bull

A gnat landed (settled) on one of the horns of a bull, and remained sitting there for a considerable (long) time. When it had rested sufficiently (enough) and was about to fly away, it said to the bull, "Do you mind if I go now?"

The bull merely (only) raised his eyes and remarked (said), without interest, "It's all the same to me; I didn't notice when you came, and I won't know when you go away."

We may often be more important in our own eyes than in the eyes of our neighbors.

Stop & Think

Did the bull care what the gnat did? Why?

KEY WORDS

- **horn** one of the hard pointed parts that grow on the heads of some animals
- **remain** to stay somewhere; to stay the same
- **considerable** large in size, amount, or degree
- **sufficiently** enough
- **merely** simply; only
- **remark** to say a few words that express what you think

- **intention** purpose
- **witness** to see something happen
- **encounter** a fight; a meeting
- **spit** to force liquid out of your mouth *spit–spat–spat
- **quench** to satisfy one's thirst
- **contents** the things that are inside something such as a box or bottle

16 The Serpent and the Eagle

An eagle flew down upon a serpent and seized (grabbed) it in his claws with the intention of carrying it off and eating it. But the serpent was too quick for him and had its coils around him (twisted its body around the eagle) in a moment. There followed a life-and-death struggle between the two.

A countryman, who witnessed the encounter, came to the assistance of the eagle, and he succeeded in freeing him from the serpent and enabling (helping) him to escape. In revenge, the serpent spat (spit-spat-spat) some of its poison into the man's drinking horn.

Heated from his efforts, the man was about to quench his thirst with a drink from the horn, when the eagle knocked it out of his hand and spilled its contents (the liquid in the drinking horn) upon the ground.

One good turn (act; deed) deserves another.

Stop & Think

What did the eagle do to thank the countryman for helping him?

serpent **drinking horn**

CHECK UP | **Choose the right words.**

1 The gnat ____________ sitting on the bull's horn for a considerable time. (remarked | remained)
2 The countryman ____________ the encounter. (witnessed | quenched)
3 The serpent ____________ some of his poison into the man's drinking horn. (spat | spilled)

GRAMMAR POINT

enable somebody / something to V

- The countryman succeeded in freeing the eagle from the serpent and **enabling him to escape.**

17 The Fir Tree and the Bramble

A fir tree was boasting to a bramble, and said, somewhat contemptuously, "You poor creature; you are of no use at all. Now, look at me. I am useful for all sorts of things, particularly when men build houses; they can't do without me then."

without respect / useless

But the bramble replied, "Ah, that's all true, but you wait till they come with axes and saws to cut you down, and then you'll wish you were a bramble, not a fir."

Better poverty without a care than wealth with its many obligations.

(a lack of skills will not attract attention from others) / duties

Stop & Think

Did the bramble think of itself as a poor creature? Why?

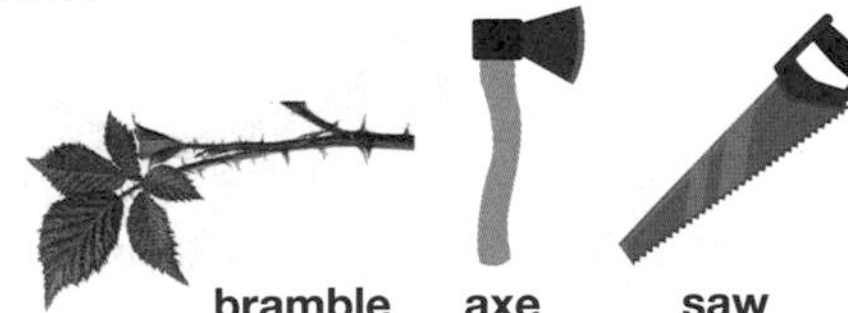

KEY WORDS

- **somewhat** to some degree
- **(of) no use** useless; in vain
- **poverty** a lack of something
- **wealth** a large amount of a useful quality or skill
- **obligation** a promise or duty

- **latter** the second of two people or things (≠ former)
- **anxious** wanting something very much; eager
- **reputation** fame
- **upset** to make one feel worried or unhappy *upset-upset-upset
- **pretend** to behave as if something were real when it's not
- **ridiculous** very silly or unreasonable

18 The Crow and the Raven 

A crow became very jealous of a raven because the latter was regarded by men as a bird which could tell the future (*predict what will happen*), and so was greatly respected by them.

The crow was very anxious (*eager*) to get the same sort of reputation herself, and one day, seeing some travelers approaching (*coming near*), she flew onto a branch of a tree at the roadside and cawed (*made a loud, unpleasant sound*) as loudly as she could. The travelers were somewhat upset (*upset-upset-upset*) by the sound, for they feared it might be a bad sign (*bad luck; something bad might happen*), till one of them, seeing the crow, said to his companions, "It's all right, my friends; we can go on without fear, for it's only a crow and that means nothing."

Those who pretend to be something they are not only make themselves ridiculous.

raven

traveler

Stop & Think

Why was the crow jealous of the raven?

CHECK UP | **Fill in the blanks with the correct words.**

reputation latter no use upset

1 The fir tree said to the bramble, "You poor creature; you are of ______________ at all."

2 A crow became very jealous of a raven because the ______________ was greatly respected by men.

3 The crow was very anxious to get the same sort of ______________ herself.

4 The travelers were somewhat ______________ by the sound.

GRAMMAR POINT

wish + S (subject) + were (something impossible or unlikely to happen)

- You'll **wish you were** a bramble, not a fir.

19 The Travelers and the Plane Tree 19

Two travelers were walking along a bare and dusty road in the heat of a summer's day. Coming up to a Plane tree, they joyfully turned aside to take shelter [find a hiding place] from the burning rays of the sun in the deep shade of its spreading branches.

As they rested, looking up into the tree, one of them remarked to his companion, "What a useless tree the Plane is! It bears [produces] no fruit and is of no service to men at all." [(people can't use Plane trees for anything)]

The Plane tree interrupted him with indignation. "You ungrateful [≠ thankful] creature!" it cried. "You come and take shelter under me from the heat of the sun, and then, in the very act of enjoying the cool shade of my leaves, you abuse me and call me good for nothing!"

Many a service is answered with ingratitude. [≠ thankfulness]

What does this fable teach people?

shade

KEY WORDS

- **bare** empty; having no trees or plants
- **dusty** covered in dust
- **aside** to one side
- **take shelter** to find a place in which one is protected from bad weather or danger
- **indignation** anger about an unfair situation
- **abuse** to speak to someone rudely or cruelly

- **wheat** a tall plant that produces grain for making flour
- **excuse** to release oneself from a requirement or request
- **seize** to grab suddenly
- **come due** (a debt) to have to be paid at a particular time

20 The Sheep, the Wolf, and the Stag

20

A stag once asked a sheep
to lend him some wheat,
saying that his friend, the wolf,
would be his surety. The sheep,
(the wolf agreed to pay back the wheat if
the stag failed to do so)
however, was afraid that they
wanted to cheat her, so she
excused herself, saying, "The
politely refused
wolf has a habit of seizing what
he wants and running off with
it without paying, and you, too,
can run much faster than I. So
how shall I be able to catch up
with either of you when the debt comes due?"
when it is time to pay the debt

Two wrongs do not make a right.
wrong behavior

wheat

debt

Stop & Think

What was the wolf's bad habit?

CHECK UP | **Answer the questions.**

1 Why did the Plane tree get mad?
   a. Because it bears no fruit. b. Because it was hot. c. Because the travelers were ungrateful.

2 What did the stag want to borrow from the sheep?
   a. Some wheat. b. A debt. c. A surety.

GRAMMAR POINT

lend someone something

- A stag once asked a sheep to **lend him some wheat**.

21 The Crow and the Pitcher

21

A thirsty crow found a pitcher with some water in it, but so little was there that, as hard as she tried, she could not reach it with her beak (a bird's mouth), and it seemed as though (as if) she would die of thirst while looking at water.

At last she thought of a clever plan. She began dropping pebbles into the pitcher, and with each pebble the water rose a little higher until at last it reached the top, and the wise bird was able to quench her thirst.

Necessity is the mother (source; cause) of invention.

beak

pebbles

Stop & Think
How did the crow solve her problem?

KEY WORDS

- **pitcher** a container for holding and pouring liquids
- **die of** to die because of
- **thirst** the feeling of needing to drink water
- **pebble** a small, smooth stone
- **necessity** need; something needed or essential
- **invention** the act of inventing something; something which has been invented

- **modestly** in a way that shows you do not want to make yourself look important (≠ proudly)
- **furiously** angrily; madly
- **spring** to jump suddenly *spring–sprang–sprung
- **glare** to look at angrily
- **heap** a large pile

22 The Lion, the Fox, and the Ass

22

A lion, a fox, and an ass went out hunting together. They had soon killed many animals, which the lion asked the ass to divide between them. The ass divided them all into three equal parts, and modestly (≠ proudly) begged the others to take their choice, at which the lion furiously sprang (spring-sprang-sprung; jumped) upon the ass and tore him to pieces.

Then, glaring at the fox, he told him to make a new division. The fox gathered most of the meat into one great heap for the lion, leaving only the smallest possible amount for himself.

"My dear friend," said the lion, "how did you understand the situation so well?" The fox replied, "Me? Oh, I learned a lesson (gained useful experience) from the ass."

Happy is he who learns from the misfortunes (bad luck) of others.

heap

furiously

Stop & Think
What did the lion do after the ass divided the food into three equal parts?

CHECK UP | **True or false?**

1 The crow could not reach the water with her beak. ________
2 The ass divided the food into three different parts. ________
3 The fox left the largest possible amount for the lion. ________

GRAMMAR POINT

divide something into
- The ass **divided them** all **into** three equal parts.

23 The Laborer and the Snake 

A laborer's little son was bitten by a snake and died from the wound. The father was extremely sad, and in his anger against the snake, he took an axe and went and stood close to the snake's hole, waiting for a chance to kill it.

Presently (Soon) the snake came out and the man struck at it, but only succeeded in cutting off the tip of its tail before it went back in again. He then tried to get it to come out a second time (one more time), pretending that he wished to apologize.

But the snake said, "I can never be your friend because of my lost tail, nor can you be mine (my friend) because of your lost child."

Injuries are never forgotten in the presence of those who caused them (when you see those who have injured you).

Stop & Think
Did the laborer really want to apologize to the snake?

KEY WORDS

- **laborer** a worker
- **die from** to die because of; to die of
- **extremely** very
- **presently** soon
- **injury** a wound on one's body; something bad done by one person to another
- **presence** a situation when someone or something is there

- **settle** to go and live in a particular place
- **meadow** a field where grass grows
- **inland** far from the sea
- **deserve** to earn something because of one's behavior or accomplishments
- **content** satisfied

24 The Crab and the Fox

A crab once left the seashore and went and settled in a meadow some way inland (far from the sea), which looked very nice and green and seemed like a good place to feed (eat) in.

But a hungry fox came along and saw the crab and caught him. Just as he was going to be eaten, the crab said, "This is just what I deserve, (the crab ended up like this because of his bad decision) for I should never have left my natural home by the sea and settled here as though I belonged to the land."

Be content (satisfied) with what you have.

seashore

meadow

Stop & Think

Why did the crab regret moving inland?

CHECK UP | Finish the sentences.

1 The laborer's little son
2 The laborer
3 The crab

a. struck at the snake.
b. left his natural home.
c. was bitten by a snake.

GRAMMAR POINT

negative statement, nor Modal + S (subject)

- I can **never** be your friend because of my lost tail, **nor can you** be mine because of your lost child.

25 The Hound and the Hare

A young hound chased a hare, and when he caught up with her, he first snapped at (bit quickly) her with his teeth as though he were about to kill her, and then let go of her and hopped about her as if he were playing with another dog.

At last the hare said, "I wish you would show yourself as you truly are! If you are my friend, why do you bite me? If you are my enemy, why do you play with me?"

He is no friend (not a true friend) who plays double (shows different personalities).

Stop & Think

How did the hare feel about the hound?

KEY WORDS

- **hound** a dog used for hunting
- **hare** an animal similar to a rabbit, but with a bigger body and longer ears and legs
- **snap at** to bite quickly

- **ought to** should
- **nuisance** something or someone that annoys people
- **awake** ≠ sleeping
- **defend** to say things to support someone or something that is being criticized
- **villain** a bad person
- **commit a crime** to do something illegal

26 The Cat and the Cock

26

A cat jumped on a cock, and tried to think of a good excuse (*reason*) for eating him, for cats don't usually eat cocks, and she knew she ought not to.

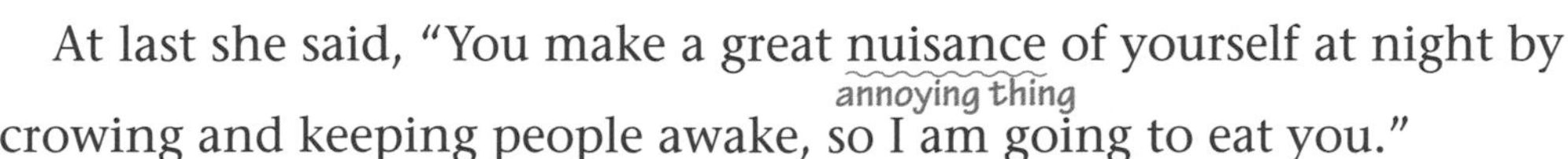

At last she said, "You make a great nuisance (*annoying thing*) of yourself at night by crowing and keeping people awake, so I am going to eat you."

But the cock defended (*said something to support*) himself by saying that he crowed so that men might wake up and start the day's work in good time (*at the correct time*), and that they really couldn't very well do without him.

"That may be," said the cat, "but whether they can or not, I'm not going without my dinner!" and she killed and ate him.

The lack of a good excuse never stopped a villain from committing a crime (*doing something illegal*).

villain

Stop & Think

What was the cat's excuse for eating the cock?

CHECK UP | Fill in the blanks with the correct words.

ought　defended　nuisance　snapped at

1 The hound ________________ the hare with his teeth as though he were about to kill her.
2 The cat knew she ________________ not to eat the cock.
3 The cock made himself a great ________________ at night by crowing and keeping people awake.
4 The cock ________________ himself by saying that he crowed to wake men up.

GRAMMAR POINT

stop someone from + V-ing

- The lack of a good excuse never **stopped a villain from committing** a crime.

27 The Blind Man and the Cub

There was once a blind man who had so fine a sense of touch that, when any animal was put into his hands, he could tell what it was merely (simply) by the feel of it.

One day the cub of a wolf was put into his hands, and he was asked what it was. He felt it for some time, and then said, "Indeed, I am not sure whether it is a wolf's cub or a fox's, but this I know: it would not be wise to trust it in a sheepfold (an area of land surrounded by a fence in which sheep are kept)."

Evil tendencies (characteristics) are shown early.

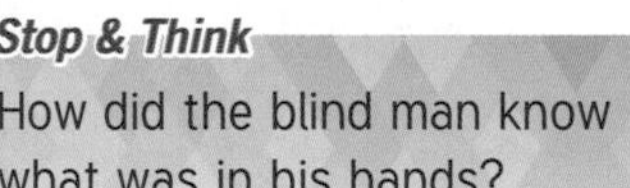

Stop & Think

How did the blind man know what was in his hands?

sheepfold

KEY WORDS

- **merely** simply; only
- **indeed** certainly; of course
- **tendency** an aspect of one's character that one shows by behaving in a particular way; characteristic

---

- **charge** to rush forward and attack someone or something
- **exhausted** very tired
- **in (a) rage** in great anger
- **roar** to make a loud deep sound
- **fume** to feel or show a lot of anger
- **battle** a fight

28 The Mouse and the Bull

A bull chased a mouse which had bitten him on the nose, but the mouse was too quick for him and slipped (slid; went quickly) into a hole in a wall. The bull charged (rushed forward and attacked) furiously into the wall again and again until he was tired out, and sank down on the ground exhausted from his efforts.

When all was quiet, the mouse ran out and bit him again. In a rage he started to get up, but by that time the mouse was back in his hole again, and the bull could do nothing but (only) roar and fume in helpless anger.

Presently he heard a high little voice say from inside the wall, "You big fellows don't always have it your own way (get what you want because you are strong), you see; sometimes we little ones come off best (win; succeed)."

The battle is not always won by the strong.

charge roar

Stop & Think

What does this fable teach people?

CHECK UP | **Choose the right words.**

1 The blind man could tell what it was ___________ by the feel of it. (indeed | merely)
2 The bull could do nothing but ___________ and fume in helpless anger. (roar | charge)
3 The ___________ is not always won by the strong. (tendency | battle)

GRAMMAR POINT

nothing but (= only)

- The bull could do **nothing but** roar and fume in helpless anger.

29 The Spendthrift and the Swallow

A spendthrift, who had wasted his fortune and had nothing left but the clothes in which he stood, saw a swallow one fine day in early spring. Thinking that summer had come, and that he could now do without his coat, he went and sold it for what he could get.

spendthrift: a person who spends his or her money carelessly
do: live

A change took place in the weather, however, and there came a sharp frost which killed the unfortunate swallow. When the spendthrift saw its dead body he cried, "Miserable bird! Thanks to you I am dying of cold myself."

took place: happened
sharp frost: freezing cold weather
Thanks to: Due to

Stop & Think
What did the spendthrift think when he first saw the swallow?

One swallow does not make summer.

spendthrift

frost

KEY WORDS

- **fortune** wealth
- **take place** to happen
- **frost** very cold weather which freezes water
- **unfortunate** unlucky (≠ fortunate)
- **miserable** extremely unhappy or uncomfortable
- **thanks to** as a result of; due to

- **dispute** an argument
- **in honor of** in order to show great respect for someone or something
- **ancestor** a member of your family who lived a long time ago
- **prominent** outstanding
- **expose** to discover and make known a hidden mistake, evil, or crime
- **detect** to notice or find out something when it is not obvious

30 The Fox and the Monkey

A fox and a monkey were on the road together, and got into a dispute as to (about) which of them was the better born (the nobler one). They kept it up for some time, till they came to a place where the road passed through a cemetery full of monuments, when the monkey stopped and looked around him and gave a great sigh.

"Why do you sigh?" said the fox.

The monkey pointed to the tombs and replied, "All the monuments that you see here were put up in honor of my ancestors, who in their days were prominent men."

The fox was speechless (≠ talkative) for a moment, but quickly recovering he said, "Oh! Tell any lie you want to, sir; you're quite safe. I'm sure none of your ancestors will rise up and expose (make your lie known to others) you."

Boasters (People who boast) boast most when they cannot be detected.

cemetery

monument

Stop & Think

Look at "They kept it up for some time." What does "it" refer to?

CHECK UP | **Answer the questions.**

1 What killed the swallow?
   a. A sharp frost. b. The hot summer. c. The spendthrift's clothes.

2 What was the dispute between the fox and the monkey about?
   a. Their ancestors. b. The monuments. c. Who was the better born.

GRAMMAR POINT

die of/die from + N (noun)

- I am **dying of cold** myself.

31 The Shepherd's Boy and the Wolf

A shepherd's boy was tending (taking care of) his flock (group of sheep) near a village, and thought it would be great fun to fool the villagers by pretending that a wolf was attacking the sheep. So he shouted out, "Wolf! Wolf!" and when the people came running over, he laughed at them for their efforts.

He did this more than once, and every time the villagers found they had been fooled, for there was no wolf at all. At last, a wolf really did come, and the boy cried, "Wolf! Wolf!" as loudly as he could, but the people were so used to (familiar with) hearing him call that they ignored his cries for help. And so the wolf had everything he wanted, and killed sheep after sheep (one by one) at his leisure (≠ in haste).

You cannot believe a liar even when he tells the truth.

shepherd

Stop & Think

Why did the villagers ignore the boy's cries for help?

KEY WORDS

- **shepherd** one whose job is to take care of sheep
- **tend** to take care of something or someone
- **flock** a group of sheep, birds, or goats
- **villager** one who lives in a village
- **at one's leisure** slowly and without hurrying (≠ in haste)
- **liar** one who tells a lie

- **envious** jealous
- **due to** because of; as a result of
- **constantly** always; regularly
- **neighborhood** the area around one's home
- **sacrifice** the act of offering something to a god

32 The Crow and the Swan

A crow was very envious (jealous) of the beautiful white feathers of a swan, and thought they were due to (a result of) the water in which the swan constantly bathed and swam.

So he left the neighborhood of the altars (special tables used in ceremonies in a church), where he survived by picking up bits of the meat offered in sacrifice (presented to the god), and went and lived among the pools and streams. But though he bathed and washed his feathers many times a day, he didn't make them any whiter, and at last died of hunger as well.

You may change your habits, but not your nature (who you really are).

altar

Stop & Think

What did the crow do to make himself look like a swan?

CHECK UP | **True or false?**

1 The shepherd's boy was attacking his sheep. ________
2 The crow was very envious of the beautiful white feathers of a swan. ________
3 The crow died by drowning. ________

GRAMMAR POINT

be used to + V-ing

- The people **were** so **used to hearing** him call that they ignored his cries for help.

33 The Wolf and the Horse

33

A wandering wolf came to a field of oats (cereal plants or their grains), but not being able to eat them, he was continuing on his way when a horse came along.

"Look," said the wolf. "Here's a fine field of oats. For your sake (benefit) I have left it untouched (uneaten), and I shall greatly enjoy the sound of your teeth chewing the ripe (ready-to-eat) grain."

But the horse replied, "If wolves could eat oats, my fine friend, you would never have pleased (satisfied) your ears instead of (rather than) your belly."

There is no virtue in giving to others what is useless to oneself.

oats

belly

Stop & Think

Why did the wolf leave the field of oats untouched?

KEY WORDS

- **wandering** walking around without an aim
- **for one's sake** for one's good or benefit
- **untouched** not handled, used, or tasted
- **chew** to bite food into small pieces while eating
- **virtue** a good moral quality

- **confine** to force someone or something to stay in a place and prevent them from leaving (≠ release)
- **have a habit of** to do something often or regularly
- **attract** to get one's attention or interest
- **prisoner** one who is locked in prison
- **precaution** care taken to avoid accidents, disease, or other dangers

34 The Caged Bird and the Bat

34

A singing bird was confined (≠ released) in a cage which hung outside a window, and had a habit of singing at night when all other birds were asleep. One night a bat came and grabbed (took hold of) the bars of the cage, and asked the bird why she was silent by day and sang only at night.

"I have a very good reason for doing so," said the bird. "It was once when I was singing in the daytime that a hunter was attracted by my voice (my voice got a hunter's attention), and set his nets for me and caught me. Since then I have never sung except by night."

But the bat replied, "It is no use doing that now, when you are a prisoner. If only (a phrase used to express a strong wish or regret) you had done so before you were caught, you might still be free."

Precautions (Care taken to avoid danger) are useless after the event.

bar

prisoner

Stop & Think

Did the bat think the caged bird's reason for singing at night sounded reasonable?

CHECK UP | Finish the sentences.

1 The wandering wolf
2 The hunter
3 The bat

a. came and grabbed the bars of the cage.
b. wasn't able to eat oats.
c. was attracted by the singing bird's voice.

GRAMMAR POINT

be attracted by

- A hunter **was attracted by** my voice.

35 The Farmer and the Fox

A farmer was greatly annoyed by a fox, which came creeping (creep-crept-crept; moving quietly and slowly) about his yard at night and carried off his hens. So he set a trap for him and caught him, and in order to take revenge upon him, the farmer tied a bunch of straw to his tail, set fire to it and let him go.

As luck would have it (as it turned out; by chance), however, the fox ran straight into the fields where the corn stood ripe and ready for cutting. It quickly caught fire and was all burnt up, and the farmer lost his whole harvest.

Revenge is a double-edged sword.
(having two different edges; one edge hurts others, while the other edge might hurt yourself)

Stop & Think
What does this fable teach people?

hen

sword

KEY WORDS

- **annoy** to make one unhappy; to upset
- **creep about** to move around a place quietly and slowly *creep–crept–crept
- **set fire to** to cause something or someone to start burning
- **harvest** the amount of a crop that is ready to be collected
- **revenge** the act of punishing one who has hurt you
- **sword** a weapon with a long pointed blade and a handle

- **sacrifice** to kill a person or animal as part of a religious ceremony
- **do one the honor** to do something that shows that one has respect for someone
- **arrangement** a way of arranging things
- **tone** the sound of someone's voice that shows what he or she is feeling
- **preparation** things that one does for a special purpose
- **victim** one who has been harmed, injured, or killed

36 The Lion and the Bull

A lion saw a fine fat bull among a herd of cattle (group of cows and bulls) and tried to think of some way of getting him into his hands (catching the bull). So he sent the bull word that he was sacrificing (killing) a sheep, and asked if he would do him the honor of dining with him. The bull accepted the invitation, but on arriving at the lion's home, he saw a great arrangement of saucepans and spits, but no sign of a sheep. So he turned on his heel and walked quietly away.

The lion called after him in an injured tone (the lion sounded hurt or sad) to ask why, and the bull turned around and said, "I have reason enough. When I saw all your preparations, I knew at once (immediately) that the victim (one who suffers) was to be a bull, not a sheep."

The net is spread in vain within sight of the bird.

Stop & Think

Why did the lion make so many preparations?

CHECK UP | **Choose the right words.**

1 The corn quickly ________________ and was all burnt up. (set fire | caught fire)
2 The farmer lost his whole ________________. (harvest | sword)
3 The bull saw a great ________________ of saucepans and spits. (tone | arrangement)

GRAMMAR POINT

"-ing" form (present participle)

- A farmer was greatly annoyed by a fox, which came **creeping** about his yard at night and carried off his hens.

37 The Hare and the Tortoise

37

One day a hare was making fun of a tortoise for being so slow upon his feet.

"Wait a bit," said the tortoise. "I'll run a race with you, and I'll bet (bet-bet-bet) that I win."

"Oh, well," replied the hare, who was much amused at the idea, "let's try it and see." It was soon agreed that the fox should set a course (arrange a plan) for the race and be the judge.

make fun of

When the time came both started off together, but the hare was soon so far ahead that he thought he might as well have a rest. So he lay down and fell fast asleep. Meanwhile (In the meantime), the tortoise kept crawling on, and in time reached the goal.

crawl

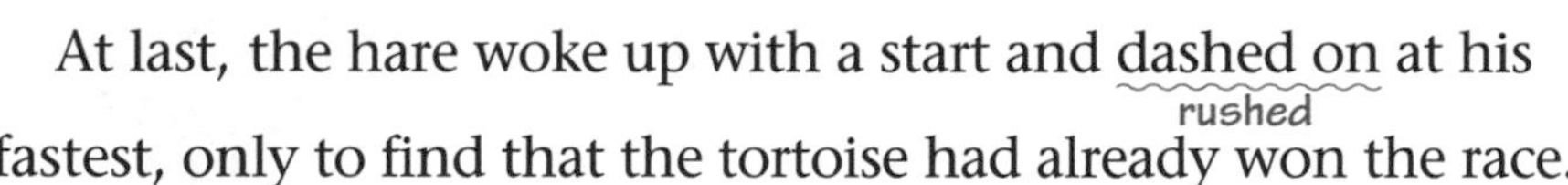

At last, the hare woke up with a start and dashed on (rushed) at his fastest, only to find that the tortoise had already won the race.

Stop & Think

Why did the hare lose the race?

Slow and steady (continuing; not giving up) wins the race.

KEY WORDS

- **bet** to say that one is sure about something *bet–bet–bet
- **amuse** to do or say something that other people think is funny
- **meanwhile** while something else is happening; in the meantime
- **crawl** to move slowly on the ground, like a tortoise or a baby
- **dash** to move hastily; to rush
- **steady** not changing; continuing to do something; regular

- **refuse to** to not do what someone wants; to say that one will not do something
- **get one to do** to persuade or force someone to do something
- **whistle** to make a high sound by forcing air through one's mouth
- **take notice** to pay attention to something
- **in despair** feeling that a situation is without hope

38 The Goatherd and the Goat

One day a goatherd was gathering his flock (group of goats) to return to the fold (an area of land surrounded by a fence in which goats are kept), when one of his goats ran off and refused to join the rest. He tried for a long time to get (make) her to return by calling and whistling to her, but the goat took no notice of him at all, so at last he threw a stone at her and broke one of her horns.

In despair (Feeling no hope), he begged her not to tell his master, but she replied, "You silly fellow, my horn would cry (shout) aloud even if I said nothing."

It's no use trying to hide what can't be hidden.

goatherd

whistle

Stop & Think

How did the goatherd break the horn of the goat?

CHECK UP | Fill in the blanks with the correct words.

dashed   notice   whistling   amused

1 The hare was much ____________ at the tortoise's idea.
2 The hare ____________ on at his fastest.
3 The goatherd tried to get the goat to return by calling and ____________ to her.
4 The goat took no ____________ of the goatherd at all.

GRAMMAR POINT

refuse to / get one to / beg one to + V

- One of the goatherd's goats ran off and **refused to join** the rest.
- The goatherd tried for a long time to **get the goat to return** by calling and whistling to her.
- The goatherd **begged** the goat **not to tell** his master.

39 The Goose That Laid the Golden Eggs

A man and his wife had the good fortune (luck) to possess (have) a goose which laid a golden egg every day. Lucky though they were, they soon began to think they were not getting rich fast enough, and imagining that the bird must be made of gold inside, they decided to kill it in order to get all of the precious metal at once.

But when they cut it open, they found it was just like any other goose. Thus, they neither got rich all at once as they had hoped, nor enjoyed any longer the daily addition (something which is added) to their wealth.

Much wants more (One wants too much) and loses all.

Stop & Think
What does this fable teach people?

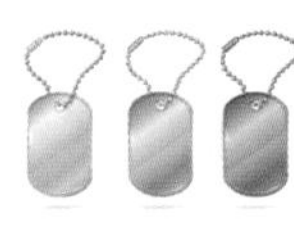

- **possess** to have; to own
- **be made of** be made of certain materials
- **precious** rare and worth a lot of money
- **addition** something which is added to something else; the process of adding things together

- **principle** a basic belief or rule that has a major influence on one's behavior
- **sometime** at a time in the future or in the past, although one does not know exactly when
- **beg for** to ask strongly for something
- **commit** to promise to do something

40 The Bat and the Weasels

40

A bat fell to the ground and was caught by a weasel, and was just about to be killed and eaten when it begged to be let go. The weasel said he couldn't do that because he was an enemy of all birds on principle. (as a rule)

"Oh," said the bat, "but I'm not a bird at all; I'm a mouse."

"So you are," said the weasel, "now that I take a closer look at you," and he let it go.

weasel

Sometime after this the bat was caught in just the same way by another weasel and, as before, begged for its life.

"No," said the weasel, "I never let a mouse go for any reason."

"But I'm not a mouse," said the bat, "I'm a bird."

"Why, so you are," said the weasel, and he too let the bat go. (Why: an interjection used to show that one is surprised or has suddenly realized something)

Look and see which way the wind blows before you commit yourself. (which way the wind blows: what the situation is; commit: promise something)

Stop & Think

Look at "it begged to be let go." What does "it" refer to?

CHECK UP | **Answer the questions.**

1 What did the man and his wife do to the goose?
   a. They cut it open. b. They fed it more food. c. They made it lay more golden eggs.

2 Why did the bat say that it was a bird and a mouse?
   a. So the weasel would be its friend. b. To escape. c. To eat the weasel.

GRAMMAR POINT

neither . . . nor . . .

- Thus, they **neither** got rich all at once as they had hoped, **nor** enjoyed any longer the daily addition to their wealth.

41 The Ass, the Cock, and the Lion

41

An ass and a cock were in a cattle pen together. Presently a lion, who had been starving for days, came along and was just about to fall upon the ass and eat him when the cock, rising to his full height and flapping his wings vigorously, let out a tremendous crow.

a small piece of land surrounded by a fence to keep farm animals in

stretching his body as much as he could

made a loud sound

Now, if there is one thing that frightens a lion, it is the crowing of a cock, and as soon as this one heard the noise, he fled.

flee–fled–fled

ran away

The ass was mightily pleased at this, and thought that if the lion couldn't face a cock, he would be still less likely to stand up to an ass. So the ass ran out and pursued him. But when the two had gotten well out of sight and hearing of the cock, the lion suddenly turned upon the ass, and ate him up.

very

False confidence often leads to disaster.

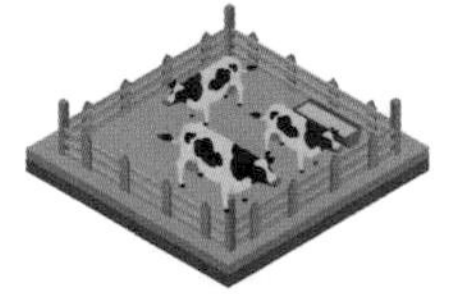

cattle pen

flap

Stop & Think

What was the lion afraid of?

KEY WORDS

- **starve** to feel very hungry; to die of hunger
- **vigorously** energetically and with force
- **tremendous** very large; huge
- **flee** to run away *flee–fled–fled
- **pursue** to follow someone or something, usually to try to catch
- **lead to** to result in; to cause
- **disaster** a horrible event

- **boasting** describing one that boasts
- **go abroad** to go to a foreign country
- **tale** a story
- **take part in** to join; to participate in

42 The Boasting Traveler

A man once went abroad (to a foreign country) on his travels, and when he came home, he had wonderful tales (stories) to tell of the things he had done in foreign countries. Among other things, he said he had taken part in (participated in) a jumping match at Rhodes, and had done a wonderful jump which no one could beat. "Just go to Rhodes and ask them," he said, "everyone will tell you it's true."

But one of those who were listening said, "If you can jump as well as all that, we needn't go to Rhodes to prove it. Let's just imagine this is Rhodes for a minute, and now, jump!"

Actions speak louder than words.

jumping match

Stop & Think

What did the man claim to have taken part in at Rhodes?

CHECK UP | True or false?

1 The ass let out a tremendous crow. ________

2 The lion heard the crowing and fled. ________

3 The man had horrible tales to tell of the things he had done in foreign countries. ________

GRAMMAR POINT

-er + than . . . (comparative)

- Actions speak **louder than** words.

43 The Lion and the Three Bulls

Three bulls were grazing (eating grass) in a meadow, and were watched by a lion, who longed to (wanted to) capture and eat them, but felt that he was no match (he can't beat them) for the three so long as (as long as) they stayed together.

So he began, by false whispers (rumors) and nasty hints, to create jealousies and distrust (≠ trust) among them. This strategy succeeded so well that before long (soon) the bulls grew (became) cold (not showing kindness and love) and unfriendly, and finally avoided each other, each one eating by himself.

As soon as the lion saw this, he fell upon them one by one and killed them in turn.

The quarrels of friends are the opportunities of enemies.

Stop & Think

When did the lion succeed in killing the three bulls?

capture

whisper

KEY WORDS

- **long to** to want to do something very much
- **capture** to catch and treat badly (≠ release)
- **hint** an indirect suggestion that shows how one feels
- **distrust** ≠ trust
- **strategy** a plan or trick designed to gain an advantage
- **unfriendly** ≠ friendly

- **mankind** human beings
- **collar** the belt, rope, or chain that is put around the neck of a pet dog
- **feast** to eat and drink a lot in order to celebrate
- **accompany** to go somewhere with someone
- **traitor** one who betrays his or her friends
- **fate** what happens to a person or thing, especially something unpleasant

44 The Wolves and the Dogs

Once upon a time the wolves said to the dogs, "Why should we continue to be enemies any longer? You are very much like us in most ways; the main difference between us is only one of training. We live a life of freedom, but you are enslaved (forced to be a slave) by mankind, who beat you, put heavy collars around your necks, and force you to keep watch over their flocks and herds for them, and, after all that, give you nothing but bones to eat. Don't put up with (tolerate) it any longer. Hand the flocks over to us, and we will all live off the fat of the land (get enough food to live comfortably without doing much work) and feast together."

The dogs allowed themselves to be persuaded by these words, and accompanied the wolves into their den (the home of some wild animals like wolves and lions). But as soon as they were well inside, the wolves fell upon them and tore them to pieces.

Traitors fully deserve their fate.

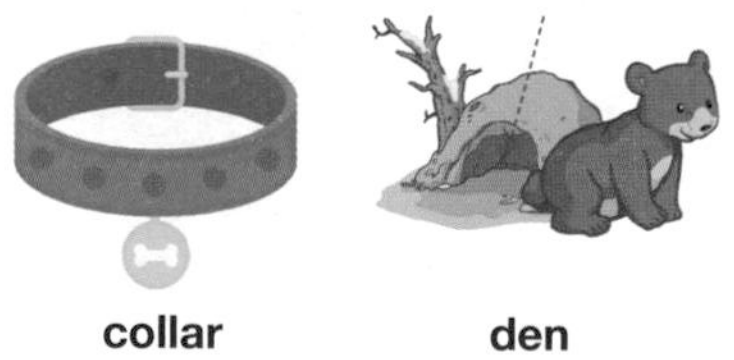

Stop & Think

What was the fate of the traitors in this story?

CHECK UP | **Choose the right words.**

1 The lion created jealousies and ________________ among them. (strategy | distrust)
2 Mankind put heavy ________________ around dogs' necks. (collars | hints)
3 The dogs ________________ the wolves into their den. (feasted | accompanied)

GRAMMAR POINT

as soon as (the moment)

- **As soon as** the lion saw this, he fell upon them one by one and killed them in turn.

45 The Ant

45

Ants were once men and made their living by farming the soil. *(using the land for growing crops)* But, not content with the results of their own work, they were always looking longingly *(in a way that showed they wanted them very much)* upon the crops and fruits of their neighbors, which the ants stole whenever they got the chance and added to their own store. *(the amount of food that the ants had kept for later use)*

At last their greed made Jupiter *(the king of the gods)* so angry that he changed them into ants. But though their forms were changed, their nature *(characteristics)* remained the same; and so, to this day, they go about among the cornfields and gather the fruits of others' labor, and store them up *(gather)* for their own use.

You may punish a thief, but his habit remains.

Stop & Think
What was the nature of the ants when they were men?

ants

Jupiter

cornfield

KEY WORDS

- **make one's living** to make money in order to live
- **soil** the land
- **whenever** anytime
- **greed** the desire for more than one needs or should have

- **arise** to happen *arise–arose–arisen
- **wrap** to cover with paper or clothes
- **beam** to shine
- **loosely** ≠ tightly
- **clad** dressed
- **persuasion** the act of persuading

46 The North Wind and the Sun 46

arise-arose-arisen
A dispute arose between the north
argument happened
wind and the sun, each claiming that he was stronger than the other. At last they agreed to test their powers upon a traveler, to see which could sooner remove his cloak.

The north wind tried first: gathering up all his force for the attack, he came blowing
furiously down upon the man, and caught up his cloak as
with lots of effort
though he would pull it from him with one single effort.
one try
But the harder he blew, the more closely the man wrapped it around himself. Then came the turn of the sun. At first he beamed gently upon the traveler, who soon opened his cloak and walked on
with it hanging loosely about his shoulders. Then he shone forth
≠ tightly
with his full strength, and the man, before he had gone many steps, was glad to throw his cloak right off and complete his journey more
lightly clad.
dressed

Persuasion is better than force.

cloak

Stop & Think

Who used a gentler method to win in this story?

CHECK UP | Finish the sentences.

1 The ants
2 The north wind
3 The sun

a. beamed gently upon the traveler.
b. gather the fruits of others' labor.
c. blew furiously down upon the man.

GRAMMAR POINT

the + -er . . . , the more + adverb / adjective . . .

- But **the harder** the north wind blew, **the more closely** the man wrapped it around himself.

47 The Stag and the Vine

47

A stag, pursued (followed) by some hunters, concealed himself behind a thick vine. The hunters lost track of (couldn't find) him and passed by his hiding place without being aware that he was anywhere near.

Supposing all danger to be over, he presently began to eat the leaves of the vine. This movement drew (attracted) the attention of the returning hunters, and one of them, supposing some animal to be hidden there, shot an arrow into the leaves. The unlucky stag was pierced to the heart, and as he died he said, "I deserve my fate for feeding on the leaves of my protector."

Ingratitude (≠ thankfulness) sometimes brings its own punishment.

Stop & Think

Where did the stag hide from the hunters?

pierce

protector

KEY WORDS

- **conceal** to hide
- **lose track of** to lose and not be able to find something or someone
- **suppose** to believe that something is probably true
- **pierce** to make a small hole in or through something with a pointed object
- **punishment** the act of punishing

- **satisfaction** the feeling of being satisfied
- **reward** a prize
- **merit** a good quality
- **on the contrary** just the opposite
- **a badge of** a sign of; an identifying mark or sign
- **disgrace** shame; embarrassment; the loss of others' respect

48 The Mischievous Dog

48

There was once a dog who used to snap at people (try to bite) and bite them for no reason, and who was a great nuisance to everyone who came to his master's house. So, his master fastened (tied) a bell around his neck to warn people of his presence.

The dog was very proud of the bell, and strutted (walked proudly with his head up) about ringing it with tremendous satisfaction.

But an old dog came up to him and said, "You shouldn't be so proud of yourself, my friend. You don't think, do you, that your bell was given to you as a reward for merit? On the contrary, it is a badge of disgrace (mark of shame)."

Notoriety (A bad reputation) is often mistaken for fame.

master

Stop & Think

What did the bell really mean in the story?

CHECK UP | Fill in the blanks with the correct words.

pierced nuisance concealed reward

1 The stag ______________ himself behind a thick vine.
2 The unlucky stag was ______________ to the heart.
3 The dog was a great ______________ to everyone who came to his master's house.
4 The bell wasn't given to the dog as a ______________ for merit.

GRAMMAR POINT

draw the attention of

- This movement **drew the attention of** the returning hunters.

49 The Farmer and Fortune

A farmer was plowing on his farm one day when he turned up a pot of golden coins with his plow. He was overjoyed at his discovery, and from that time forth made an offering daily at the shrine of the Goddess of the Earth.

from that time forth: from that point in time forward
made an offering: gave something as a gift
shrine: a small temple
Goddess of the Earth: the female god who protects the earth

Fortune was displeased at this, and came to him and said, "My man, why do you give Earth the credit for the gift which I gave you? You never thought of thanking me for your good luck, but should you be unlucky enough to lose what you have gained, I know very well that I, Fortune, will then get all the blame."

should: if

Show gratitude where gratitude is due.

due: owed

Stop & Think
What did the farmer find when he was plowing on his farm?

shrine

plow

KEY WORDS

- **plow** to break up land with a plow; a farming tool used to dig into and turn over soil
- **discovery** something found or discovered by someone
- **credit** praise; approval
- **gratitude** the feeling of being grateful to someone for something; thankfulness
- **due** owed

- **keeper** one who is responsible for taking care of something
- **hive** a structure where bees live
- **upset** unhappy
- **stare** to look at angrily
- **overturn** to turn over
- **sting** the small, sharp tail of a bee; (animals) to hurt or kill someone or something with a sting

50 The Beekeeper

A thief found his way into an apiary while the beekeeper was away, and stole all the honey. When the keeper returned and found the hives empty, he was very upset and stood staring at them for some time.

a place where people keep bees for producing honey

Before long the bees came back from gathering honey and, finding their hives overturned and the keeper standing by, they attacked him with their stings.

After a short time

At this he became furious and cried, "You ungrateful creatures! You let the thief who stole my honey get away, and then you sting me who has always taken such good care of you!"

≠ thankful

When you hit back, make sure you have got the right man.

apiary

Stop & Think

Look at the title "The Beekeeper." Is a "beekeeper" a place, person, or thing?

CHECK UP | Answer the questions.

1 Why was Fortune displeased?
a. Because the farmer scolded her.
b. Because the farmer was lazy.
c. Because the farmer didn't thank her.

2 Who did the bees mistake the beekeeper for?
a. The thief.
b. The one who fed them.
c. The one who gathered honey for them.

GRAMMAR POINT

who (relative pronoun)

- You let the thief **who** stole my honey get away.
- You sting me **who** has always taken such good care of you!

51 The Boy and the Filberts

51

A boy put his hand into a jar of filberts (nuts), and grasped (held tightly) as many as his fist could possibly hold. But when he tried to pull it out again, he found he couldn't do so, for the neck of the jar was too small to allow for the passage of so large a handful (pulling out of a large handful of filberts).

Not wanting to lose his nuts, but unable to withdraw his hand, he burst into tears (started to cry). A man standing nearby, who saw what the problem was, said to him, "Come, my boy; don't be so greedy. Be content with half the amount, and you'll be able to get your hand out without difficulty."

Do not attempt (try to do) too much at once (one time).

Stop & Think

What was the boy's problem?

filberts

jar

KEY WORDS

- **grasp** to hold something very firmly
- **passage** the movement of passing through
- **handful** the amount of something that fills one's hand
- **unable** ≠ able
- **withdraw** to take out
  *withdraw–withdrew–withdrawn
- **attempt** to try to do something

- **rear** to take care of a child or young animal until the child or animal grows up; to raise
- **abandon** to give up
- **pursuit** the action of pursuing
- **overtake** to catch up with
  *overtake–overtook–overtaken
- **suspicion** a feeling that someone or something cannot be trusted
- **breed** to develop
  *breed–bred–bred

52 The Shepherd and the Wolf

A shepherd found a wolf's cub wandering (walking around) in his pastures (lands covered with grass), and took him home and reared (raised) him along with his dogs. When the cub grew to his full size, if ever a wolf stole a sheep from the flock, he would join the dogs in hunting the wolf down.

It sometimes happened that the dogs failed to catch the thief and, abandoning the pursuit (giving up the chase), returned home. The wolf would on such occasions continue the chase by himself, and when he overtook the thief, would stop and share the feast with him, and then return to the shepherd.

But if some time passed without a sheep being carried off by the wolves, he would steal one himself and share it with the dogs. The shepherd's suspicions were aroused (The shepherd became suspicious), and one day he caught the wolf in the act (when the wolf stole sheep). Then, fastening a rope around his neck, the shepherd hung him from the nearest tree.

wolf's cub

pasture

(One shows his true nature by his actions.)

What's bred in the bone is sure to come out in the flesh.

Stop & Think

What would the wolf do if the dogs failed to catch a thief?

CHECK UP | **True or false?**

1 The boy was able to withdraw his hand from the jar. ________

2 The boy attempted too much at once. ________

3 The shepherd reared the wolf's cub along with his dogs. ________

GRAMMAR POINT

too . . . to . . . = so . . . that . . .

- The neck of the jar was **too** small **to** allow for the passage of so large a handful.
  (= The neck of the jar was **so** small **that** it could not allow for the passage of so large a handful.)

53 The Stag at the Pool

A thirsty stag went down to a pool to drink. As he bent over the surface, he saw his own reflection in the water, and was struck with (suddenly had a feeling or an idea) admiration for his fine spreading antlers (a deer's horns), but at the same time he felt nothing but disgust for the weakness and slenderness (the state of being too thin) of his legs.

While he stood there looking at himself, he was seen and attacked by a lion, and in the chase which followed the stag soon got ahead of his pursuer, and kept his lead (ran ahead of the lion) as long as the ground over which he ran was open and free of trees. But coming presently to a forest, he was caught by his antlers in the branches, and fell victim to the teeth and claws of his enemy.

"Woe is me!" (an expression used to show great sadness and that one feels sorry for oneself) he cried with his last breath. "I despised my legs, which might have saved my life, but I gloried in my horns, and they have ruined me."

Stop & Think
What caused the stag to get stuck in the branches?

What is worth most is often valued least.

antlers

KEY WORDS

- **reflection** an image reflected from a mirror or water
- **admiration** respect and approval
- **disgust** dislike
- **weakness** a fault or problem that makes someone less effective or attractive (≠ strength)
- **fall victim to** to be hurt or killed because of something or someone
- **glory in** to feel very proud of something

- **grateful** thankful
- **rob someone of** to take something away from someone by force
- **displeased** ≠ pleased
- **request** an act of asking for something in a polite or formal way
- **give one's word** to tell someone that you will do something; to promise

54 The Bee and Jupiter

A queen bee from Hymettus flew up to Olympus with some fresh honey from the hive as a present for Jupiter, who was so pleased with the gift that he promised to give her anything she wanted. She said she would be very grateful if he would give stings to the bees, to kill people who robbed them of their honey.
took away by force

Jupiter was greatly displeased with this request, for he loved mankind, but he had given his word, so he said that stings they
human beings promised
should have. The stings he gave them, however, were of such a kind that whenever a bee stings a man, the sting remains in the wound
the sting separates from the bee
and the bee dies.

Evil wishes, like chickens, come home to roost.
(a phrase meaning that the bad things one has done will return to cause problems for him or her)

rob

Stop & Think
Why was Jupiter greatly displeased with the queen bee's request?

CHECK UP | Choose the right words.

1 The stag felt __________ for the weakness and slenderness of his legs. (admiration | disgust)
2 The stag __________ in his horns. (gloried | bent)
3 The queen bee wanted to kill people who __________ the bees of their honey. (robbed | displeased)

GRAMMAR POINT

fall victim to

- The stag was caught by his antlers in the branches, and **fell victim to** the teeth and claws of his enemy.

55 Hercules and the Wagon Driver

55

A wagon driver was driving his team (animals used to pull a wagon) along a muddy lane with a full load behind them, when the wheels of his wagon sank so deep in the mud that no efforts of his horses could move them. (his horses could not move the wagon)

As he stood there looking helplessly on, and calling loudly at intervals upon Hercules (the god who is famous for his strength) for assistance, the god himself appeared and said to him, "Put your shoulder to the wheel, man, and order your horses to pull, and then you may call on Hercules to assist you. If you won't lift a finger to help yourself, you can't expect Hercules or anyone else to come to your aid (help you)."

Heaven helps those who help themselves.

Stop & Think
What does this fable teach people?

wagon

muddy

KEY WORDS

- **muddy** covered with mud
- **lane** a narrow road
- **load** something that a person or animal carries
- **at intervals** repeated after a particular period of time
- **assistance** help
- **call on (upon)** to ask someone in a formal way to do something
- **assist** to help

- **newcomer** one who has only recently arrived somewhere
- **hand over** to give
- **company** the people one spends time with

56 The Ass and His Purchaser

A man who wanted to buy an ass went to a market and, coming across (finding unexpectedly) a likely-looking (appearing to be suitable) beast, arranged with the owner that he should be allowed to take him home for a try to see what he was like.

purchaser

When the man reached home, he put him into his stable along with the other asses.

stable

The newcomer took a look around, and immediately went and chose a place next to the laziest and greediest beast in the stable. When the man saw this, he put a rope on him at once, led him back to the market and handed him over (gave him back) to his owner again.

The latter was a good deal (a lot; very) surprised to see him back so soon, and said, "Do you mean to say you have tested him already?" "I don't want to put him through any more tests," replied the other. "I can see what sort of beast he is from the companion he chose for himself."

A man is known by the company (the people one spends time with) he keeps.

CHECK UP | **Finish the sentences.**

1 The wagon driver
2 The wagon
3 The purchaser

a. sank very deep into the mud.
b. handed the ass over to his owner again.
c. called loudly upon Hercules for assistance.

GRAMMAR POINT

expect someone to V

- If you won't lift a finger to help yourself, you can't **expect Hercules** or **anyone** else **to come** to your aid.

57 The Bear and the Travelers

Two travelers were on the road together, when a bear suddenly appeared on the scene (a phrase used to say someone or something is involved in the situation). As he observed them, one ran to a tree at the side of the road, and climbed up into the branches and hid there.

The other was not as fast as his companion, and as he could not escape, he threw himself on the ground (lay down) and pretended to be dead. The bear came up and sniffed all around him, but he kept perfectly still (not moving) and held his breath, for they say that a bear will not touch a dead body. The bear took him for a corpse (regarded him as a dead body), and went away.

When the coast was clear (a phrase used to say that one can do something without being caught), the traveler in the tree came down, and asked the other what it was the bear had whispered (spoken quietly) to him when the bear put his mouth to his ear. The other replied, "He told me never again to travel with a friend who deserts (leaves without helping) you at the first sign of danger."

Misfortune tests the sincerity of friendship.

Stop & Think

What did the second traveler do when he could not run away?

sniff

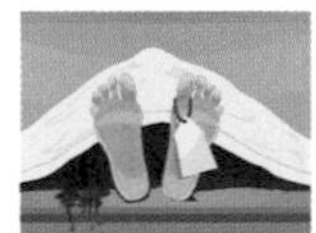

corpse

KEY WORDS

- **observe** to watch closely for some time
- **escape** to get away; to run away
- **sniff** to smell quickly
- **hold one's breath** to stop breathing for a short time
- **take . . . for** to consider; to regard . . . as
- **sincerity** honesty

- **idly** without any purpose or reason
- **acquaintance** someone whom you know, but not very well
- **comfort** the thing that makes one's life easier and more pleasant
- **costly** expensive
- **dubious** feeling doubt (≠ certain)
- **blessing** something that is lucky or makes one happy

58 The Pack Ass and the Wild Ass

A wild ass, who was wandering idly about, one day came upon (came across) a pack ass (an ass who is owned by a farmer or wagon driver) lying at full length in a sunny spot and thoroughly (completely) enjoying himself. Going up to him, the wild ass said, "What a lucky beast you are! Your shiny coat (fur) shows how well you live. How I envy you!"

Not long after this, the wild ass saw his acquaintance (the pack ass) again, but this time he was carrying a heavy load, and his driver was following behind and beating him with a thick stick.

pack ass

"Ah, my friend," said the wild ass, "I don't envy you anymore, for I see now you pay dearly (very much) for your comforts."

stick

Costly advantages are dubious (doubtful; ≠ certain) blessings.

Stop & Think

Did the wild ass envy the pack ass when he saw him again? Why?

CHECK UP | Fill in the blanks with the correct words.

observed comforts idly escape

1 The bear ______________ the two travelers.
2 The second traveler could not ______________ from the bear.
3 The wild ass was wandering ______________ about.
4 The pack ass paid dearly for his ______________.

GRAMMAR POINT

What . . . ! / How . . . ! (exclamation)

- **What** a lucky beast you are! (= **How** lucky a beast you are!)

59 The Frogs and the Well

Two frogs lived together in a pond, but one hot summer the pond dried up, and they left it to look for another place to live, for frogs like damp places if they can find them.

After a while they came to a deep well, and one of them looked down into it and said to the other, "This looks like a nice cool place; let us jump in and settle here."

But the other one, who was wiser, replied, "Not so fast, my friend. Supposing this well dried up like the pond, how should we get out again?"

Think twice before you act.

well

damp

Stop & Think

What does this fable teach people?

KEY WORDS

- **dry up** to become completely dry
- **look for** to search for
- **damp** wet and humid (≠ dry)
- **Suppose . . . ?** What if . . . ?

- **scraps** small pieces of food left over after a meal; leftovers
- **agreement** a situation in which people agree on things; a deal between people
- **coolly** calmly, without getting excited or angry

60 The Dog and the Wolf

A dog was lying in the sun before a farmyard gate, when a wolf jumped upon him and was just about to eat him up. But the dog begged for his life and said, "You see how thin I am and what a poor meal I should be for you now, but if you will only wait a few days, my master is going to have a feast. All the rich scraps (tasty leftovers) will come to me, and I shall get nice and fat. Then will be the time for you to eat me."

scraps

The wolf thought this was a very good plan, and went away. Sometime afterwards he came to the farmyard again, and found the dog lying out of reach (unable to be reached) on the stable roof.

"Come down," he called, "and be eaten. Don't you remember our agreement?"

But the dog said coolly, "My friend, if you ever catch me lying down by the gate there again, don't you wait for any feast (don't wait anymore)."

Once bitten, twice shy (frightened).

Stop & Think

Why didn't the wolf eat the dog the first time he caught him?

CHECK UP | Answer the questions.

1 Why did the two frogs leave the pond?
a. Because it dried up. b. Because it was damp. c. Because it was deep.

2 What should the wolf do the next time he catches the dog lying by the gate?
a. Just leave him there. b. Wait till he gets fat. c. Just eat him.

GRAMMAR POINT

find + O (object) + V-ing

- The wolf came to the farmyard again, and **found the dog lying** out of reach on the stable roof.

Step
2

61 The Peasant and the Apple Tree

peasant

sparrows

grasshopper

A peasant had an apple tree growing in his garden, which bore (produced) no fruit, but merely served to provide a shelter (hiding place) from the heat for the sparrows and grasshoppers which sat and sang in its branches. Disappointed at its uselessness (≠ usefulness), the peasant determined to cut it down, and went and fetched his axe for the purpose.

But when the sparrows and the grasshoppers saw what he was about to do, they begged him to spare it (not to hurt it), and said to him, "If you destroy the tree, we shall have to seek shelter elsewhere, and you will no longer have our merry singing to accompany (be there with) your work in the garden."

Stop & Think
Where was the sparrows' and grasshoppers' shelter?

- **peasant** a poor farmer
- **disappointed** displeased because one has failed to get what he or she wants
- **determine to** to decide what will happen
- **spare** to not to hurt; to leave one alone
- **merry** happy; joyful
- **set to work** to begin doing something actively
- **stroke** a cut; the action of hitting
- **hollow** empty
- **a swarm of** a large group of insects living or flying together
- **delighted** very happy; very pleased
- **utility** usefulness

He, however, refused to listen to them, and set to work (began working) with a will (determination) to cut through the trunk. A few strokes showed that it was hollow inside and contained a swarm (very large group) of bees and a large store of honey. Delighted with his find, he threw down his axe, saying, "The old tree is worth keeping after all."

Utility (Usefulness) is most men's test of worth (value).

Stop & Think

What was inside the apple tree's trunk?

CHECK UP | **True or false?**

1 The apple tree bore no fruit. ________
2 The apple tree provided a shelter from the heat for the peasant. ________
3 The peasant was delighted with what he found inside the tree. ________

GRAMMAR POINT

worth + V-ing

- The old tree is **worth keeping** after all.

62 The Bat, the Bramble, and the Seagull

A bat, a bramble, and a seagull went into partnership (became partners) and determined to go on a trading voyage together. The bat borrowed a sum of money for his venture; the bramble gathered a stock of clothes of various kinds; the seagull took a quantity of lead (a soft heavy gray metal used on roofs). And so they set out (started the journey).

By and by (After a short time) a great storm came on, and their boat with all its cargo went to the bottom of the sea, but the three travelers managed to reach land.

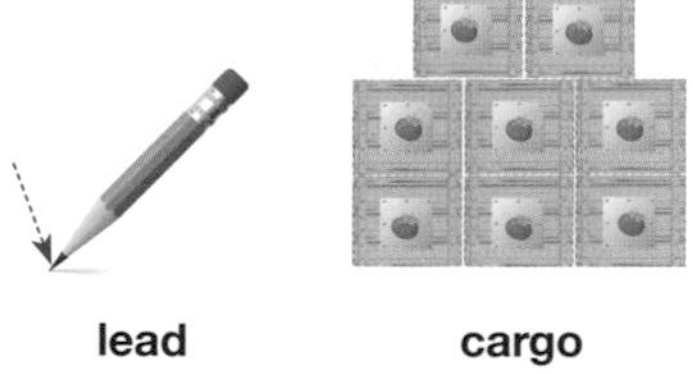

Stop & Think
What happened during the trading voyage?

KEY WORDS

- **partnership** the state of being partners involved in an activity together
- **voyage** a long journey, especially by sea
- **sum** an amount
- **venture** a new business or activity that involves risk
- **stock** a supply of goods
- **various** different
- **cargo** a load of goods carried by a ship
- **manage to** to succeed in doing something, but with difficulty
- **every now and then** sometimes
- **dive** to go under water *dive–dove–dived
- **recognize** to know who or what someone or something is
- **acquire** to get

Ever since then the seagull flies to and fro (back and forth) over the sea, and every now and then dives (dive-dove-dived) below the surface, looking for the lead he's (he has) lost; the bat is so afraid of meeting his creditors (people who lent him money) that he hides away by day and only comes out at night to feed, and the bramble catches hold of (holds) the clothes of everyone who passes by, hoping someday to recognize and recover (get back) its lost garments.

All men are more concerned (care more) to recover what they lose than to acquire what they lack.

garments

Stop & Think

Why does the bat only come out at night to feed?

CHECK UP | **Choose the right words.**

1 The bat, bramble, and seagull went on a ____________ together. (partnership | voyage)

2 The bat borrowed a sum of money for his ____________. (stock | venture)

3 Their boat with all its ______________ went to the bottom of the sea. (cargo | sum)

GRAMMAR POINT

manage to

- The three travelers **managed to** reach land.

63 The Mice and the Weasels

There was a war between the mice and the weasels in which the mice always got the worst of it, large numbers of them being killed and eaten by the weasels. So they called a council of war, in which an old mouse got up and said, "It's no wonder we are always beaten, for we have no generals to plan our battles and direct our movements in the field."

It's no wonder: It isn't surprising

generals: the highest-ranking officers in an army

Stop & Think

What did the mice decide to do after the council?

KEY WORDS

- **council** a meeting at which a group of people discuss and give advice on a topic
- **battle** a fight between armies in a war
- **distinguish** to make one person or thing seem different from others
- **rank** one's position in an organization
- **helmet** a hard hat worn to protect one's head
- **defeat** to win; to beat
- **hamper** to make it difficult for someone to do something
- **penalty** a disadvantage caused by a situation or action; a punishment

Acting on his advice, they chose the biggest mice to be their leaders, and these leaders, in order to be distinguished from the rank and file (ordinary soldiers), provided themselves with helmets decorated with straw.

They then led the mice out to battle, confident of victory, but they were defeated (beaten) as usual and were soon running as fast as they could to their holes. All made their way to safety (safely escaped) without difficulty except the leaders, who were so hampered by their helmets that they could not get into their holes, and easily fell victim to their pursuers (the weasels that pursued the mice).

Greatness (power; authority) carries its own penalties.

general

battle

helmet

Stop & Think

What happened to the leaders of the mice?

CHECK UP | **Finish the sentences.**

1 Large numbers of mice
2 The old mouse
3 The leaders of the mice

a. suggested choosing generals.
b. wore helmets decorated with straw.
c. were eaten by the weasels.

GRAMMAR POINT

choose someone to be

- They **chose the biggest mice to be** their leaders.

64 The Ass, the Fox, and the Lion

An ass and a fox went into partnership and set out (started a journey) to search for food together. They hadn't gone far before they saw a lion coming their way, at which they were both dreadfully (extremely) frightened.

But the fox thought he saw a way of saving his own skin (saving his life), and went boldly up to the lion and whispered in his ear, "I'll help you get hold of the ass without the trouble of pursuing him if you promise to let me go free."

The lion agreed to this, and the fox then rejoined his companion and before long (in a short time) led him by a hidden pit, which some hunter had dug as a trap for wild animals, and into which the ass fell.

When the lion saw that the ass was safely caught and couldn't get away, it was to the fox that the lion first turned his attention, and he soon finished him off, and then at his leisure (≠ in haste) proceeded to feast upon (eat a large amount of) the ass.

Betray a friend and you'll often find you have ruined yourself.

Stop & Think
How did the fox try to save himself?

companion

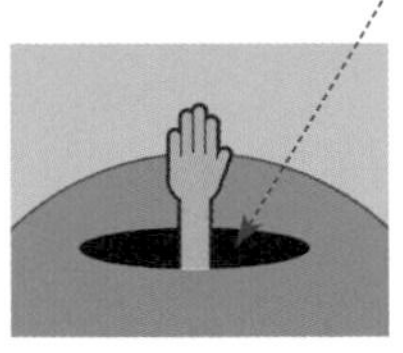

pit

hunter

KEY WORDS

- **dreadfully** extremely; terribly
- **frightened** very scared
- **save one's own skin** to escape death or harm, usually at someone else's expense
- **boldly** bravely
- **get hold of** to catch; to grab
- **pit** a very large hole dug in the ground
- **proceed** to do something after you have done something else
- **betray** to hurt a friend or someone else who trusts you, especially by giving information to an enemy

Stop & Think

What does this fable teach people?

CHECK UP | Fill in the blanks with the correct words.

boldly proceeded dreadfully pit

1 The ass and the fox were both ______________ frightened.
2 The fox went ______________ up to the lion and whispered in his ear.
3 The ass fell into a hidden ______________.
4 The lion ______________ to feast upon the ass.

GRAMMAR POINT

a way of + V-ing

- The fox saw **a way of saving** his own skin.

65 The Impostor

65

A certain man fell ill [became], and being in a very bad way, he made a promise that he would sacrifice a hundred oxen [singular: ox] to the gods if they would make him healthy again. Wishing to see how he would keep his promise, the gods caused him to recover in a short time.

Now, he hadn't [didn't have] an ox in the world, so he made a hundred little oxen out of [by using] wax and offered them up on an altar, at the same time saying, "Oh gods, I call on you to witness [see and know] that I have kept my promise."

The gods were determined to get even with [take revenge on] him, so they sent him a dream in which he was told to go to the seashore and fetch a hundred gold coins which he would find there. Hurrying in great excitement to the shore, he fell in with [met] a band [group] of robbers, who seized [caught] him and carried him off to sell as a slave, and when they sold him, a hundred gold coins was the price they received.

Do not promise more than you can perform [do].

Stop & Think

What did the man do to keep his promise?

KEY WORDS

- **impostor** one who tricks others; one who pretends to be someone else in order to deceive others
- **make a promise** to promise
- **sacrifice** to kill a person or animal to honor a god
- **wax** a soft substance that is used for making candles and models
- **get even with** to take revenge on
- **a band of** a group of people who do something together, especially criminals
- **robber** one who takes money or property illegally, often by using threats or violence
- **slave** one who is owned by another person and works for no money
- **perform** to do; to carry out

wax

robber

slaves

Stop & Think

Were the gods satisfied with the man's wax oxen? How do you know?

CHECK UP | **Answer the questions.**

1 How many oxen did the man have?

a. A hundred. b. One. c. None.

2 What happened in the man's dream?

a. He seized robbers. b. He became a slave. c. He got even with the gods.

GRAMMAR POINT

cause someone to

- The gods **caused him to** recover in a short time.

66 The Cat and the Mice

There was once a house that was full of mice. A cat heard of this and said to herself, “That’s the place for me.” Then off she went to live in the house, and caught the mice one by one and ate them.

At last the mice could stand (tolerate) it no longer, and they decided to take to (go into) their holes and stay there.

“That’s awkward,” said the cat to herself, “the only thing to do is to lure them out (persuade the mice to come out) by a trick.”

So she considered a while, and then climbed up the wall and let herself hang down by her back legs from a peg, and pretended to be dead. By and by (After a while) a mouse peeped out and saw the cat hanging there.

Stop & Think

What was the cat’s trick?

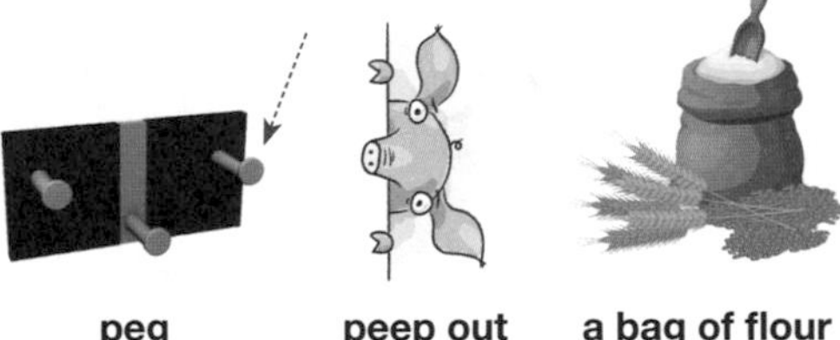

peg **peep out** **a bag of flour**

KEY WORDS

- **stand** to put up with; to tolerate
- **awkward** difficult to deal with; weird
- **lure** to persuade one to do something dangerous or wrong
- **peg** an object that is attached to a wall and from which things can hang
- **peep out** to secretly look at something
- **madam** a polite or respectful way to address a woman
- **turn . . . into** to change . . . into
- **innocent** harmless (≠ guilty)
- **appearance** the way someone or something looks

"Aha!" it cried. "You're very clever, madam, no doubt, but you may turn (change) yourself into a bag of flour hanging there if you like, yet you won't catch us coming anywhere near you."

If you are wise, you won't be deceived (tricked) by the innocent appearance of those whom you have once found to be dangerous.

Stop & Think

Did the cat succeed in deceiving the mice?

CHECK UP | **True or false?**

1 The cat went to live in the house full of cats. ________
2 A mouse peeped out and saw the cat hanging there. ________
3 The cat was really dead. ________

GRAMMAR POINT

see + O (object) + V-ing

- By and by a mouse peeped out and **saw the cat hanging** there.

67 The Eagle, the Jackdaw, and the Shepherd

67

One day a jackdaw saw an eagle fly down onto a lamb and carry it off in its claws.
baby sheep

"My word," said the jackdaw. "I'll do that myself."
Wow!

So it flew high up into the air, and then came shooting down with a great whistling of wings onto the back of a big ram. As soon as it had landed, its claws got caught in the wool, and nothing it could do was of any use; there it stuck, flapping away, and only making things worse instead of better.
sound of wings moving rapidly
male sheep
(the jackdaw couldn't do anything to free itself)
stick-stuck-stuck

jackdaw

lamb

Stop & Think
What was the jackdaw's problem?

KEY WORDS

- **wool** thick hair that grows on sheep
- **stick** to be unable to move
  *stick–stuck–stuck
- **clip** to cut
- **odd** unusual; strange
- **make of** to know what something is; to understand something
- **beyond one's power** beyond one's ability; more than one can do (≠ within one's power)
- **risk** to take a dangerous chance
- **ridicule** unkind laughter or words that make someone or something sound stupid

By and by up came the shepherd. "Oh," he said, "so that's what you'd be doing, is it?" And he took the jackdaw, clipped its wings and carried it home to his children. It looked so odd that they didn't know what to make of it. (what to make of it: what it was)

"What sort of bird is it, father?" they asked.

"It's a jackdaw," he replied, "and nothing but a jackdaw, but it wants to be taken for an eagle." (taken for: regarded as)

If you attempt what is beyond your power, your effort will be wasted and you risk not only misfortune but ridicule. (attempt: try to do; ridicule: unkind laughter or words)

ram

wool

Stop & Think

What does this fable teach people?

CHECK UP | **Finish the sentences.**

1 The eagle
2 The jackdaw
3 The shepherd

a. clipped the jackdaw's wings.
b. carried the lamb off in its claws.
c. got caught in the ram's wool.

GRAMMAR POINT

not only . . . but (also) . . .

- You risk **not only** misfortune **but** ridicule.

68 The Lark and the Farmer

A lark nested (built a nest) in a field of corn, and was raising her young under cover of the ripening (becoming ripe) grain. One day, before the young were fully grown, the farmer came to look at the crop, and finding it turning yellow fast, he said, "I must send word to my neighbors to come and help me harvest this field."

One of the young larks heard him, and was very much frightened, and asked her mother to move house at once.

"There's no hurry," she replied, "a man who looks to (relies on) his friends for help will take his time about a thing (do a thing at his leisure)." In a few days the farmer came by again, and saw that the grain was overripe (too ripe) and falling upon the ground.

Stop & Think

Where did the lark raise her young?

lark

harvest

frightened

KEY WORDS

- **grain** the seeds from crops such as wheat that are used for food
- **harvest** to collect crops that are ripe
- **look to** to rely on
- **take one's time** to do something at one's leisure
- **overripe** too ripe
- **put . . . off** to delay doing something
- **no longer** not . . . anymore
- **in hand** under control

"I must put it off no longer," he said. "This very day I'll hire the men and set them to work at once." The lark heard him and said to her young, "Come, my children, we must be off. He talks no more of his friends now, but is going to take things in hand himself."

delay / away / under control

Self-help is the best help.

Stop & Think

Why did the lark decide to move after the farmer came back?

CHECK UP | **Fill in the blanks with the correct words.**

no longer   look to   in hand   overripe

1 The farmer planned to ____________ his friends for help.
2 The grain was ____________ and falling upon the ground.
3 The farmer said, "I must put it off ____________."
4 The farmer was going to take things ____________ himself.

GRAMMAR POINT

no longer
- I must put it off **no longer**.

69 The Miser

Stop & Think

How did the miser lose his lump of gold?

A miser sold everything he had, and melted down his store of gold (all of the gold that he had saved) into a single lump, which he buried secretly in a field. Every day he went to look at it, and would sometimes spend long hours admiring his treasure.

One of his workers noticed his frequent visits to the spot, (he visited the spot very often) and one day watched him and discovered his secret. Awaiting (Waiting for) an opportunity, the worker went one night and dug up the gold and stole it.

The next day the miser visited the place as usual (like he always did) and finding his treasure gone, fell to (began) tearing (violently pulling) his hair out and groaning over his loss.

KEY WORDS

- **miser** one who wants to keep all of his or her money and is unwilling to spend any of it
- **melt** to turn something solid into liquid
- **lump** a solid pile or piece of something
- **bury** to put something in the ground and cover it with dirt
- **frequent** happening often
- **await** to wait for
- **groan** to make a deep sound showing pain or worry
- **condition** situation
- **tell someone of something** to inform someone about something
- **worse off** less fortunate

In this condition (situation) he was seen by one of his neighbors, who asked him what his trouble was. The miser told him of his misfortune, but the other replied, "Don't take (think about) it so badly, my friend. Put a brick into the hole, and take a look at it every day. You won't be any worse off (less fortunate) than before, for even when you had your gold, it was of no use to you."

The true value of money is not in having it, but in using it wisely.

lumps of gold **bury** **treasure** **bricks**

Stop & Think

What was the neighbor's advice?

CHECK UP | Answer the questions.

1 Where did the miser bury his lump of gold?
   a. Next to a store. b. In a field. c. Under his house.

2 How was the worker able to find out the miser's secret?
   a. He saw the miser visiting the same spot all the time.
   b. The miser told him about the gold.
   c. The miser tore his hair out and groaned over his loss.

GRAMMAR POINT

spend . . . + V-ing

- Every day the miser went to look at it, and would sometimes **spend** long hours **admiring** his treasure.

70 The Lion and the Mouse

lair

paw

gnaw

set free

A lion asleep in his lair (a place where a lion lives) was woken up by a mouse running over his face. Losing his temper, he seized it with his paw (foot) and was about to kill it.

The mouse, terrified, begged him to spare its life (let it live). "Please let me go," it cried, "and one day I will repay you for your kindness."

The idea of so small a creature ever being able to do anything for him amused the lion (the lion felt the mouse's idea was funny) so much that he laughed aloud, and happily let it go.

But the mouse's chance came after all. One day the lion got caught in a net which had been spread by some hunters, and the mouse heard and recognized his roars (shouts) of anger and ran to the spot. Immediately it set to work (began working) gnawing (repeatedly biting) the ropes with its teeth, and before long succeeded in setting the lion free (releasing the lion).

Stop & Think

Why did the lion lose his temper?

KEY WORDS

- **lose one's temper** to suddenly get angry
- **paw** the foot of some animals such as cats, dogs, and lions
- **repay** to pay back; to reward someone who has been kind to you
- **kindness** the act of being kind
- **roar** a loud noise made by an animal, machine, or person
- **gnaw** to bite something hard repeatedly
- **succeed in** ≠ fail to
- **set one free** to let one go free; to release one

"There!" said the mouse. "You laughed at me when I promised I would repay you, but now you see that even a mouse can help a lion."

Kindness is never wasted.

Stop & Think

What does this fable teach people?

CHECK UP | **Put the events in order by marking them 1, 2, 3, and 4.**

_____ The lion seized the mouse with his paw and was about to kill it.
_____ The mouse succeeded in setting the lion free.
_____ The lion got caught in a net.
_____ The lion, asleep in his lair, was woken up by a mouse running over his face.

GRAMMAR POINT

repay someone for something

- I will **repay you for** your **kindness**.

71 The Milkmaid and Her Pail

A farmer's daughter had been out to milk the cows (get milk from the cows), and was returning to the dairy carrying her pail of milk upon her head.

As she walked along, she started thinking in this way: "The milk in this pail will provide me with cream, which I will make into (turn into) butter and take to the market to sell. With the money I will buy a number of (several) eggs, and these, when hatched, will produce chickens, and by and by I shall have quite a large poultry yard (a yard where birds that are used for food are raised). Then I shall sell some of my chickens, and with the money which they bring in I will buy myself a new gown, which I shall wear when I go to the fair (festival). And all the young fellows will admire it, and fall in love with me, but I shall toss my head and have nothing to say to them."

(the milkmaid pretended to ignore the young fellows in her mind)

Stop & Think

Where did the milkmaid put her pail of milk?

milkmaid

pail

poultry yard

KEY WORDS

- **dairy** a place on a farm where milk is kept or cheese is made
- **pail** a bucket
- **make . . . into** to turn . . . into
- **a number of** several
- **hatch** (eggs) to break open so that a baby bird, fish, etc. can come out
- **poultry** birds such as chickens that are used for meat or eggs
- **gown** a long dress
- **toss** to turn one's head quickly up and to the side
- **fantasy** something one imagines; a daydream
- **vanish** to disappear

Lost in her thoughts and forgetting all about the pail, she tossed her head. Down went the pail, all the milk was spilled (came out), and all her fine fantasies vanished (the pleasant things she thought about disappeared) in a moment!

Do not count your chickens before they are hatched.

egg hatched **gown** **spill**

Stop & Think

Did the milkmaid's dream come true?

CHECK UP | True or false?

1 The milkmaid had been out to milk the cows. ________
2 The milkmaid carried her pail of milk in her arms. ________
3 The milkmaid forgot all about the pail. ________

GRAMMAR POINT

have nothing to V

- I shall toss my head and **have nothing to say** to them.

72 The Woman and the Farmer

A woman, who had recently lost her husband, used to go every day to his grave and weep over her loss. A farmer, who was plowing not far from the spot, saw the woman and desired to have her for his wife, so he left his plow and came and sat by her side, and began to shed tears himself.

weep-wept-wept

shed-shed-shed

cry; weep

She asked him why he wept, and he replied, "I have just lost my wife, who was very dear to me, and tears ease my grief." "And I," she said, "have just lost my husband." And so for a while they mourned in silence.

help me feel less sad

Then he said, "Since you and I are in the same situation, why don't we marry and live together? I shall take the place of your dead husband, and you that of my dead wife." The woman agreed to the plan, which indeed seemed reasonable enough, and they dried their tears.

replace

Stop & Think
Do you think that the farmer had really lost his wife? Why?

grave

mourn

breast

KEY WORDS

- **used to** did often or regularly in the past, but not anymore now
- **grave** a place where a dead body has been put underground
- **weep** to cry *weep–wept–wept
- **shed tears** to cry; to weep *shed–shed–shed
- **ease** to make things less difficult, unpleasant, or painful
- **grief** great sadness
- **mourn** to feel or express great sadness, especially because of someone's death
- **take the place of** to replace
- **reasonable** making good sense; easy to agree with (≠ unreasonable)
- **theft** the action or crime of stealing
- **breast** chest; the part of one's body above the stomach

Meanwhile, a thief had come and stolen the oxen which the farmer had left with his plow. On discovering the theft, the farmer beat his breast and cried loudly over his loss.

In the meantime

singular: ox

When the woman heard his cries, she came and said, "Oh! Are you weeping still?" to which he replied, "Yes, and I mean it this time."

(the farmer was really crying over his lost oxen, not pretending to cry as he had done with the woman)

Stop & Think

What does this fable teach people?

CHECK UP | Finish the sentences.

1 The woman
2 The farmer
3 A thief

a. desired to have the woman for his wife.
b. came and stole the farmer's oxen.
c. had recently lost her husband.

GRAMMAR POINT

used to V

- A woman, who had recently lost her husband, **used to go** every day to his grave and weep over her loss.

73 The Monkey and the Dolphin

73

When people go on a voyage, they often take with them small dogs or monkeys as pets to while away the time. Thus it happened that a man returning to Athens from the east had a pet monkey on board with him.

long journey by sea / spend time doing something pleasant / the capital city of Greece

As they neared the coast of Attica, a great storm burst upon them, and the ship sank. All on board were thrown into the water, and tried to save themselves by swimming, the monkey among them. A dolphin saw him and, assuming him to be a man, took him on his back and began swimming toward the shore.

approached / burst-burst-burst / interrupted / thinking / human being

When they got near the Piraeus, which is the port of Athens, the dolphin asked the monkey if he was an Athenian. The monkey replied that he was, and added that he came from a very distinguished family.

citizen of Athens / successful and respected

Stop & Think

What happened when the ship was near the coast of Attica?

KEY WORDS

- **burst upon** to interrupt someone or something very suddenly *burst–burst–burst
- **assume** to think something is true
- **port** a harbor
- **distinguished** successful and respected by many people
- **refer to** to mean
- **official** one in an important position in a government
- **dishonesty** ≠ honesty
- **disgusted** feeling very angry and upset

"Then of course you know the Piraeus," continued the dolphin. The monkey thought he was referring to some high official or other, and replied, "Oh, yes; he's a very old friend of mine."

a; not specific

At that, detecting the monkey's dishonesty, the dolphin was so disgusted that he dove below the surface, and the unfortunate monkey was quickly drowned.

finding out

≠ honesty

died quickly under the water

dolphin

port

Athenians

official

Stop & Think

Why did the dolphin dive down into the sea?

CHECK UP | **Choose the right words.**

1 The dolphin __________ the monkey to be a man. (burst upon | assumed)
2 The monkey thought the dolphin was ______________ some high official. (referring to | detecting)
3 The monkey said that he came from a very _________________ family. (disgusted| distinguished)

GRAMMAR POINT

begin + V-ing (= begin to V)

- A dolphin saw the monkey and, assuming him to be a man, took him on his back and **began swimming** toward the shore.
  (= A dolphin saw the monkey and, assuming him to be a man, took him on his back and **began to swim** toward the shore.)

74 The Ass and His Burdens

74

A peddler who owned an ass one day bought a quantity of salt, and loaded up his beast with as much as he could carry. On the way home, the ass slipped as he was crossing a stream and fell into the water. The salt got thoroughly wet and much of it melted and drained away, so that when he got on his legs again, the ass found his load had become much lighter.

His master, however, drove him back to town and bought more salt, which he added to what remained in the baskets, and started out again. As soon as they had reached the stream, the ass lay down in it and rose, as before, with a much lighter load.

Stop & Think
What did the peddler load the ass up with?

- **peddler** a traveling trader who sells small goods
- **a quantity of** an amount of
- **load up** to put a load on or in something or someone
- **drain away** to be carried away by water
- **sponge** a soft item which absorbs water, used for cleaning things
- **soak up** to take in; to absorb
- **burden** something heavy that one has to carry

But his master detected (found out) the trick and turning back once more, bought a large number of sponges and piled them on the back of the ass. When they came to the stream the ass again lay down, but this time, as the sponges soaked up (absorbed) large quantities of water, the ass found when he got up on his legs that he had a heavier burden to carry than ever.

You may play a good card (use a clever trick) once too often (once or twice).

peddler

slip

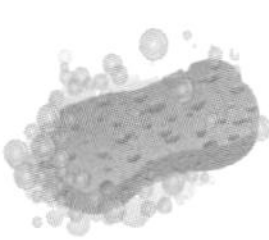

sponge

Stop & Think

Was the peddler nice to the ass?

CHECK UP | **Fill in the blanks with the correct words.**

drained soaked burden peddler

1 A ____________ who owned an ass one day bought a quantity of salt.
2 The salt got thoroughly wet and much of it melted and ____________ away.
3 The sponges ____________ up large quantities of water.
4 The ass had a heavier ____________ to carry than ever.

GRAMMAR POINT

as much as one can / could

- A peddler who owned an ass one day bought a quantity of salt, and loaded up his beast with **as much as he could** carry.

75 The Farmer, His Boy, and the Rooks

A farmer had just sown (planted) a field of wheat, and was keeping a careful watch over it, for large numbers of rooks and starlings kept settling on it and eating up the grain. Along with him went his boy, carrying a sling, and whenever (anytime) the farmer asked for the sling, the starlings understood what he said and warned the rooks and they all flew off in a moment. So the farmer thought of a trick. "My boy," he said, "we must get the better of (beat) these birds somehow. After this, when I want the sling, I won't say 'sling,' but just 'Humph!' and you must then hand (give) me the sling quickly."

Presently the whole flock (group of birds) came back. "Humph!" said the farmer, but the starlings took no notice, and he had time to sling (shoot) several stones among them, hitting one on the head, another in the legs, and another on the wing, before they got out of range (too far away to be shot).

Stop & Think
Why did the farmer keep a careful watch over his wheat?

rook

starling

sling

KEY WORDS

- **keep a watch over** to pay close attention to something in order to protect it
- **warn** to tell someone about something dangerous so that he or she can avoid it
- **fly off** to fly away
- **get the better of** to beat or defeat
- **hand** to give
- **out of range** too far away to be hit or shot
- **rascal** a dishonest person; a troublemaker

As they quickly flew away, they met some cranes, who asked them what the matter was. "Matter?" said one of the rooks. "It's those rascals, men, that are the matter. Don't you go near them. They have a way of saying one thing and meaning another, which has just been the death of several of our poor friends."

what the problem was

dishonest humans

(what the farmer and his boy did)

a flock of birds

Stop & Think

What was the farmer's new way of asking for his sling?

CHECK UP | Answer the questions.

1 What was the farmer shooting at?

a. His boy. b. Cranes. c. Starlings.

2 How did the farmer successfully solve his problem?

a. He got a gun. b. He changed what he said. c. He killed the cranes.

GRAMMAR POINT

ask someone wh- S (subject) + V (verb) (indirect question)

- As they quickly flew away, they met some cranes, who **asked them what the matter was.**

76 The Owl and the Birds

The owl is a very wise bird, and once, long ago, when the first oak appeared in the forest, she called all the other birds together and said to them, "You see this tiny tree? If you take my advice, you will destroy it now, while it is small, for when it grows big, mistletoe (a bush that produces small white fruits) will appear upon it, from which birdlime (a sticky substance that is spread on branches to catch small birds) will be prepared for your destruction (death)."

Again, when the first flax (a plant whose stem is used to make a strong cloth) was sown, she said to them, "Go and eat up that seed, for it is the seed of the flax, out of which men will one day make nets to catch you."

Stop & Think

How did the other birds react to the owl's advice?

KEY WORDS

- **take one's advice** to do as one suggests
- **destruction** complete ruin or damage; death
- **deadly** able or likely to kill people or animals
- **turn out** to happen; to end up; to become
- **wisdom** the ability to make good decisions by using one's knowledge and experience
- **hence** therefore; thus
- **ponder** to think deeply
- **foolishness** the state of being foolish

Once more, when she saw the first hunter, she warned the birds that he was their deadly enemy, who would wing his arrows with their own feathers (use their own feathers to make his arrows) and shoot them.

But the birds took no notice of what she said; in fact, they thought she was rather mad (crazy) and laughed at her. When, however, everything turned out (ended up) just as she had said, they changed their minds and developed (came to have) a great respect for her wisdom. Hence (Thus), whenever she appears, the birds pay attention to her in the hope of hearing something that may be useful to them. She, however, no longer gives them advice, but just sits sadly pondering the foolishness of her kind (other birds).

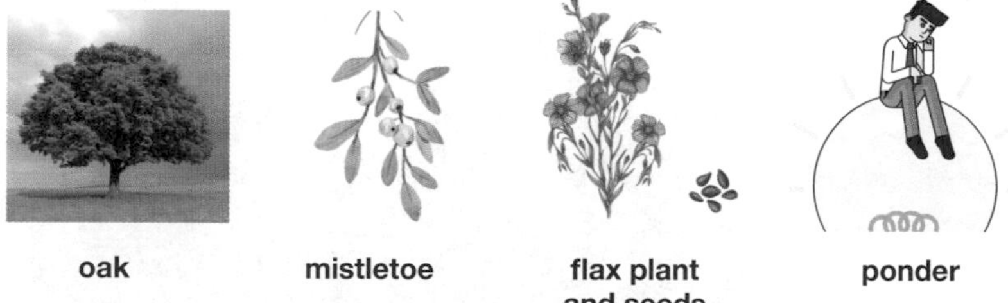

oak | mistletoe | flax plant and seeds | ponder

Stop & Think

What does this fable teach people?

CHECK UP | **True or false?**

1 The owl is not a wise bird. ________

2 The birds took the owl's advice. ________

3 The owl no longer gives other birds advice. ________

GRAMMAR POINT

warn that S (subject) + V (verb) . . .

- The owl **warned** the birds **that the hunter was** their deadly enemy.

77 The Dog and the Cook

77

A rich man once invited a number of his friends and acquaintances (people the rich man knew) to a feast. His dog thought it would be a good opportunity to invite another dog, a friend of his, so he went to him and said, "My master is giving a feast. There'll be plenty of fine food, so come and dine (eat) with me tonight." The dog thus invited came, and when he saw the preparations being made in the kitchen, he said to himself, "My word, I'm in luck (lucky); I'll make sure to eat enough tonight to last me (keep my stomach full) two or three days."

Stop & Think
What did the cook do to the dog that had been invited to the feast?

KEY WORDS

- **plenty** a large amount of something
- **last** to continue to be enough for a period of time
- **wag** (dogs) to move the tail quickly from side to side
- **briskly** fast, swiftly
- **nasty** serious; bad
- **limp** to walk with difficulty because one's foot or leg is hurt
- **howl** (animals) to make a long loud sound
- **splendid** excellent; wonderful; very rich and grand
- **expense** cost; loss

At the same time, he wagged his tail briskly to show his friend how delighted he was to have been asked. But just then the cook noticed him and, in his anger at seeing a strange dog in the kitchen, grabbed him by his back legs and threw him out the window. The dog had a nasty (serious) fall and limped away as quickly as he could, howling miserably.

Presently some other dogs met him and said, "Well, what sort of a dinner did you get?" to which he replied, "I had a splendid (wonderful) time. The wine was so good, and I drank so much of it, that I really don't remember how I got out of the house!"

Be shy (careful) of favors offered at the expense of others (making another person look silly).

feast

limp

howling

Stop & Think

Why did the poor dog lie to the other dogs about what had happened at the feast?

CHECK UP | **Finish the sentences.**

1 The rich man
2 The rich man's dog
3 The cook

a. was angry to see a strange dog.
b. gave a feast.
c. invited another dog to the feast.

GRAMMAR POINT

make sure to

- I'll **make sure to** eat enough tonight to last me two or three days.

78 The Lion, the Wolf, and the Fox

A lion, ill with age, lay sick in his den, and all the beasts of the forest came to inquire after his health with the exception of the fox.

getting sick as he got old / except for

The wolf thought this was a good opportunity for some revenge against the fox, so he called the lion's attention to his absence and said, "You see, sire, that we have all come to see how you are except the fox, who hasn't come near you, and doesn't care whether you are well or ill."

≠ presence / (an old word used for talking to a king; the lion was the king here)

Just then the fox came in and heard the last words of the wolf. The lion roared at him in deep displeasure, but he begged to be allowed to explain his absence and said, "Not one of them cares for you so much as I, sire, for all this time I have been going around to the doctors and trying to find a cure for your illness."

made a loud, deep sound

Stop & Think
Which animal was the last to visit the ill lion?

ill

beasts

KEY WORDS

- **inquire after** to ask about the health or condition of someone
- **exception** someone or something that is not included in a group
- **absence** the fact of being absent (≠ presence)
- **displeasure** a feeling of unhappiness (≠ pleasure)
- **cure** treatment
- **illness** sickness
- **prescription** a particular treatment or medicine which a doctor has told one to take
- **stir up** to arouse feelings; to provoke

"And may I ask if you have found one?" said the lion. "I have, sire," said the fox, "and it is this: you must skin (*remove the skin of*) a wolf and wrap (*cover*) yourself in his skin while it is still warm." The lion thus turned to the wolf and struck him dead with one blow of his paw, in order to try the fox's prescription (*medicine; treatment*). But the fox laughed and said to himself, "That's what you get for stirring up ill will (*a feeling of dislike or hatred*)."

wrap

prescription

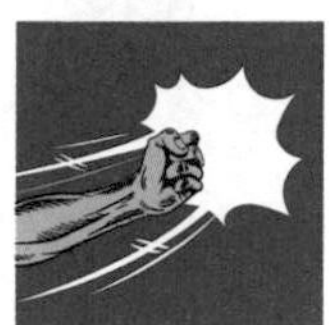

strike

Stop & Think

Was there really a doctor's prescription for the lion?

CHECK UP | Choose the right words.

1 All the beasts of the forest came to ________________ the lion's health. (inquire after | stir up)

2 The lion roared at the fox in deep ________________. (absence | displeasure)

3 The fox said he had been trying to find a cure for the lion's ____________. (prescription | illness)

GRAMMAR POINT

with the exception of + N (noun)

- All the beasts of the forest came to inquire after his health **with the exception of the fox.**

79 The Eagle and the Beetle

79

An eagle was chasing (pursuing) a hare, who was running for dear life (as fast as she could) and didn't know where to turn for help. Eventually she saw a beetle, and begged it to aid her. So when the eagle flew up, the beetle warned her not to touch the hare, which was under its protection.

But the eagle never noticed the beetle because it was so small, and seized the hare and ate her up. The beetle never forgot this, and kept an eye on (closely watched) the eagle's nest, and whenever the eagle laid an egg, the beetle climbed up and rolled it out of the nest and broke it.

At last the eagle got so worried over the loss of her eggs that she

Stop & Think

Who did the hare turn to for help?

hare

beetle

roll

KEY WORDS

- **for dear life** with as much effort as possible, usually to avoid danger
- **eventually** finally
- **beetle** an insect with a smooth hard back
- **protection** the act of protecting
- **keep an eye on** to watch something or someone closely
- **protector** one who protects others
- **lap** the upper part of one's legs when one sits down
- **dirt** small pieces of soil or mud
- **deposit** to put something somewhere
- **robe** a long loose piece of clothing
- **insult** an action or comment that seriously hurts someone's feelings

went up to Jupiter, who is the special protector of eagles, and begged him to give her a safe place to nest in. So he let her lay her eggs in his lap. But the beetle noticed this and made a ball of dirt the size of an eagle's egg, then flew up and deposited it in Jupiter's lap.

nest in: build a nest

deposited: put

When Jupiter saw the dirt, he stood up to shake it out of his robe and forgetting about the eggs, he shook them out too, and so they were broken just as before. Ever since then, they say, eagles never lay their eggs during the season when beetles are about.

about: nearby

The weak will sometimes find ways to avenge an insult, even upon the strong.

The weak: Weak people or animals

avenge an insult: get revenge when something bad is done or said to them

Stop & Think

How did Jupiter accidentally break the eagle's eggs?

CHECK UP | **Fill in the blanks with the correct words.**

protector lap protection dirt

1 The beetle warned the eagle that the hare was under its ____________.
2 Jupiter is the special ____________ of eagles.
3 The beetle made a ball of ____________ the size of an eagle's egg.
4 The beetle deposited the dirt in Jupiter's ____________.

GRAMMAR POINT

who (relative pronoun)

- An eagle was chasing a hare, **who** was running for dear life and didn't know where to turn for help.
- The eagle went up to Jupiter, **who** is the special protector of eagles.

80 The Old Woman and the Doctor

80

An old woman became almost totally blind from a disease of the eyes and, after consulting a doctor, made an agreement with him in the presence of witnesses (when witnesses were there in person) that she would pay him a high fee if he cured (successfully treated) her, while if he failed, he was to receive nothing.

The doctor therefore prescribed a course of treatment (said or wrote down what medicine she should take), and every time he paid the old woman a visit, he took away with him something from her house until at last, when he visited her for the last time and the cure (treatment) was complete, there was nothing left.

Stop & Think

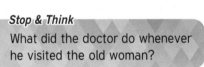

What did the doctor do whenever he visited the old woman?

KEY WORDS

- **disease** an illness
- **consult** to ask for advice from someone who has special knowledge about a subject
- **witness** one who watches you sign an official document
- **cure** to treat successfully
- **prescribe** (a doctor) to say or write down what medicine or other treatment one should take
- **pay one a visit** to visit someone
- **refusal** the act of refusing to do something
- **sue** to make a legal claim against someone in court
- **payment** the amount of money one has to pay
- **defense** an excuse or reason one gives in court for doing or not doing something
- **state** to express something in a formal way
- **according to** based on

When the old woman saw that her house was empty, she refused to pay the doctor his fee, and after repeated refusals on her part, he sued her before the judges for payment of her debt. On being brought into court, she was ready with her defense.

reason for not paying her debt

"The doctor," she said, "has stated the facts of our agreement correctly. I agreed to pay him a fee if he cured me, and he, on his part, promised to charge nothing if he failed. Now he says I am cured, but I say that I am blinder than ever, and I can prove what I say. When my eyes were bad, I could still see well enough to be aware that my house contained a certain amount of furniture and other things. But now, when according to him I am cured, I am entirely unable to see anything there at all."

expressed / ask for no money / completely

blind

consulting a doctor

court

furniture

Stop & Think

What was the real reason why the old woman refused to pay for the treatment?

CHECK UP | **Put the events in order by marking them 1, 2, 3, and 4.**

_____ The doctor sued the old woman before the judges for payment of her debt.
_____ The old woman refused to pay the doctor his fee.
_____ The old woman became almost totally blind.
_____ The doctor prescribed a course of treatment.

GRAMMAR POINT

sue someone for something

- The doctor **sued the old woman** before the judges **for payment** of her debt.

81 The Fox and the Goat

81

A fox fell into a well and was unable to get out again. By and by a thirsty goat came by and, seeing the fox in the well, asked him if the water was good.

"Good?" said the fox. "It's the best water I've ever tasted in all my life. Come down and try it yourself." The goat thought of nothing but *(only)* the prospect *(opportunity; chance)* of quenching his thirst *(satisfying his need to drink water)*, and jumped in at once.

When he had had enough to drink, he looked about, like the fox, for some way of getting out, but could find none. Then the fox said, "I have an idea. You stand on your back legs, plant your front legs firmly *(press your front legs strongly)* against the side of the well, and then I'll climb onto your back and, from there, by stepping on your horns, I can get out. And when

Stop & Think

Do you think that the fox will help the goat out? Why?

quench one's thirst

beard

KEY WORDS

- **prospect** opportunity; chance; possibility; expectation
- **plant** to press; to put
- **firmly** strongly; with force
- **remind one of** to tell one that he or she should do or remember something
- **sense** good judgment
- **make certain** to check that something is correct or true; to make sure
- **leap** to jump *leap–leapt–leapt

I'm out, I'll help you out too." The goat did as he was requested (asked), the fox climbed onto the goat's back and so out of the well, and then he coolly (without showing any emotion) walked away.

The goat called loudly after him and reminded him of his promise to help him out, but the fox merely (simply) turned and said, "If you had as much sense (good judgment) in your head as you have hair in your beard, you wouldn't have jumped into the well without making certain that you could get out again."

Look before you leap (jump; leap-leapt-leapt).

leap

Stop & Think

What does this fable teach people?

CHECK UP | **Answer the questions.**

1 Why did the goat jump into the well?

a. To save the fox. b. To drink water. c. To plant his front legs.

2 What should the goat have done before he jumped into the well?

a. He should have discussed it with the fox. b. He should have made sure he could get out.
c. He should have walked coolly away.

GRAMMAR POINT

remind someone of something

- The goat called loudly after him and **reminded him of his promise** to help him out.

82 The Town Mouse and the Country Mouse

82

A town mouse and a country mouse were acquaintances, and the country mouse one day invited his friend to come and see him at his home in the fields.

The town mouse came, and they sat down to a dinner of barleycorns (a type of grain) and roots, the latter of which had a distinctly earthy (smelling or tasting like soil) flavor. The fare was not much to the taste of the guest, (the town mouse did not like the food) and after a while he said, "My poor dear friend, you live here no better than (just like) the ants. Now, you should just see how I fare (do)! My larder is a regular treasure chest. You must come and stay with me, and I promise you you shall live off the fat of the land (get enough food to live comfortably without doing much work)."

Stop & Think

Did the town mouse like the dinner that the country mouse offered him?

barleycorns

root

KEY WORDS

- **distinctly** clearly; very
- **flavor** taste
- **fare** food that is available; to do well or badly in a situation
- **to the taste of someone** to one's liking
- **chest** a large strong box
- **luxury** something one enjoys but does not need, especially something expensive or fancy
- **uncomfortable** ≠ comfortable
- **venture** to go somewhere that could be dangerous
- **in the lap of luxury** having an easy and comfortable life with a lot of valuable things
- **surround** to be all around someone or something
- **whereas** but; while

So when he returned to town, he took the country mouse with him, and showed him into a larder containing flour and oatmeal and figs and honey and dates (a type of fruits). The country mouse had never seen anything like it, and sat down to enjoy the luxuries (delicious and excellent food) his friend provided. But before they had well begun, the door of the larder opened and someone came in. The two mice ran off and hid themselves in a narrow and extremely uncomfortable hole. A short time later, when all was quiet, they ventured out (came out) again, but someone else came in, and off they hurried again. This was too much for the visitor. (the country mouse couldn't put up with it anymore)

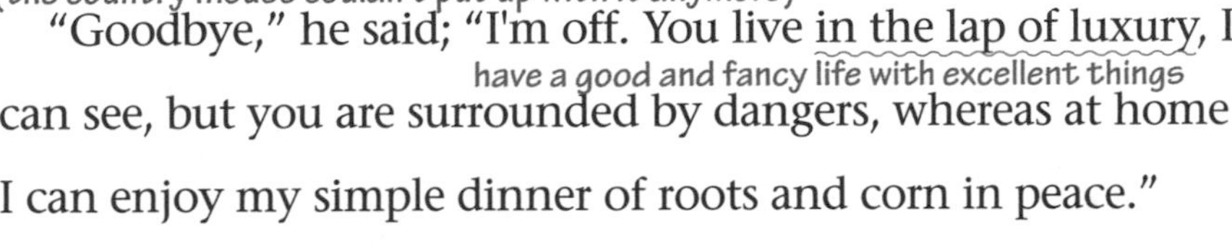

"Goodbye," he said; "I'm off. You live in the lap of luxury (have a good and fancy life with excellent things), I can see, but you are surrounded by dangers, whereas at home I can enjoy my simple dinner of roots and corn in peace."

larder

oatmeal

figs

dates

Better a simple meal in peace than a fancy meal in fear.

Stop & Think

Why did the country mouse decide to leave his friend's home?

CHECK UP | True or false?

1 The barleycorns had a distinctly earthy flavor. ________
2 The country mouse's fare was not much to the taste of the town mouse. ________
3 The two mice ran off and hid in a large hole. ________

GRAMMAR POINT

no better than

- You live here **no better than** the ants.

83 The Eagle and the Fox

An eagle and a fox became great friends and decided to live near one another. They thought that the more they saw of each other, the better friends they would be. So the eagle built a nest at the top of a tall tree, while the fox settled in a grove at the foot of it and produced a litter of cubs.
gave birth to a group of baby foxes

One day the fox went out searching for food, and the eagle, who also wanted food for her young, flew down into the grove, took the fox's cubs, and carried them up into the tree as a meal for herself and her family.

When the fox came back and found out what had happened, she was not so much sorry for the loss of her cubs as furious
(her anger at the eagle was greater than her sadness over the loss of her babies)

Stop & Think
What terrible thing did the eagle do to the fox?

KEY WORDS

- **grove** a small wood or group of trees
- **get at** to reach or touch someone or something
- **pay back** to take revenge on; to get even with
- **nearby** not far away
- **curse** to say bad things about someone so that he or she will have bad luck
- **flesh** meat
- **chick** a baby bird
- **roasted** cooked by fire
- **faith** loyalty; friendship; belief
- **divine** relating to or coming from a god or gods

because she couldn't get at the eagle and pay her back for her treachery. So she sat down nearby and cursed the eagle. But it wasn't long before she had her revenge.

reach / take revenge on her / behavior that betrays or is not loyal to someone who trusts you

Some villagers happened to be sacrificing a goat on a neighboring altar, and the eagle flew down and carried off a piece of the burning flesh to her nest. There was a strong wind blowing and the nest caught fire, with the result that her chicks fell half-roasted to the ground. Then the fox ran to the spot and ate them all in full sight of the eagle.

people who live in a village / killing to honor gods / meat / while the eagle watched

False faith may escape human punishment, but cannot escape the divine.

friendship

grove

fox's cub

flesh

chicks

Stop & Think

What does this fable teach people?

CHECK UP | **Fill in the blanks with the correct words.**

get at faith chicks grove

1 The fox settled in a ______________ at the foot of the tall tree.
2 The fox was furious because she couldn't ______________ the eagle.
3 The eagle's ______________ fell half-roasted to the ground.
4 False ______________ cannot escape divine punishment.

GRAMMAR POINT

not so much . . . as . . .

- The fox was **not so much** sorry for the loss of her cubs **as** furious.

84 Mercury and the Woodcutter

A woodcutter was chopping down a tree on the bank (side) of a river when his axe, glancing off (lightly hitting and bouncing off) the trunk, flew out of his hands and fell into the water.

As he stood by the water's edge despairing (feeling hopeless) over his loss, Mercury (the god of travelers) appeared and asked him the reason for his grief. On learning what had happened, out of (because of) pity for the man he dove into the river and, bringing up a golden axe, asked him if that was the one he had lost. The woodcutter replied that it was not, so Mercury then dove a second time and bringing up a silver axe, asked if that was his.

"No, that is not mine either," said the woodcutter.

Stop & Think
How many times did Mercury dive into the river for the poor woodcutter?

Once more Mercury dove into the river, and brought up the missing axe. The woodcutter was overjoyed at recovering (getting back his axe)

KEY WORDS

- **chop down** to cut down (a tree)
- **glance off** to hit something lightly and then move quickly in another direction
- **despair** to feel that there is no hope at all
- **property** something that one owns
- **try one's luck** to take a chance and hope to succeed
- **previous** last; the time, thing or person right before the present one
- **occasion** an event
- **stretch** to pull one's body or a part of one's body to full length
- **eagerly** showing a strong desire or will; excitedly
- **decline** to refuse

his property, and thanked Mercury warmly. And the latter was so pleased with the man's honesty that he made the woodcutter a present of the other two axes.

woodcutter

When the woodcutter told this story to his companions, one of them was filled with envy of his good fortune (luck), and decided to try his own luck (do the same thing and hope it works). So he went and began to chop down a tree at the edge of the river, and soon let his axe drop into the water.

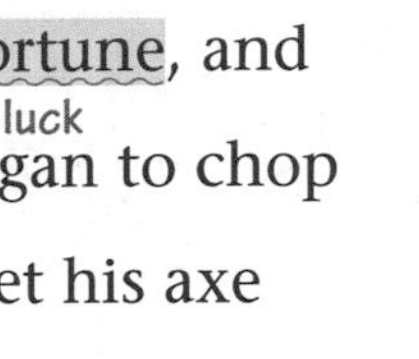

golden and silver axes

Mercury appeared as before and, on learning that the fellow's axe had fallen in, he dove and brought up a golden axe, just as he had done on the previous occasion (the last time). Without waiting to be asked whether it was his or not, the fellow cried, "That's mine! That's mine!" and stretched out his hands eagerly for the prize. But Mercury was so disgusted (upset) at his dishonesty that he not only declined (refused) to give him the golden axe, but also refused to recover for him the one he had let fall into the stream.

stretch out one's hand

Stop & Think

What does this fable teach people?

Honesty is the best policy.

CHECK UP | Put the events in order by marking them 1, 2, 3, and 4.

_____ The poor woodcutter's axe flew out of his hands and fell into the water.
_____ The woodcutter's companion let his axe drop into the water.
_____ Mercury dove into the river and brought up a golden axe for the first woodcutter.
_____ Mercury gave the woodcutter the golden and silver axes as a present.

GRAMMAR POINT

be filled with

- One of the woodcutter's companions **was filled with** envy of his good fortune.

英文閱讀聽力素養訓練課

伊｜索｜寓｜言｜故｜事

作者

原著 Aesop

英譯 V.S. Vernon Jones

改寫 Richard Luhrs

英英解釋與測驗題 Olanda Lin

譯者 羅竹君／林晨禾

編輯 林晨禾

插畫 幸品瑄／楊雅媛／楊盟玉
夏萱／宋雅圓／高嘉玟

校對 黃詩韻

內文排版 林書玉（課本）／謝青秀（訓練書）

封面設計 林書玉

製程管理 洪巧玲

發行人 黃朝萍

出版者 語言工場出版有限公司

電話 +886-(0)2-2365-9739

傳真 +886-(0)2-2365-9835

網址 www.icosmos.com.tw

讀者服務 onlineservice@icosmos.com.tw

出版日期 2024 年04月 初版二刷 （寂天雲隨身聽APP版）

作者簡介

V.S. Vernon Jones

為二十世紀之翻譯家，於1912 年完成多篇《伊索寓言》之翻譯。

Richard Luhrs

紐約州立大學（State University of New York）英語寫作系與哲學系（BA in English Composition and Philosophy）雙學士，於日本、台灣、韓國等地從事英語教學二十餘年，曾替LTTC財團法人語言訓練測驗中心及各出版社編寫英語教材。

國家圖書館出版品預行編目(CIP)資料

英文閱讀聽力素養訓練課：伊索寓言故事(寂天雲隨身聽APP版) / Aesop原著；Richard Luhrs改寫；V.S. Vernon Jones英譯.-- 初版. --
[臺北市]：語言工場, 2024.04
面； 公分
ISBN 978-986-6963-88-9 (20K平裝)

1.CST: 英語 2.CST: 讀本
805.18 113003947

劃撥帳號 1998620-0 寂天文化事業股份有限公司
訂書金額未滿 1000 元，請外加運費 100 元。
【若有破損，請寄回更換，謝謝】

英文閱讀聽力素養訓練課

伊|索|寓|言|故|事

TRAINING BOOK + MP3

Table of Contents

Vocabulary & Listening Practice

1 The Bear and the Fox

2 The Lion and the Wild Ass pp. 2–3

❶ Vocabulary Practice: Match.

______	1	**deceive**	A	the act of being kind or giving willingly
______	2	**confine**	B	one who pretends to behave better than he or she really does
______	3	**hypocrite**	C	to keep within limits
______	4	**generosity**	D	to fool other people
______	5	**boast about**	E	to speak too proudly of yourself; to brag
______	6	**portion**	F	to be left after other things or people are gone
______	7	**remain**	G	qualified to get something
______	8	**prey**	H	a part
______	9	**entitled**	I	except if
______	10	**superior**	J	animals that are hunted by other animals for food
______	11	**unless**	K	better (≠ inferior)

Answers ❶

1. D 2. C 3. B 4. A 5. E
6. H 7. F 8. J 9. G 10. K 11. I

❷ Listen and fill in the blanks with the correct words. Remember to change the form of verbs or nouns if necessary.

01

The Bear and the Fox

A bear was once boasting about his 1.______________ and saying how good he was compared with other animals. (There is, in fact, a belief that a bear will never touch a dead body.)

A fox, who heard him talking in this way, smiled and said, "My friend, when you are hungry, please 2.______________ your attention to the dead and leave the living alone."

A hypocrite 3.______________ no one but himself.

02

The Lion and the Wild Ass

A lion and a wild ass went out hunting together. The ass would run down the prey with his 4.______________ speed, and the lion would then come up and kill it. They were very successful, and when it came to sharing the meat the lion divided it all into three equal portions.

"I will take the first," he said, "because I am the king of the beasts. I will also take the second because, as your partner, I am 5.______________ to half of what remains. As for the third, well, 6.______________ you give it up to me and run off pretty quickly, the third, believe me, will make you feel very sorry for yourself!"

Might makes right.

Answers ❷

1. generosity 2. confine 3. deceives 4. superior
5. entitled 6. unless

3 The Butcher and His Customers

4 The Lioness and the Vixen

pp. 4–5

1 Vocabulary Practice: Match.

______	1 **avoid**	A	a group of baby animals that are born at the same time
______	2 **butcher**	B	someone who cuts and sells meat
______	3 **grimly**	C	seriously
______	4 **accuse someone of**	D	a stand or counter at which things are displayed for sale
______	5 **nastily**	E	unkindly
______	6 **stall**	F	to say that someone has done something wrong
______	7 **litter**	G	to stay away from; to try not to do something
______	8 **cub**	H	a young bear, lion, fox, wolf, or other wild animal

Answers

1

1. G 2. B 3. C 4. F 5. E
6. D 7. A 8. H

❷ Listen and fill in the blanks with the correct words. Remember to change the form of verbs or nouns if necessary.

03

The Butcher and His Customers

Two men were buying meat at a butcher's stall in the market and, while the butcher's back was turned for a moment, one of them picked up a 1.______________ and quickly put it inside the other's coat, where it could not be seen.

When the butcher turned around, he noticed the missing meat at once, and 2.______________ the men of having stolen it. But the one who had taken it said he didn't have it, and the one who had it said he hadn't taken it.

The butcher felt sure they were deceiving him, but he only said, "You may cheat me with your lying, but you can't cheat the gods, and they won't let you go so easily."

3.______________ the truth is often the same as lying.

04

The Lioness and the Vixen

A lioness and a vixen were talking together about their children, as mothers will, and saying how healthy and well-grown they were, what beautiful 4.______________ they had, and how they looked just like their parents.

"My litter of cubs is a joy to see," said the fox. Then she added rather 5.______________, "But I notice you never have more than one."

"No," said the lioness grimly, "but that one is a lion."

Quality beats 6.______________.

Answers ❷

1. joint 2. accused 3. Avoiding 4. coats
5. nastily 6. quantity

5 Father and Sons

6 The Fox and the Grapes pp. 6–7

1 Vocabulary Practice: Match.

______	1	**undo**	A	joined together as a group (≠ separate)
______	2	**unity**	B	to argue with others
______	3	**quarrel**	C	one's opinions and behavior
______	4	**convince**	D	to say that something or someone is bad or wrong
______	5	**out of one's reach**	E	in peace
______	6	**in harmony**	F	no use (≠ successful)
______	7	**united**	G	to make others think that something is true
______	8	**in vain**	H	unable to be touched
______	9	**criticize**	I	to open something that is tied
______	10	**attitude**	J	the situation when people are united
______	11	**ripe**	K	pride
______	12	**dignity**	L	(fruits) ready to eat or use

Answers

1

1. I 2. J 3. B 4. G 5. H 6. E
7. A 8. F 9. D 10. C 11. L 12. K

❷ Listen and fill in the blanks with the correct words. Remember to change the form of verbs or nouns if necessary.

05

Father and Sons

A certain man had several sons who were always quarreling with one another, and though he tried very hard, he could not get them to live together 1.______________. So, he decided to convince them of their error by the following means.

Telling them to fetch a bundle of sticks, he asked each in turn to break it across his knee. All tried and all failed. Then he 2.______________ the bundle and handed them the sticks one by one, so that they had no difficulty at all in breaking them.

"There, my boys," he said. "3.______________ you will be more than a match for your enemies, but if you quarrel and separate, you will be weaker than those who attack you."

Unity is strength.

06

The Fox and the Grapes

A hungry fox saw some fine bunches of grapes hanging from a vine that ran along a high wall, and did his best to 4.______________ them by jumping as high as he could into the air.

But it was all in vain, for they were just out of his reach, so he gave up and walked away with an 5.______________ of dignity and unconcern, saying, "I thought those grapes were ripe, but I see now they are quite sour."

It is easy to 6.______________ what you cannot get.

Answers ❷

1. in harmony **2.** undid **3.** United **4.** reach
5. attitude **6.** criticize

7 The Stag with One Eye

8 The Wolf, the Fox, and the Ape pp. 8–9

1 Vocabulary Practice: Match.

______	1	**misfortune**	A	coming closer to something or someone
______	2	**charge someone with**	B	belief; respect
______	3	**graze**	C	surprising; not planned
______	4	**credit**	D	even though; despite
______	5	**suspect**	E	to eat grass
______	6	**evidence**	F	the act of stealing
______	7	**approach**	G	to think something may be true, especially bad things
______	8	**in spite of**	H	a fact or object that helps prove something
______	9	**threaten**	I	to put one in danger; to endanger
______	10	**denial**	J	to accuse someone of
______	11	**unexpected**	K	a terrible event
______	12	**theft**	L	a statement that something that has been said is not true

Answers

1

1.K 2.J 3.E 4.B 5.G 6.H

7.A 8.D 9.I 10.L 11.C 12.F

❷ Listen and fill in the blanks with the correct words. Remember to change the form of verbs or nouns if necessary.

07

The Stag with One Eye

A stag, blind in one eye, was grazing close to the seashore and kept his good eye turned towards the land so that he would be able to see the 1.______________ of any hounds, while the blind eye he turned towards the sea, never suspecting that any danger would 2.______________ him from that side.

As it happened, however, some sailors who were sailing along the shore saw him and shot an arrow at him, by which he was killed. As he lay dying, he said to himself, "What a fool I am! I thought only of the dangers of the land, from where none attacked me, but I feared no danger from the sea, and my ruin has come from there."

Misfortune often attacks us from an 3.______________ direction.

The Wolf, the Fox, and the Ape

A wolf charged a fox with theft, which the fox denied, and the case was brought before an ape to be tried.

When he had heard the 4.______________ from both sides, the ape gave this judgment: "I do not think," he said, "that you, wolf, ever lost what you claim, but I still believe that you, fox, are guilty of the theft, 5.______________ all your denials."

The dishonest get no 6.______________, even if they act honestly.

Answers ❷

1. approach 2. threaten 3. unexpected 4. evidence
5. in spite of 6. credit

9 The Three Tradesmen

10 The Man and the Lion

pp. 10–11

1 Vocabulary Practice: Match.

______	1	**companion**	A the skin of an animal prepared for making clothes or luggage
______	2	**security**	B safety from harm
______	3	**recommend**	C a human or animal image that is made of a material such as stone, metal or wood
______	4	**statue**	D to disagree with
______	5	**situation**	E the condition that exists at a particular time
______	6	**carpenter**	F someone whose job is to make and repair wooden objects
______	7	**journey**	G a long trip
______	8	**object to**	H to say that someone or something is good; to suggest
______	9	**strength**	I to kill a person or an animal by squeezing his, her, or its throat
______	10	**leather**	J a person or animal one spends a lot of time with
______	11	**strangle**	K power

Answers

1. 1. J 2. B 3. H 4. C 5. E 6. F 7. G 8. D 9. K 10. A 11. I

❷ Listen and fill in the blanks with the correct words. Remember to change the form of verbs or nouns if necessary.

09

The Three Tradesmen

The citizens of a certain city were debating about the best material to use for the walls which were about to be built for the greater 1.______________ of the town.

A carpenter got up and advised the use of wood, which he said was easy to get and easy to work with. A stonemason 2.________________ wood because it could burn so easily, and recommended stones instead. Then a tanner got up and said, "In my opinion, there's nothing like 3.______________."

Every man for himself.

10

The Man and the Lion

A man and a lion were companions on a journey, and while talking they both began to 4.________________ their abilities, and each claimed to be superior to the other in strength and courage. They were still arguing angrily when they came to a crossroad where there was a statue of a man 5.______________ a lion.

"There!" said the man proudly. "Look at that! Doesn't that prove to you that we are stronger than you?"

"Not so fast, my friend," said the lion. "That is only your view of the 6.______________. If we lions could make statues, you may be sure that in most of them you would see the man losing."

There are two sides to every story.

Answers ❷

1. security **2.** objected to **3.** leather **4.** boast about
5. strangling **6.** situation

11 The Farmer and the Stork

12 The Boy Bathing pp. 12–13

❶ Vocabulary Practice: Match.

______	1	**suffer**	A to die under water
______	2	**sow**	B doing no harm (≠ harmful)
______	3	**drown**	C to plant seeds in the ground
______	4	**crisis**	D to feel pain in one's body or mind
______	5	**beg**	E help
______	6	**make (an) attempt**	F the things that cover a bird's body
______	7	**feathers**	G to swim; to wash one's body
______	8	**scold**	H to ask strongly for something
______	9	**harmless**	I a plant grown for food
______	10	**bathe**	J to talk angrily about someone's behavior
______	11	**crop**	K a difficult or dangerous situation
______	12	**assistance**	L to make an effort to do something

Answers

❶ **1.** D **2.** C **3.** A **4.** K **5.** H **6.** L **7.** F **8.** J **9.** B **10.** G **11.** I **12.** E

❷ Listen and fill in the blanks with the correct words. Remember to change the form of verbs or nouns if necessary.

11

The Farmer and the Stork

A farmer set some traps in a field which he had recently 1.______________ with corn, in order to catch the cranes which came to eat the seeds. When he returned to look at his traps, he found several cranes caught, and among them a stork, which 2.______________ to be let go and said, "You shouldn't kill me; I am not a crane, but a stork, as you can easily see by my feathers, and I am the most honest and 3.______________ of birds."

But the farmer replied, "I don't care what you are; I find you among these cranes, who ruin my crops, and like them you shall suffer."

If you choose bad companions, no one will believe that you are not bad yourself.

12

The Boy Bathing

A boy was bathing in a river and got into deep water, and was in great danger of 4.______________. A man who was passing along the road heard his cries for help. He went to the riverside and began to scold him for being so careless as to get into deep water, but made no 5.______________ to help him.

"Oh, sir," cried the boy, "please help me first and scold me afterwards."

Give assistance, not advice, in a 6.______________.

Answers ❷

1. sown **2.** begged **3.** harmless **4.** drowning
5. attempt **6.** crisis

13 The Eagle and the Cocks

14 The Flea and the Man

pp. 14–15

❶ Vocabulary Practice: Match.

______	1	**rival**	A completely; carefully
______	2	**creature**	B small in degree, size, or amount
______	3	**cock**	C a place where horses are kept
______	4	**crow**	D a person or thing that competes with another
______	5	**do . . . harm to**	E an adult male chicken; a rooster
______	6	**slight**	F a living thing
______	7	**thoroughly**	G to kill or ruin completely
______	8	**stable**	H (a cock) to make a loud high noise
______	9	**immediately**	I a feeling that you are better than other people
______	10	**destroy**	J to hurt
______	11	**pride**	K without delay; at once
______	12	**terrified**	L extremely afraid; frightened

Answers ❶

1.D 2.F 3.E 4.H 5.J 6.B

7.A 8.C 9.K 10.G 11.I 12.L

❷ Listen and fill in the blanks with the correct words. Remember to change the form of verbs or nouns if necessary.

13

The Eagle and the Cocks

There were two cocks in the same farmyard, and they fought to decide who should be the 1.______________. When the fight was over, the beaten one went and hid himself in a dark corner, while the winner flew up onto the roof of the stable and 2.______________ happily.

But an eagle noticed him from high up in the sky, and flew down and carried him off. Immediately the other cock came out of his corner and ruled the roost without a 3.______________.

Pride comes before a fall.

14

The Flea and the Man

A flea bit a man, and bit him again, and again, till the man could stand it no longer and searched 4.______________ for the flea until at last he succeeded in catching it.

Holding it between his finger and thumb, he said—or rather shouted, so angry was he—"Who are you, you horrible little creature, that you attack me so freely?"

The flea, 5.______________, replied in a weak little voice, "Oh, sir, please let me go; don't kill me! I am such a little thing that I can't do you much harm."

But the man laughed and said, "I am going to kill you right now. Whatever is bad has got to be 6.______________, no matter how slight the harm it does."

Do not waste your pity on a troublemaker.

Answers ❷

1. master **2.** crowed **3.** rival **4.** thoroughly
5. terrified **6.** destroyed

15 The Gnat and the Bull

16 The Serpent and the Eagle pp. 16–17

❶ Vocabulary Practice: Match.

______	**1 merely**	**A** enough
______	**2 encounter**	**B** simply; only
______	**3 contents**	**C** to see something happen
______	**4 horn**	**D** to satisfy one's thirst
______	**5 sufficiently**	**E** one of the hard pointed parts that grow on the heads of some animals
______	**6 witness**	**F** to stay somewhere; to stay the same
______	**7 remain**	**G** to say a few words that express what you think
______	**8 remark**	**H** a fight; a meeting
______	**9 considerable**	**I** large in size, amount, or degree
______	**10 intention**	**J** purpose
______	**11 spit**	**K** to force liquid out of your mouth
______	**12 quench**	**L** the things that are inside something such as a box or bottle

Answers ❶

1.B 2.H 3.L 4.E 5.A 6.C
7.F 8.C 9.I 10.J 11.K 12.D

❷ Listen and fill in the blanks with the correct words. Remember to change the form of verbs or nouns if necessary.

15

The Gnat and the Bull

A gnat landed on one of the horns of a bull, and remained sitting there for a considerable time. When it had rested 1.______________ and was about to fly away, it said to the bull, "Do you mind if I go now?"

The bull merely raised his eyes and 2.______________, without interest, "It's all the same to me; I didn't notice when you came, and I won't know when you go away."

We may often be more important in our own eyes than in the eyes of our 3.______________.

16

The Serpent and the Eagle

An eagle flew down upon a serpent and seized it in his claws with the 4.______________ of carrying it off and eating it. But the serpent was too quick for him and had its coils around him in a moment. There followed a life-and-death struggle between the two.

A countryman, who 5.______________ the encounter, came to the assistance of the eagle, and he succeeded in freeing him from the serpent and enabling him to escape. In revenge, the serpent spat some of his poison into the man's drinking horn.

Heated from his efforts, the man was about to 6.______________ his thirst with a drink from the horn, when the eagle knocked it out of his hand and spilled its 7.______________ upon the ground.

One good turn deserves another.

Answers ❷
1. sufficiently **2.** remarked **3.** neighbors **4.** intention
5. witnessed **6.** quench **7.** contents

17 The Fir Tree and the Bramble

18 The Crow and the Raven

pp. 18–19

1 Vocabulary Practice: Match.

______	**1 obligation**	**A** wanting something very much; eager
______	**2 reputation**	**B** very silly or unreasonable
______	**3 somewhat**	**C** to some degree
______	**4 poverty**	**D** to make one feel worried or unhappy
______	**5 ridiculous**	**E** useless; in vain
______	**6 wealth**	**F** a promise or duty
______	**7 latter**	**G** to behave as if something were real when it's not
______	**8 pretend**	**H** a lack of something
______	**9 (of) no use**	**I** fame
______	**10 anxious**	**J** a large amount of a useful quality or skill
______	**11 upset**	**K** the second of two people or things (≠ former)

Answers

1 1.F 2.I 3.C 4.H 5.B 6.J 7.K 8.G 9.E 10.A 11.D

❷ Listen and fill in the blanks with the correct words. Remember to change the form of verbs or nouns if necessary.

17

The Fir Tree and the Bramble

A fir tree was boasting to a bramble, and said, somewhat contemptuously, "You poor 1.______________; you are of no use at all. Now, look at me. I am useful for all sorts of things, particularly when men build houses; they can't do without me then."

But the bramble replied, "Ah, that's all true, but you wait till they come with 2.______________ and saws to cut you down, and then you'll wish you were a bramble, not a fir."

Better poverty without a care than wealth with its many 3.______________.

18

The Crow and the Raven

A crow became very jealous of a raven because the latter was regarded by men as a bird which could tell the future, and so was greatly respected by them.

The crow was very anxious to get the same sort of 4.______________ herself, and one day, seeing some travelers approaching, she flew onto a branch of a tree at the roadside and cawed as loudly as she could. The travelers were somewhat 5.______________ by the sound, for they feared it might be a bad sign, till one of them, seeing the crow, said to his 6.______________, "It's all right, my friends; we can go on without fear, for it's only a crow and that means nothing."

Those who pretend to be something they are not only make themselves 7.______________.

Answers ❷
1. creature **2.** axes **3.** obligations **4.** reputation
5. upset **6.** companions **7.** ridiculous

19 The Travelers and the Plane Tree

20 The Sheep, the Wolf, and the Stag

pp. 20–21

❶ Vocabulary Practice: Match.

______	**1**	**abuse**	A covered in dust
______	**2**	**wheat**	B empty; having no trees or plants
______	**3**	**take shelter**	C to one side
______	**4**	**dusty**	D to speak to someone rudely or cruelly
______	**5**	**bare**	E to release oneself from a requirement or request
______	**6**	**excuse**	F (a debt) to have to be paid at a particular time
______	**7**	**come due**	G to find a place in which one is protected from bad weather or danger
______	**8**	**aside**	H a tall plant that produces grain for making flour
______	**9**	**seize**	I anger about an unfair situation
______	**10**	**indignation**	J to grab suddenly

Answers

❶ 1. D 2. H 3. G 4. A 5. B
6. E 7. F 8. C 9. J 10. I

❷ Listen and fill in the blanks with the correct words. Remember to change the form of verbs or nouns if necessary.

19

The Travelers and the Plane Tree

Two travelers were walking along a bare and dusty road in the heat of a summer's day. Coming up to a Plane tree, they joyfully turned aside to take shelter from the burning rays of the sun in the deep 1.______________ of its spreading branches.

As they rested, looking up into the tree, one of them remarked to his companion, "What a useless tree the Plane is! It bears no fruit and is of no service to men at all."

The Plane tree interrupted him with 2.__________________. "You ungrateful creature!" it cried. "You come and take shelter under me from the heat of the sun, and then, in the very act of enjoying the cool shade of my leaves, you 3.______________ me and call me good for nothing!"

Many a service is answered with 4.______________.

20

The Sheep, the Wolf, and the Stag

A stag once asked a sheep to lend him some 5.______________, saying that his friend, the wolf, would be his surety. The sheep, however, was afraid that they wanted to cheat her, so she 6.______________ herself, saying, "The wolf has a habit of seizing what he wants and running off with it without paying, and you, too, can run much faster than I. So how shall I be able to catch up with either of you when the debt 7.__________________?"

Two wrongs do not make a right.

Answers ❷

1. shade **2.** indignation **3.** abuse **4.** ingratitude
5. wheat **6.** excused **7.** comes due

21 The Crow and the Pitcher

22 The Lion, the Fox, and the Ass

pp. 22–23

1 Vocabulary Practice: Match.

______	1	**glare**	A	a large pile
______	2	**thirst**	B	to jump suddenly
______	3	**heap**	C	in a way that shows you do not want to make yourself look important (≠ proudly)
______	4	**pitcher**	D	need; something needed or essential
______	5	**invention**	E	a small, smooth stone
______	6	**spring**	F	a container for holding and pouring liquids
______	7	**die of**	G	to look at angrily
______	8	**modestly**	H	angrily; madly
______	9	**pebble**	I	the act of inventing something
______	10	**furiously**	J	the feeling of needing to drink water
______	11	**necessity**	K	to die because of

Answers 1

1. G **2.** J **3.** A **4.** F **5.** I

6. B **7.** K **8.** C **9.** E **10.** H **11.** D

2 Listen and fill in the blanks with the correct words. Remember to change the form of verbs or nouns if necessary.

21

The Crow and the Pitcher

A thirsty crow found a pitcher with some water in it, but so little was there that, as hard as she tried, she could not reach it with her 1.______________, and it seemed as though she would 2.______________ thirst while looking at water.

At last she thought of a clever plan. She began dropping pebbles into the pitcher, and with each pebble the water rose a little higher until at last it reached the top, and the wise bird was able to quench her thirst.

3.______________ is the mother of invention.

22

The Lion, the Fox, and the Ass

A lion, a fox, and an ass went out hunting together. They had soon killed many animals, which the lion asked the ass to divide between them. The ass divided them all into three equal parts, and 4.______________ begged the others to take their choice, at which the lion furiously sprang upon the ass and tore him to pieces.

Then, 5.______________ at the fox, he told him to make a new division. The fox gathered most of the meat into one great heap for the lion, leaving only the smallest possible amount for himself.

"My dear friend," said the lion, "how did you understand the situation so well?" The fox replied, "Me? Oh, I learned a lesson from the ass."

Happy is he who learns from the 6.______________ of others.

Answers **2**

1. beak **2.** die of **3.** Necessity **4.** modestly
5. glaring **6.** misfortunes

23 The Laborer and the Snake

24 The Crab and the Fox

pp. 24–25

❶ Vocabulary Practice: Match.

______	1	**presently**	A	satisfied
______	2	**settle**	B	a field where grass grows
______	3	**deserve**	C	a wound on one's body; something bad done by one person to another
______	4	**laborer**	D	to die because of
______	5	**presence**	E	to earn something because of one's behavior or accomplishments
______	6	**die from**	F	to go and live in a particular place
______	7	**meadow**	G	soon
______	8	**content**	H	a worker
______	9	**extremely**	I	very
______	10	**inland**	J	a situation when someone or something is there
______	11	**injury**	K	far from the sea

Answers

❶ 1. G 2. F 3. E 4. H 5. J 6. D 7. B 8. A 9. I 10. K 11. C

❷ Listen and fill in the blanks with the correct words. Remember to change the form of verbs or nouns if necessary.

23

The Laborer and the Snake

A laborer's little son was bitten by a snake and died from the wound. The father was 1.______________ sad, and in his anger against the snake, he took an axe and went and stood close to the snake's hole, waiting for a chance to kill it.

Presently the snake came out and the man 2.______________ at it, but only succeeded in cutting off the tip of its tail before it went back in again. He then tried to get it to come out a second time, pretending that he wished to apologize.

But the snake said, "I can never be your friend because of my lost tail, 3.______________ can you be mine because of your lost child."

Injuries are never forgotten in the 4.______________ of those who caused them.

24

The Crab and the Fox

A crab once left the seashore and went and settled in a meadow some way 5.______________, which looked very nice and green and seemed like a good place to feed in.

But a hungry fox came along and saw the crab and caught him. Just as he was going to be eaten, the crab said, "This is just what I deserve, for I should never have left my 6.__________________ by the sea and settled here as though I belonged to the land."

Be 7.______________ with what you have.

Answers ❷
1. extremely **2.** struck **3.** nor **4.** presence
5. inland **6.** natural home **7.** content

25 The Hound and the Hare

26 The Cat and the Cock pp. 26–27

1 Vocabulary Practice: Match.

______	**1**	**ought to**	A	to say things to support someone or something that is being criticized
______	**2**	**nuisance**	B	should
______	**3**	**defend**	C	something or someone that annoys people
______	**4**	**awake**	D	a bad person
______	**5**	**snap at**	E	an animal similar to a rabbit, but with a bigger body and longer ears and legs
______	**6**	**hare**	F	to bite quickly
______	**7**	**commit a crime**	G	a dog used for hunting
______	**8**	**villain**	H	to do something illegal
______	**9**	**hound**	I	≠ sleeping

Answers

1 1. B 2. C 3. A 4. I 5. F 6. E 7. H 8. D 9. G

2 Listen and fill in the blanks with the correct words. Remember to change the form of verbs or nouns if necessary.

25

The Hound and the Hare

A young hound chased a hare, and when he caught up with her, he first **1.**________________ her with his teeth as though he were about to kill her, and then let go of her and hopped about her as if he were playing with another dog.

At last the hare said, "I wish you would show yourself as you truly are! If you are my friend, why do you bite me? If you are my **2.**______________, why do you play with me?"

He is no friend who **3.**________________.

26

The Cat and the Cock

A cat jumped on a cock, and tried to think of a good excuse for eating him, for cats don't usually eat cocks, and she knew she ought not to.

At last she said, "You make a great **4.**______________ of yourself at night by crowing and keeping people awake, so I am going to eat you."

But the cock **5.**______________ himself by saying that he crowed so that men might wake up and start the day's work in good time, and that they really couldn't very well do without him.

"That may be," said the cat, "but whether they can or not, I'm not going without my dinner!" and she killed and ate him.

The lack of a good excuse never stopped a villain from **6.**________________________.

Answers **2**

1. snapped at **2.** enemy **3.** plays double **4.** nuisance
5. defended **6.** committing a crime

27 The Blind Man and the Cub

28 The Mouse and the Bull

pp. 28–29

1 Vocabulary Practice: Match.

______	1	**fume**	A to make a loud deep sound
______	2	**exhausted**	B an aspect of one's character that one shows by behaving in a particular way; characteristic
______	3	**indeed**	C to feel or show a lot of anger
______	4	**merely**	D a fight
______	5	**battle**	E certainly; of course
______	6	**in (a) rage**	F simply; only
______	7	**tendency**	G to rush forward and attack someone or something
______	8	**charge**	H in great anger
______	9	**roar**	I very tired

Answers

1

1. C 2. I 3. E 4. F 5. D
6. H 7. B 8. G 9. A

❷ Listen and fill in the blanks with the correct words. Remember to change the form of verbs or nouns if necessary.

27

The Blind Man and the Cub

There was once a blind man who had so fine a sense of touch that, when any animal was put into his hands, he could tell what it was 1.____________ by the feel of it.

One day the cub of a wolf was put into his hands, and he was asked what it was. He felt it for some time, and then said, "2.____________, I am not sure whether it is a wolf's cub or a fox's, but this I know: it would not be wise to trust it in a sheepfold."

Evil 3.____________ are shown early.

The Mouse and the Bull

A bull chased a mouse which had bitten him on the nose, but the mouse was too quick for him and slipped into a hole in a wall. The bull charged furiously into the wall again and again until he was tired out, and sank down on the ground 4.____________ from his efforts.

When all was quiet, the mouse ran out and bit him again. 5.____________ he started to get up, but by that time the mouse was back in his hole again, and the bull could do nothing but 6.____________ and fume in helpless anger.

Presently he heard a high little voice say from inside the wall, "You big fellows don't always have it your own way, you see; sometimes we little ones 7.____________ best."

The battle is not always won by the strong.

Answers ❷
1. merely **2.** Indeed **3.** tendencies **4.** exhausted
5. In a rage **6.** roar **7.** come off

29 The Spendthrift and the Swallow

30 The Fox and the Monkey pp. 30–31

1 Vocabulary Practice: Match.

______	1	**fortune**	A	a member of your family who lived a long time ago
______	2	**take place**	B	as a result of; due to
______	3	**unfortunate**	C	to happen
______	4	**dispute**	D	outstanding
______	5	**in honor of**	E	to discover and make known a hidden mistake, evil, or crime
______	6	**prominent**	F	wealth
______	7	**detect**	G	unlucky
______	8	**miserable**	H	extremely unhappy or uncomfortable
______	9	**ancestor**	I	an argument
______	10	**thanks to**	J	in order to show great respect for someone or something
______	11	**expose**	K	very cold weather which freezes water
______	12	**frost**	L	to notice or find out something when it is not obvious

Answers **1**

1. F 2. C 3. G 4. I 5. J 6. D
7. L 8. H 9. A 10. B 11. E 12. K

❷ Listen and fill in the blanks with the correct words. Remember to change the form of verbs or nouns if necessary.

29

The Spendthrift and the Swallow

A spendthrift, who had wasted his fortune and had nothing left but the clothes in which he stood, saw a swallow one fine day in early spring. Thinking that summer had come, and that he could now do 1.______________ his coat, he went and sold it for what he could get.

A change 2.______________ in the weather, however, and there came a sharp frost which killed the unfortunate swallow. When the spendthrift saw its dead body he cried, "Miserable bird! 3.______________ you I am dying of cold myself."

One swallow does not make summer.

30

The Fox and the Monkey

A fox and a monkey were on the road together, and got into a 4.______________ as to which of them was the better born. They kept it up for some time, till they came to a place where the road passed through a cemetery full of 5.______________, when the monkey stopped and looked around him and gave a great sigh.

"Why do you sigh?" said the fox.

The monkey pointed to the tombs and replied, "All the monuments that you see here were put up in honor of my ancestors, who in their days were 6.______________ men."

The fox was speechless for a moment, but quickly recovering he said, "Oh! Tell any lie you want to, sir; you're quite safe. I'm sure none of your ancestors will rise up and expose you."

Boasters boast most when they cannot be 7.______________.

Answers ❷
1. without **2.** took place **3.** Thanks to **4.** dispute
5. monuments **6.** prominent **7.** detected

31 The Shepherd's Boy and the Wolf

32 The Crow and the Swan pp. 32–33

1 Vocabulary Practice: Match.

______	**1 envious**	A	jealous
______	**2 liar**	B	slowly and without hurrying (≠ in haste)
______	**3 sacrifice**	C	to take care of something or someone
______	**4 flock**	D	a group of sheep, birds, or goats
______	**5 tend**	E	always; regularly
______	**6 villager**	F	the act of offering something to a god
______	**7 shepherd**	G	because of; as a result of
______	**8 neighborhood**	H	the area around one's home
______	**9 at one's leisure**	I	one whose job is to take care of sheep
______	**10 due to**	J	one who tells a lie
______	**11 constantly**	K	one who lives in a village

Answers

1 1. A 2. J 3. F 4. D 5. C 6. K 7. I 8. H 9. B 10. G 11. E

❷ Listen and fill in the blanks with the correct words. Remember to change the form of verbs or nouns if necessary.

31

The Shepherd's Boy and the Wolf

A shepherd's boy was tending his flock near a village, and thought it would be great fun to fool the villagers by pretending that a wolf was attacking the sheep. So he shouted out, "Wolf! Wolf!" and when the people came running over, he laughed at them for their **1.**______________.

He did this more than once, and every time the villagers found they had been fooled, for there was no wolf at all. At last, a wolf really did come, and the boy cried, "Wolf! Wolf!" as loudly as he could, but the people were so **2.**______________ hearing him call that they ignored his cries for help. And so the wolf had everything he wanted, and killed sheep after sheep **3.**____________________.

You cannot believe a liar even when he tells the truth.

The Crow and the Swan

A crow was very envious of the beautiful white feathers of a swan, and thought they were **4.**______________ the water in which the swan constantly bathed and swam.

So he left the neighborhood of the altars, where he survived by picking up bits of the meat offered **5.**______________, and went and lived among the pools and streams. But though he bathed and washed his feathers many times a day, he didn't make them any whiter, and at last died of hunger as well.

You may change your habits, but not your **6.**______________.

Answers ❷
1. efforts **2.** used to **3.** at his leisure
4. due to **5.** in sacrifice **6.** nature

33 The Wolf and the Horse

34 The Caged Bird and the Bat

pp. 34–35

1 Vocabulary Practice: Match.

______	1	**precaution**	A a good moral quality
______	2	**attract**	B to bite food into small pieces while eating
______	3	**untouched**	C walking around without an aim
______	4	**prisoner**	D not handled, used, or tasted
______	5	**have a habit of**	E to get one's attention or interest
______	6	**confine**	F for one's good or benefit
______	7	**chew**	G to force someone or something to stay in a place and prevent them from leaving (≠ release)
______	8	**virtue**	H to do something often or regularly
______	9	**for one's sake**	I care taken to avoid accidents, disease, or other dangers
______	10	**wandering**	J one who is locked in prison

Answers 1

1. I 2. E 3. D 4. J 5. H
6. G 7. B 8. A 9. F 10. C

❷ Listen and fill in the blanks with the correct words. Remember to change the form of verbs or nouns if necessary.

33

The Wolf and the Horse

A wandering wolf came to a field of oats, but not being able to eat them, he was continuing on his way when a horse came along.

"Look," said the wolf. "Here's a fine field of oats. 1.________________ I have left it untouched, and I shall greatly enjoy the sound of your teeth chewing the ripe grain."

But the horse replied, "If wolves could eat oats, my fine friend, you would never have 2.________________ your ears instead of your belly."

There is no 3.________________ in giving to others what is useless to oneself.

34

The Caged Bird and the Bat

A singing bird was confined in a cage which hung outside a window, and had a habit of singing at night when all other birds were asleep. One night a bat came and 4.________________ the bars of the cage, and asked the bird why she was silent by day and sang only at night.

"I have a very good reason for doing so," said the bird. "It was once when I was singing in the daytime that a hunter was 5.________________ by my voice, and set his nets for me and caught me. Since then I have never sung except by night."

But the bat replied, "It is no use doing that now, when you are a 6.________________. If only you had done so before you were caught, you might still be free."

7.________________ are useless after the event.

Answers ❷

1. For your sake 2. pleased 3. virtue 4. grabbed
5. attracted 6. prisoner 7. Precautions

35 The Farmer and the Fox

36 The Lion and the Bull

pp. 36–37

1 Vocabulary Practice: Match.

______	1	**creep about**	A	things that one does for a special purpose
______	2	**do one the honor**	B	to make one unhappy; to upset
______	3	**sword**	C	to cause something or someone to start burning
______	4	**harvest**	D	one who has been harmed, injured, or killed
______	5	**tone**	E	to move around a place quietly and slowly
______	6	**arrangement**	F	to kill a person or animal as part of a religious ceremony
______	7	**sacrifice**	G	the sound of someone's voice that shows what he or she is feeling
______	8	**annoy**	H	the amount of a crop that is ready to be collected
______	9	**set fire to**	I	a weapon with a long pointed blade and a handle
______	10	**preparation**	J	a way of arranging things
______	11	**victim**	K	to do something that shows that one has respect for someone
______	12	**revenge**	L	the act of punishing one who has hurt you

Answers

1

1. E 2. K 3. I 4. H 5. G 6. J

7. F 8. B 9. C 10. A 11. D 12. L

❷ Listen and fill in the blanks with the correct words. Remember to change the form of verbs or nouns if necessary.

35

The Farmer and the Fox

A farmer was greatly annoyed by a fox, which came 1.________________ his yard at night and carried off his hens. So he set a trap for him and caught him, and in order to take revenge upon him, the farmer tied a bunch of straw to his tail, 2.______________ it and let him go.

As luck would have it, however, the fox ran straight into the fields where the corn stood ripe and ready for cutting. It quickly caught fire and was all burnt up, and the farmer lost his whole 3.______________.

Revenge is a double-edged sword.

The Lion and the Bull

A lion saw a fine fat bull among a herd of cattle and tried to think of some way of getting him into his hands. So he sent the bull word that he was sacrificing a sheep, and asked if he would do him the 4.______________ of dining with him. The bull accepted the invitation, but on arriving at the lion's home, he saw a great arrangement of saucepans and spits, but no sign of a sheep. So he turned on his heel and walked quietly away.

The lion called after him in an 5.________________ to ask why, and the bull turned around and said, "I have reason enough. When I saw all your 6.______________, I knew at once that the victim was to be a bull, not a sheep."

The net is spread 7.______________ within sight of the bird.

Answers ❷

1. creeping about **2.** set fire to **3.** harvest **4.** honor
5. injured tone **6.** preparations **7.** in vain

37 The Hare and the Tortoise

38 The Goatherd and the Goat pp. 38–39

1 Vocabulary Practice: Match.

______	**1 bet**	A	to say that one is sure about something
______	**2 dash**	B	to pay attention to something
______	**3 whistle**	C	to move hastily; to rush
______	**4 amuse**	D	to persuade or force someone to do something
______	**5 in despair**	E	while something else is happening; in the meantime
______	**6 get one to do**	F	not changing; continuing to do something; regular
______	**7 crawl**	G	to not do what someone wants; to say that one will not do something
______	**8 refuse to**	H	to move slowly on the ground, like a tortoise or a baby
______	**9 take notice**	I	feeling that a situation is without hope
______	**10 steady**	J	to make a high sound by forcing air through one's mouth
______	**11 meanwhile**	K	to do or say something that other people think is funny

Answers

1 1. A 2. C 3. J 4. K 5. I 6. D 7. H 8. G 9. B 10. F 11. E

❷ Listen and fill in the blanks with the correct words. Remember to change the form of verbs or nouns if necessary.

37

The Hare and the Tortoise

One day a hare was making fun of a tortoise for being so slow upon his feet.

"Wait a bit," said the tortoise. "I'll run a race with you, and I'll bet that I win."

"Oh, well," replied the hare, who was much 1.______________ the idea, "let's try it and see." It was soon agreed that the fox should set a course for the race and be the judge.

When the time came both started off together, but the hare was soon so far ahead that he thought he might as well have a rest. So he lay down and fell fast asleep. 2.______________, the tortoise kept crawling on, and in time reached the goal.

At last, the hare woke up with a start and 3.______________ on at his fastest, only to find that the tortoise had already won the race.

Slow and 4.______________ wins the race.

The Goatherd and the Goat

One day a goatherd was gathering his flock to return to the fold, when one of his goats ran off and 5.______________ join the rest. He tried for a long time to get her to return by calling and whistling to her, but the goat took no 6.______________ of him at all, so at last he threw a stone at her and broke one of her horns.

7.______________, he begged her not to tell his master, but she replied, "You silly fellow, my horn would cry aloud even if I said nothing."

It's no use trying to hide what can't be hidden.

Answers ❷
1. amused at **2.** Meanwhile **3.** dashed **4.** steady
5. refused to **6.** notice **7.** In despair

39 The Goose That Laid the Golden Eggs

40 The Bat and the Weasels

pp. 40–41

1 Vocabulary Practice: Match.

____	**1 commit**	A	rare and worth a lot of money
____	**2 be made of**	B	at a time in the future or in the past, although one does not know exactly when
____	**3 possess**	C	to have; to own
____	**4 principle**	D	a basic belief or rule that has a major influence on one's behavior
____	**5 precious**	E	to promise to do something
____	**6 beg for**	F	to ask strongly for something
____	**7 addition**	G	be made of certain materials
____	**8 sometime**	H	something which is added to something else; the process of adding things together

Answers

1

1. E **2.** G **3.** C **4.** D

5. A **6.** F **7.** H **8.** B

❷ Listen and fill in the blanks with the correct words. Remember to change the form of verbs or nouns if necessary.

39

The Goose That Laid the Golden Eggs

A man and his wife had the good fortune to **1.**______________ a goose which laid a golden egg every day. Lucky though they were, they soon began to think they were not getting rich fast enough, and imagining that the bird must be made of gold inside, they decided to kill it in order to get all of the **2.**__________________ at once.

But when they cut it open, they found it was just like any other goose. Thus, they neither got rich all at once as they had hoped, nor enjoyed any longer the daily **3.**______________ to their wealth.

Much wants more and loses all.

40

The Bat and the Weasels

A bat fell to the ground and was caught by a weasel, and was just about to be killed and eaten when it begged to be let go. The weasel said he couldn't do that because he was an enemy of all birds **4.**________________.

"Oh," said the bat, "but I'm not a bird at all; I'm a mouse."

"So you are," said the weasel, "now that I take a closer look at you," and he let it go.

Sometime after this the bat was caught in just the same way by another weasel and, as before, **5.**______________ its life.

"No," said the weasel, "I never let a mouse go for any reason."

"But I'm not a mouse," said the bat, "I'm a bird."

"Why, so you are," said the weasel, and he too let the bat go.

Look and see which way the wind blows before you **6.**______________ yourself.

Answers ❷

1. possess **2.** precious metal **3.** addition **4.** on principle **5.** begged for **6.** commit

41 The Ass, the Cock, and the Lion

42 The Boasting Traveler pp. 42–43

1 Vocabulary Practice: Match.

______	**1 lead to**	A	a story
______	**2 flee**	B	a horrible event
______	**3 pursue**	C	to result in; to cause
______	**4 tale**	D	to feel very hungry; to die of hunger
______	**5 disaster**	E	to go to a foreign country
______	**6 take part in**	F	energetically and with force
______	**7 starve**	G	to run away
______	**8 boasting**	H	to join; to participate in
______	**9 go abroad**	I	describing one that boasts
______	**10 vigorously**	J	to follow someone or something, usually to try to catch
______	**11 tremendous**	K	very large; huge

Answers

1

1. C 2. G 3. J 4. A 5. B
6. H 7. D 8. I 9. E 10. F 11. K

❷ Listen and fill in the blanks with the correct words. Remember to change the form of verbs or nouns if necessary.

41

The Ass, the Cock, and the Lion

An ass and a cock were in a cattle pen together. Presently a lion, who had been 1.______________ for days, came along and was just about to fall upon the ass and eat him when the cock, rising to his full height and flapping his wings 2.______________, let out a tremendous crow.

Now, if there is one thing that frightens a lion, it is the crowing of a cock, and as soon as this one heard the noise, he 3.______________.

The ass was mightily pleased at this, and thought that if the lion couldn't face a cock, he would be still less likely to stand up to an ass. So the ass ran out and pursued him. But when the two had gotten well out of sight and hearing of the cock, the lion suddenly turned upon the ass, and ate him up.

False confidence often 4.______________ disaster.

42

The Boasting Traveler

A man once went 5.______________ on his travels, and when he came home, he had wonderful tales to tell of the things he had done in foreign countries. Among other things, he said he had 6.________________ a jumping match at Rhodes, and had done a wonderful jump which no one could beat. "Just go to Rhodes and ask them," he said, "everyone will tell you it's true."

But one of those who were listening said, "If you can jump as well as all that, we needn't go to Rhodes to prove it. Let's just imagine this is Rhodes for a minute, and now, jump!"

7.______________ speak louder than words.

Answers ❷

1. starving **2.** vigorously **3.** fled **4.** leads to **5.** abroad **6.** taken part in **7.** Actions

43 The Lion and the Three Bulls

44 The Wolves and the Dogs

pp. 44–45

1 Vocabulary Practice: Match.

______	**1 fate**	**A**	the belt, rope, or chain that is put around the neck of a pet dog
______	**2 mankind**	**B**	to catch and treat badly (≠ release)
______	**3 capture**	**C**	what happens to a person or thing, especially something unpleasant
______	**4 hint**	**D**	≠ friendly
______	**5 long to**	**E**	to eat and drink a lot in order to celebrate
______	**6 accompany**	**F**	≠ trust
______	**7 unfriendly**	**G**	a plan or trick designed to gain an advantage
______	**8 feast**	**H**	to go somewhere with someone
______	**9 strategy**	**I**	to want to do something very much
______	**10 traitor**	**J**	human beings
______	**11 collar**	**K**	one who betrays his or her friends
______	**12 distrust**	**L**	an indirect suggestion that shows how one feels

Answers 1

1. C **2.** J **3.** B **4.** L **5.** I **6.** H
7. D **8.** E **9.** G **10.** K **11.** A **12.** F

❷ Listen and fill in the blanks with the correct words. Remember to change the form of verbs or nouns if necessary.

43

The Lion and the Three Bulls

Three bulls were grazing in a meadow, and were watched by a lion, who 1.______________ capture and eat them, but felt that he was no match for the three so long as they stayed together.

So he began, by false whispers and 2.______________, to create jealousies and distrust among them. This 3.______________ succeeded so well that before long the bulls grew cold and unfriendly, and finally avoided each other, each one eating by himself.

As soon as the lion saw this, he fell upon them one by one and killed them in turn.

The 4.______________ of friends are the opportunities of enemies.

44

The Wolves and the Dogs

Once upon a time the wolves said to the dogs, "Why should we continue to be enemies any longer? You are very much like us in most ways; the main difference between us is only one of training. We live a life of freedom, but you are enslaved by 5.______________, who beat you, put heavy collars around your necks, and force you to keep watch over their flocks and herds for them, and, after all that, give you nothing but bones to eat. Don't 6.________________ it any longer. Hand the flocks over to us, and we will all live off the fat of the land and feast together."

The dogs allowed themselves to be persuaded by these words, and 7.______________ the wolves into their den. But as soon as they were well inside, the wolves fell upon them and tore them to pieces.

8.______________ fully deserve their fate.

Answers ❷

1. longed to **2.** nasty hints **3.** strategy **4.** quarrels
5. mankind **6.** put up with **7.** accompanied **8.** Traitors

45 The Ant

46 The North Wind and the Sun pp. 46–47

1 Vocabulary Practice: Match.

______	**1**	**persuasion**	**A** dressed
______	**2**	**whenever**	**B** ≠ tightly
______	**3**	**loosely**	**C** the act of persuading
______	**4**	**beam**	**D** to shine
______	**5**	**soil**	**E** anytime
______	**6**	**make one's living**	**F** to cover with paper or clothes
______	**7**	**arise**	**G** the desire for more than one needs or should have
______	**8**	**wrap**	**H** to happen
______	**9**	**greed**	**I** the land
______	**10**	**clad**	**J** to make money in order to live

Answers **1**

1. C **2.** E **3.** B **4.** D **5.** I
6. J **7.** H **8.** F **9.** G **10.** A

❷ **Listen and fill in the blanks with the correct words. Remember to change the form of verbs or nouns if necessary.**

45

The Ant

Ants were once men and 1.________________ by farming the soil. But, not content with the results of their own work, they were always looking longingly upon the crops and fruits of their neighbors, which the ants stole whenever they got the chance and added to their own store.

At last their 2.____________ made Jupiter so angry that he changed them into ants. But though their forms were changed, their nature remained the same; and so, to this day, they go about among the 3.____________ and gather the fruits of others' labor, and store them up for their own use.

You may punish a thief, but his habit remains.

46

The North Wind and the Sun

A dispute arose between the north wind and the sun, each claiming that he was stronger than the other. At last they agreed to test their powers upon a traveler, to see which could sooner remove his cloak.

The north wind tried first: gathering up all his force for the attack, he came blowing 4.____________ down upon the man, and caught up his cloak as though he would pull it from him with one single effort. But the harder he blew, the more closely the man 5.____________ it around himself. Then came the turn of the sun. At first he beamed gently upon the traveler, who soon opened his cloak and walked on with it hanging 6.____________ about his shoulders. Then he shone forth with his full strength, and the man, before he had gone many steps, was glad to throw his cloak right off and complete his journey more lightly clad.

7.____________ is better than force.

Answers ❷
1. made their living **2.** greed **3.** cornfields **4.** furiously
5. wrapped **6.** loosely **7.** Persuasion

47 The Stag and the Vine

48 The Mischievous Dog 

❶ Vocabulary Practice: Match.

_____	**1 on the contrary**	A to hide
_____	**2 satisfaction**	B to lose and not be able to find something or someone
_____	**3 punishment**	C to believe that something is probably true
_____	**4 conceal**	D to make a small hole in or through something with a pointed object
_____	**5 suppose**	E the act of punishing
_____	**6 disgrace**	F the feeling of being satisfied
_____	**7 merit**	G a prize
_____	**8 lose track of**	H a good quality
_____	**9 a badge of**	I just the opposite
_____	**10 reward**	J a sign of; an identifying mark or sign
_____	**11 pierce**	K shame; embarrassment; the loss of others' respect

Answers ❶
1. I 2. F 3. E 4. A 5. C 6. K 7. H 8. B 9. J 10. G 11. D

❷ Listen and fill in the blanks with the correct words. Remember to change the form of verbs or nouns if necessary.

47

The Stag and the Vine

A stag, pursued by some hunters, concealed himself behind a thick vine. The hunters 1.__________________ him and passed by his hiding place without being aware that he was anywhere near.

Supposing all danger to be over, he presently began to eat the leaves of the vine. This movement drew the attention of the returning hunters, and one of them, supposing some animal to be hidden there, shot an arrow into the leaves. The unlucky stag was 2.______________ to the heart, and as he died he said, "I deserve my fate for feeding on the leaves of my protector."

3.______________ sometimes brings its own punishment.

48

The Mischievous Dog

There was once a dog who used to snap at people and bite them for no reason, and who was a great nuisance to everyone who came to his master's house. So, his master 4.______________ a bell around his neck to warn people of his presence.

The dog was very proud of the bell, and strutted about ringing it with 5.______________ satisfaction.

But an old dog came up to him and said, "You shouldn't be so proud of yourself, my friend. You don't think, do you, that your bell was given to you as a reward for merit? 6.____________________, it is a badge of disgrace."

Notoriety is often mistaken for 7.______________.

Answers ❷

1. lost track of 2. pierced 3. Ingratitude 4. fastened
5. tremendous 6. On the contrary 7. fame

49 The Farmer and Fortune

50 The Beekeeper pp. 50–51

❶ Vocabulary Practice: Match.

______	**1 sting**	A the feeling of being grateful to someone for something; thankfulness
______	**2 gratitude**	B owed
______	**3 overturn**	C one who is responsible for taking care of something
______	**4 discovery**	D to turn over
______	**5 upset**	E something found or discovered by someone
______	**6 keeper**	F to look at angrily
______	**7 stare**	G to break up land with a plow; a farming tool used to dig into and turn over soil
______	**8 hive**	H the small, sharp tail of a bee
______	**9 credit**	I unhappy
______	**10 due**	J a structure where bees live
______	**11 plow**	K praise; approval

Answers

❶ 1.H 2.A 3.D 4.E 5.I 6.C 7.F 8.J 9.K 10.B 11.G

❷ Listen and fill in the blanks with the correct words. Remember to change the form of verbs or nouns if necessary.

49

The Farmer and Fortune

A farmer was plowing on his farm one day when he turned up a pot of golden coins with his plow. He was overjoyed at his 1.______________, and from that time forth made an offering daily at the shrine of the Goddess of the Earth.

Fortune was displeased at this, and came to him and said, "My man, why do you give Earth the 2.______________ for the gift which I gave you? You never thought of thanking me for your good luck, but should you be unlucky enough to lose what you have gained, I know very well that I, Fortune, will then get all the 3.______________."

Show gratitude where gratitude is due.

50

The Beekeeper

A thief found his way into an apiary while the beekeeper was away, and stole all the honey. When the keeper returned and found the hives empty, he was very upset and stood 4.______________ at them for some time.

Before long the bees came back from gathering honey and, finding their hives 5.______________ and the keeper standing by, they attacked him with their stings.

At this he became furious and cried, "You ungrateful creatures! You let the thief who stole my honey 6.______________, and then you sting me who has always taken such good care of you!"

When you hit back, make sure you have got the right man.

Answers

❷ 1. discovery 2. credit 3. blame 4. staring
5. overturned 6. get away

51 The Boy and the Filberts

52 The Shepherd and the Wolf pp. 52–53

❶ Vocabulary Practice: Match.

______	1 **handful**	A	the action of pursuing
______	2 **overtake**	B	the amount of something that fills one's hand
______	3 **passage**	C	the movement of passing through
______	4 **rear**	D	to develop
______	5 **suspicion**	E	to take out
______	6 **withdraw**	F	to try to do something
______	7 **unable**	G	to catch up with
______	8 **pursuit**	H	≠ able
______	9 **abandon**	I	to take care of a child or young animal until the child or animal grows up; to raise
______	10 **attempt**	J	to give up
______	11 **grasp**	K	to hold something very firmly
______	12 **breed**	L	a feeling that someone or something cannot be trusted

Answers ❶

1. B 2. C 3. C 4. I 5. L 6. E
7. H 8. A 9. J 10. F 11. K 12. D

❷ Listen and fill in the blanks with the correct words. Remember to change the form of verbs or nouns if necessary.

51

The Boy and the Filberts

A boy put his hand into a jar of filberts, and grasped as many as his fist could possibly hold. But when he tried to pull it out again, he found he couldn't do so, for the neck of the jar was too small to allow for the 1.______________ of so large a handful.

Not wanting to lose his nuts, but unable to withdraw his hand, he 2.______________________. A man standing nearby, who saw what the problem was, said to him, "Come, my boy; don't be so greedy. Be content with half the amount, and you'll be able to get your hand out without difficulty."

Do not 3.______________ too much at once.

52

The Shepherd and the Wolf

A shepherd found a wolf's cub wandering in his pastures, and took him home and 4.______________ him along with his dogs. When the cub grew to his full size, if ever a wolf stole a sheep from the flock, he would join the dogs in hunting the wolf down.

It sometimes happened that the dogs failed to catch the thief and, 5.______________ the pursuit, returned home. The wolf would on such occasions continue the chase by himself, and when he 6.______________ the thief, would stop and share the feast with him, and then return to the shepherd.

But if some time passed without a sheep being carried off by the wolves, he would steal one himself and share it with the dogs. The shepherd's 7.______________ were aroused, and one day he caught the wolf in the act. Then, fastening a rope around his neck, the shepherd hung him from the nearest tree.

What's bred in the bone is sure to come out in the flesh.

Answers ❷

1. passage 2. burst into tears 3. attempt 4. reared
5. abandoning 6. overtook 7. suspicions

53 The Stag at the Pool

54 The Bee and Jupiter

pp. 54–55

❶ Vocabulary Practice: Match.

______	1	**grateful**	A	a fault or problem that makes someone less effective or attractive (≠ strength)
______	2	**disgust**	B	to feel very proud of something
______	3	**admiration**	C	an act of asking for something in a polite or formal way
______	4	**request**	D	thankful
______	5	**reflection**	E	to be hurt or killed because of something or someone
______	6	**rob someone of**	F	≠ pleased
______	7	**weakness**	G	respect and approval
______	8	**give one's word**	H	to tell someone that you will do something; to promise
______	9	**fall victim to**	I	an image reflected from a mirror or water
______	10	**glory in**	J	dislike
______	11	**displeased**	K	to take something away from someone by force

Answers

❶ 1. D 2. J 3. G 4. C 5. I
6. K 7. A 8. H 9. E 10. B 11. F

❷ Listen and fill in the blanks with the correct words. Remember to change the form of verbs or nouns if necessary.

53

The Stag at the Pool

A thirsty stag went down to a pool to drink. As he bent over the surface, he saw his own reflection in the water, and was struck with 1.______________ for his fine spreading antlers, but at the same time he felt nothing but disgust for the 2.______________ and slenderness of his legs.

While he stood there looking at himself, he was seen and attacked by a lion, and in the chase which followed the stag soon got ahead of his pursuer, and kept his lead as long as the ground over which he ran was open and free of trees. But coming presently to a forest, he was caught by his antlers in the branches, and 3.____________________ the teeth and claws of his enemy.

"Woe is me!" he cried with his last breath. "I despised my legs, which might have saved my life, but I gloried in my horns, and they have ruined me."

What is worth most is often valued least.

54

The Bee and Jupiter

A queen bee from Hymettus flew up to Olympus with some fresh honey from the hive as a present for Jupiter, who was so pleased with the gift that he 4.______________ give her anything she wanted. She said she would be very grateful if he would give stings to the bees, to kill people who 5.________________________ their honey.

Jupiter was greatly displeased with this 6.______________, for he loved mankind, but he had given his word, so he said that stings they should have. The stings he gave them, however, were of such a kind that whenever a bee stings a man, the sting remains in the wound and the bee dies.

Evil wishes, like chickens, come home to roost.

Answers ❷

1. admiration **2.** weakness **3.** fell victim to **4.** promised to
5. robbed them of **6.** request

55 Hercules and the Wagon Driver

56 The Ass and His Purchaser

pp. 56–57

1 Vocabulary Practice: Match.

______	1 **load**	A	one who has only recently arrived somewhere
______	2 **newcomer**	B	something that a person or animal carries
______	3 **assistance**	C	help
______	4 **hand over**	D	repeated after a particular period of time
______	5 **muddy**	E	to give
______	6 **company**	F	to ask someone in a formal way to do something
______	7 **call on (upon)**	G	to help
______	8 **assist**	H	the people one spends time with
______	9 **lane**	I	a narrow road
______	10 **at intervals**	J	covered with mud

Answers

1

1. B 2. A 3. C 4. E 5. J 6. H 7. F 8. C 9. I 10. D

❷ Listen and fill in the blanks with the correct words. Remember to change the form of verbs or nouns if necessary.

55

Hercules and the Wagon Driver

A wagon driver was driving his team along a 1.______________ lane with a full load behind them, when the wheels of his wagon sank so deep in the mud that no efforts of his horses could move them.

As he stood there looking helplessly on, and calling loudly 2.______________ upon Hercules for assistance, the god himself appeared and said to him, "Put your shoulder to the wheel, man, and order your horses to pull, and then you may call on Hercules to 3.______________ you. If you won't lift a finger to help yourself, you can't expect Hercules or anyone else to come to your aid."

Heaven helps those who help themselves.

56

The Ass and His Purchaser

A man who wanted to buy an ass went to a market and, coming across a likely-looking beast, 4.______________ with the owner that he should be allowed to take him home for a try to see what he was like.

When the man reached home, he put him into his stable along with the other asses. The 5.______________ took a look around, and immediately went and chose a place next to the laziest and greediest beast in the stable. When the man saw this, he put a rope on him at once, led him back to the market and 6.______________________ to his owner again.

The latter was a good deal surprised to see him back so soon, and said, "Do you mean to say you have tested him already?" "I don't want to put him through any more tests," replied the other. "I can see what sort of beast he is from the companion he chose for himself."

A man is known by the 7.______________ he keeps.

Answers ❷

1. muddy **2.** at intervals **3.** assist **4.** arranged
5. newcomer **6.** handed him over **7.** company

57 The Bear and the Travelers

58 The Pack Ass and the Wild Ass pp. 58–59

❶ Vocabulary Practice: Match.

______	1	**sniff**	A to consider; to regard . . . as
______	2	**take . . . for**	B to stop breathing for a short time
______	3	**comfort**	C the thing that makes one's life easier and more pleasant
______	4	**costly**	D to get away; to run away
______	5	**idly**	E to smell quickly
______	6	**hold one's breath**	F someone whom you know, but not very well
______	7	**observe**	G something that is lucky or makes one happy
______	8	**acquaintance**	H expensive
______	9	**blessing**	I honesty
______	10	**escape**	J without any purpose or reason
______	11	**sincerity**	K feeling doubt (≠ certain)
______	12	**dubious**	L to watch closely for some time

Answers ❶

1.E 2.A 3.C 4.H 5.J 6.B
7.L 8.F 9.G 10.D 11.I 12.K

❷ Listen and fill in the blanks with the correct words. Remember to change the form of verbs or nouns if necessary.

57

The Bear and the Travelers

Two travelers were on the road together, when a bear suddenly appeared on the scene. As he 1.______________ them, one ran to a tree at the side of the road, and climbed up into the branches and hid there.

The other was not as fast as his companion, and as he could not escape, he threw himself on the ground and pretended to be dead. The bear came up and sniffed all around him, but he kept perfectly still and 2.______________________, for they say that a bear will not touch a dead body. The bear took him for a corpse, and went away.

When the coast was clear, the traveler in the tree came down, and asked the other what it was the bear had whispered to him when the bear put his mouth to his ear. The other replied, "He told me never again to travel with a friend who 3.______________ you at the first sign of danger."

Misfortune tests the 4.______________ of friendship.

58

The Pack Ass and the Wild Ass

A wild ass, who was wandering 5.______________ about, one day came upon a pack ass lying at full length in a sunny spot and thoroughly enjoying himself. Going up to him, the wild ass said, "What a lucky beast you are! Your shiny coat shows how well you live. How I envy you!"

Not long after this, the wild ass saw his acquaintance again, but this time he was carrying a heavy load, and his driver was following behind and beating him with a 6.______________________.

"Ah, my friend," said the wild ass, "I don't envy you anymore, for I see now you 7.______________ for your comforts."

Costly advantages are 8.______________ blessings.

Answers ❷

1. observed	**2.** held his breath	**3.** deserts	**4.** sincerity
5. idly	**6.** thick stick	**7.** pay dearly	**8.** dubious

59 The Frogs and the Well

60 The Dog and the Wolf

pp. 60–61

❶ Vocabulary Practice: Match.

______	1 **look for**	A	to search for
______	2 **Suppose**	B	What if
______	3 **scraps**	C	wet and humid (≠ dry)
______	4 **agreement**	D	calmly, without getting excited or angry
______	5 **coolly**	E	small pieces of food left over after a meal; leftovers
______	6 **damp**	F	a situation in which people agree on things; a deal between people
______	7 **dry up**	G	to become completely dry

Answers ❶

1. A **2.** B **3.** E **4.** F
5. D **6.** C **7.** G

❷ Listen and fill in the blanks with the correct words. Remember to change the form of verbs or nouns if necessary.

59

The Frogs and the Well

Two frogs lived together in a pond, but one hot summer the pond dried up, and they left it to look for another place to live, for frogs like **1.**______________ places if they can find them.

After a while they came to a deep well, and one of them looked down into it and said to the other, "This looks like a nice cool place; let us jump in and settle here."

But the other, who was wiser, replied, "Not so fast, my friend. **2.**______________ this well dried up like the pond, how should we get out again?"

Think twice before you **3.**______________.

60

The Dog and the Wolf

A dog was lying in the sun before a farmyard gate, when a wolf jumped upon him and was just about to eat him up. But the dog begged for his life and said, "You see how thin I am and what a poor meal I should be for you now, but if you will only wait a few days, my master is going to have a feast. All the rich **4.**______________ will come to me, and I shall get nice and fat. Then will be the time for you to eat me."

The wolf thought this was a very good plan, and went away. Sometime afterwards he came to the farmyard again, and found the dog lying out of reach on the stable roof.

"Come down," he called, "and be eaten. Don't you remember our **5.**______________?"

But the dog said **6.**______________, "My friend, if you ever catch me lying down by the gate there again, don't you wait for any feast."

Once bitten, twice shy.

Answers ❷

1. damp **2.** Supposing **3.** act **4.** scraps
5. agreement **6.** coolly

61 The Peasant and the Apple Tree pp. 64–65

❶ Vocabulary Practice: Match.

______	**1 stroke**	A	happy; joyful
______	**2 delighted**	B	very happy; very pleased
______	**3 disappointed**	C	to decide what will happen
______	**4 a swarm of**	D	usefulness
______	**5 determine to**	E	a cut; the action of hitting
______	**6 hollow**	F	a poor farmer
______	**7 set to work**	G	empty
______	**8 peasant**	H	a large group of insects living or flying together
______	**9 merry**	I	displeased because one has failed to get what he or she wants
______	**10 utility**	J	to treat one kindly; to leave one alone
______	**11 spare**	K	to begin doing something actively

Answers

❶ 1. E 2. B 3. I 4. H 5. C
6. G 7. K 8. F 9. A 10. D 11. J

❷ Listen and fill in the blanks with the correct words. Remember to change the form of verbs or nouns if necessary.

61

The Peasant and the Apple Tree

A peasant had an apple tree growing in his garden, which 1.______________ no fruit, but merely served to provide a shelter from the heat for the sparrows and grasshoppers which sat and sang in its branches. Disappointed at its uselessness, the peasant 2.______________ cut it down, and went and fetched his axe for the purpose.

But when the sparrows and the grasshoppers saw what he was about to do, they begged him to 3.______________ it, and said to him, "If you destroy the tree, we shall have to seek shelter elsewhere, and you will no longer have our merry singing to 4.______________ your work in the garden."

He, however, refused to listen to them, and 5.______________ with a will to cut through the trunk. A few strokes showed that it was 6.______________ inside and contained a swarm of bees and a large store of honey. 7.______________ with his find he threw down his axe, saying, "The old tree is worth keeping after all."

8.______________ is most men's test of worth.

Answers ❷

1. bore 2. determined to 3. spare 4. accompany
5. set to work 6. hollow 7. Delighted 8. Utility

62 The Bat, the Bramble, and the Seagull pp. 66–67

❶ Vocabulary Practice: Match.

______	1	**dive**	A	sometimes
______	2	**acquire**	B	an amount
______	3	**recognize**	C	to succeed in doing something, but with difficulty
______	4	**sum**	D	a load of goods carried by a ship
______	5	**partnership**	E	different
______	6	**every now and then**	F	to go under water
______	7	**voyage**	G	a supply of goods
______	8	**manage to**	H	a long journey, especially by sea
______	9	**stock**	I	a new business or activity that involves risk
______	10	**various**	J	the state of being partners involved in an activity together
______	11	**cargo**	K	to know who or what someone or something is
______	12	**venture**	L	to get

Answers ❶

1. F 2. L 3. K 4. B 5. J 6. A
7. H 8. C 9. G 10. E 11. D 12. I

❷ Listen and fill in the blanks with the correct words. Remember to change the form of verbs or nouns if necessary.

62

The Bat, the Bramble, and the Seagull

A bat, a bramble, and a seagull went into 1.______________ and determined to go on a trading voyage together. The bat borrowed a sum of money for his venture; the bramble gathered 2.______________ clothes of various kinds; the seagull took a quantity of lead. And so they set out.

By and by a great storm came on, and their boat with all its cargo went to the bottom of the sea, but the three travelers 3.______________ reach land.

Ever since then the seagull flies to and fro over the sea, and 4.____________________________ dives below the surface, looking for the lead he's lost; the bat is so afraid of meeting his 5.______________ that he hides away by day and only comes out at night to feed, and the bramble catches hold of the clothes of everyone who passes by, hoping someday to 6.______________ and recover its lost garments.

All men are more concerned to recover what they lose than to 7.______________ what they lack.

Answers ❷
1. partnership 2. a stock of 3. managed to
4. every now and then 5. creditors 6. recognize 7. acquire

63 The Mice and the Weasels

pp. 68–69

1 Vocabulary Practice: Match.

______	1 **rank**	A	a disadvantage caused by a situation or action; a punishment
______	2 **distinguish**	B	a fight between armies in a war
______	3 **battle**	C	to win; to beat
______	4 **helmet**	D	to make one person or thing seem different from others
______	5 **defeat**	E	a hard hat worn to protect one's head
______	6 **hamper**	F	a meeting at which a group of people discuss and give advice on a topic
______	7 **council**	G	to make it difficult for someone to do something
______	8 **penalty**	H	one's position in an organization

Answers

1

1. H 2. D 3. B 4. E
5. C 6. G 7. F 8. A

❷ Listen and fill in the blanks with the correct words. Remember to change the form of verbs or nouns if necessary.

63

The Mice and the Weasels

There was a war between the mice and the weasels in which the mice always got the worst of it, large numbers of them being killed and eaten by the weasels. So they called a 1.______________ of war, in which an old mouse got up and said, "It's no wonder we are always beaten, for we have no 2.______________ to plan our battles and direct our movements in the field."

Acting on his advice, they chose the biggest mice to be their leaders, and these leaders, in order to be 3.____________________ from the rank and file, provided themselves with helmets decorated with straw.

They then led the mice out to battle, confident of victory, but they were 4.______________ as usual and were soon running as fast as they could to their holes. All made their way to 5.______________ without difficulty except the leaders, who were so 6.______________ by their helmets that they could not get into their holes, and easily fell victim to their pursuers.

Greatness carries its own 7.______________.

Answers ❷

1. council **2.** generals **3.** distinguished **4.** defeated
5. safety **6.** hampered **7.** penalties

64 The Ass, the Fox, and the Lion pp. 70–71

❶ Vocabulary Practice: Match.

______	1	**frightened**	A	a very large hole dug in the ground
______	2	**pit**	B	very scared
______	3	**save one's own skin**	C	bravely
______	4	**proceed**	D	to escape death or harm, usually at someone else's expense
______	5	**dreadfully**	E	extremely; terribly
______	6	**betray**	F	to hurt a friend or someone else who trusts you, especially by giving information to an enemy
______	7	**boldly**	G	to catch; to grab
______	8	**get hold of**	H	to do something after you have done something else

Answers ❶

1. B 2. A 3. D 4. H
5. E 6. F 7. C 8. G

❷ Listen and fill in the blanks with the correct words. Remember to change the form of verbs or nouns if necessary.

64

The Ass, the Fox, and the Lion

An ass and a fox went into partnership and 1.______________ to search for food together. They hadn't gone far before they saw a lion coming their way, at which they were both 2.______________ frightened.

But the fox thought he saw a way of saving his own skin, and went 3.______________ up to the lion and whispered in his ear, "I'll help you get hold of the ass without the trouble of pursuing him if you promise to let me go free."

The lion agreed to this, and the fox then rejoined his companion and before long led him by a 4.______________, which some hunter had dug as a trap for wild animals, and into which the ass fell.

When the lion saw that the ass was safely caught and couldn't get away, it was to the fox that the lion first turned his 5.______________, and he soon finished him off, and then 6.______________________ proceeded to feast upon the ass.

Betray a friend and you'll often find you have 7.______________ yourself.

Answers ❷

1. set out 2. dreadfully 3. boldly 4. hidden pit
5. attention 6. at his leisure 7. ruined

65 The Impostor

pp. 72–73

1 Vocabulary Practice: Match.

______	**1**	**wax**	A	to promise
______	**2**	**get even with**	B	one who is owned by another person and works for no money
______	**3**	**impostor**	C	to kill a person or animal to honor a god
______	**4**	**perform**	D	to take revenge on
______	**5**	**a band of**	E	one who tricks others; one who pretends to be someone else in order to deceive others
______	**6**	**sacrifice**	F	one who takes money or property illegally, often by using threats or violence
______	**7**	**slave**	G	a soft substance that is used for making candles and models
______	**8**	**robber**	H	a group of people who do something together, especially criminals
______	**9**	**make a promise**	I	to do; to carry out

Answers

1
1. G 2. D 3. E 4. I 5. H
6. C 7. B 8. F 9. A

❷ Listen and fill in the blanks with the correct words. Remember to change the form of verbs or nouns if necessary.

65

The Impostor

A certain man fell ill, and being in a very bad way, he made a promise that he would 1.______________ a hundred oxen to the gods if they would make him healthy again. Wishing to see how he would keep his promise, the gods caused him to 2.______________ in a short time.

Now, he hadn't an ox in the world, so he made a hundred little oxen out of wax and offered them up on an 3.______________, at the same time saying, "Oh gods, I call on you to witness that I have kept my promise."

The gods were determined to 4.________________ him, so they sent him a dream in which he was told to go to the seashore and fetch a hundred gold coins which he would find there. Hurrying in great excitement to the shore, he fell in with a band of 5.______________, who seized him and carried him off to sell as a slave, and when they sold him, a hundred gold coins was the price they 6.______________.

Do not promise more than you can 7.______________.

Answers
❷
1. sacrifice 2. recover 3. altar 4. get even with
5. robbers 6. received 7. perform

66 The Cat and the Mice

pp. 74–75

1 Vocabulary Practice: Match.

______	1 **peep out**	A	to persuade one to do something dangerous or wrong
______	2 **awkward**	B	to change . . . into
______	3 **appearance**	C	the way someone or something looks
______	4 **lure**	D	difficult to deal with; weird
______	5 **turn . . . into**	E	to secretly look at something
______	6 **madam**	F	to put up with; to tolerate
______	7 **stand**	G	an object that is attached to a wall and from which things can hang
______	8 **innocent**	H	a polite or respectful way to address a woman
______	9 **peg**	I	harmless (≠ guilty)

Answers

1

1. E 2. D 3. C 4. A 5. B
6. H 7. F 8. I 9. G

❷ Listen and fill in the blanks with the correct words. Remember to change the form of verbs or nouns if necessary.

66

The Cat and the Mice

There was once a house that was full of mice. A cat heard of this and said to herself, "That's the place for me." Then off she went to live in the house, and caught the mice one by one and ate them.

At last the mice could 1.______________ it no longer, and they decided to take to their holes and stay there.

"That's awkward," said the cat to herself, "the only thing to do is to 2.______________ them out by a trick."

So she considered a while, and then climbed up the wall and let herself 3.______________ by her back legs from a peg, and pretended to be dead. By and by a mouse 4.______________ and saw the cat hanging there.

"Aha!" it cried. "You're very clever, madam, no doubt, but you may 5.____________________ a bag of flour hanging there if you like, yet you won't catch us coming anywhere near you."

If you are wise, you won't be deceived by the 6.______________ appearance of those whom you have once found to be dangerous.

Answers ❷

1. stand **2.** lure **3.** hang down **4.** peeped out

5. turn yourself into **6.** innocent

67 The Eagle, the Jackdaw, and the Shepherd

pp. 76–77

❶ Vocabulary Practice: Match.

______	1	**odd**	A	thick hair that grows on sheep
______	2	**stick**	B	unusual; strange
______	3	**beyond one's power**	C	to cut
______	4	**wool**	D	beyond one's ability; more than one can do
______	5	**risk**	E	to take a dangerous chance
______	6	**ridicule**	F	to be unable to move
______	7	**clip**	G	to know what something is; to understand something
______	8	**make of**	H	unkind laughter or words that make someone or something sound stupid

Answers ❶

1. B 2. F 3. D 4. A
5. E 6. H 7. C 8. G

❷ Listen and fill in the blanks with the correct words. Remember to change the form of verbs or nouns if necessary.

67

The Eagle, the Jackdaw, and the Shepherd

One day a jackdaw saw an eagle fly down onto a 1.______________ and carry it off in its claws.

"My word," said the jackdaw. "I'll do that myself."

So it flew high up into the air, and then came shooting down with a great whistling of wings onto the back of a big ram. 2.______________ it had landed, its claws got caught in the wool, and nothing it could do was of any use; there it 3.______________, flapping away, and only making things worse instead of better.

By and by up came the shepherd. "Oh," he said, "so that's what you'd be doing, is it?" And he took the jackdaw, 4.______________ its wings and carried it home to his children. It looked so odd that they didn't know what to 5.______________ it.

"What sort of bird is it, father?" they asked.

"It's a jackdaw," he replied, "and nothing but a jackdaw, but it wants to be 6.______________ an eagle."

If you attempt what is beyond your power, your effort will be wasted and you risk not only misfortune but 7.______________.

Answers ❷

1. lamb **2.** As soon as **3.** stuck **4.** clipped **5.** make of **6.** taken for **7.** ridicule

68 The Lark and the Farmer pp. 78–79

❶ Vocabulary Practice: Match.

______	1 **in hand**	A	to do something at one's leisure
______	2 **overripe**	B	not . . . anymore
______	3 **look to**	C	to collect crops that are ripe
______	4 **put . . . off**	D	to delay doing something
______	5 **no longer**	E	too ripe
______	6 **harvest**	F	to rely on
______	7 **grain**	G	under control
______	8 **take one's time**	H	the seeds from crops such as wheat that are used for food

Answers

❶ 1. G 2. E 3. F 4. D 5. B 6. C 7. H 8. A

❷ **Listen and fill in the blanks with the correct words. Remember to change the form of verbs or nouns if necessary.**

68

The Lark and the Farmer

A lark nested in a field of corn, and was raising her young under cover of the **1.**____________________. One day, before the young were fully grown, the farmer came to look at the crop and finding it turning yellow fast, he said, "I must send word to my neighbors to come and help me **2.**________________ this field."

One of the young larks heard him, and was very much **3.**________________, and asked her mother to move house at once.

"There's no hurry," she replied, "a man who **4.**________________ his friends for help will take his time about a thing." In a few days the farmer came by again, and saw that the grain was overripe and falling upon the ground.

"I must **5.**________________ no longer," he said. "This very day I'll hire the men and set them to work at once." The lark heard him and said to her young, "Come, my children, we must be off. He talks no more of his friends now, but is going to take things **6.**________________ himself."

Self-help is the best help.

Answers ❷

1. ripening grain **2.** harvest **3.** frightened
4. looks to **5.** put it off **6.** in hand

69 The Miser pp. 80–81

❶ Vocabulary Practice: Match.

______	1 **await**	A	to put something in the ground and cover it with dirt
______	2 **miser**	B	to make a deep sound showing pain or worry
______	3 **lump**	C	less fortunate
______	4 **frequent**	D	to turn something solid into liquid
______	5 **worse off**	E	situation
______	6 **condition**	F	a solid pile or piece of something
______	7 **melt**	G	to inform someone about something
______	8 **bury**	H	to wait for
______	9 **tell someone of something**	I	one who wants to keep all of his or her money and is unwilling to spend any of it
______	10 **groan**	J	happening often

Answers

❶ 1. H 2. I 3. F 4. J 5. C
6. E 7. D 8. A 9. G 10. B

❷ Listen and fill in the blanks with the correct words. Remember to change the form of verbs or nouns if necessary.

69

The Miser

A miser sold everything he had, and 1.________________ his store of gold into a single lump, which he buried secretly in a field. Every day he went to look at it, and would sometimes spend long hours 2.______________ his treasure.

One of his workers noticed his 3.______________ visits to the spot, and one day watched him and discovered his secret. Awaiting an opportunity, the worker went one night and dug up the gold and stole it.

The next day the miser visited the place 4.______________ and, finding his treasure gone, fell to tearing his hair out and groaning over his loss.

5.____________________ he was seen by one of his neighbors, who asked him what his trouble was. The miser told him of his misfortune, but the other replied, "Don't take it so badly, my friend. Put a brick into the hole, and take a look at it every day. You won't be any 6.______________ than before, for even when you had your gold, it was of no use to you."

The true value of money is not in having it, but in using it 7.______________.

Answers ❷
1. melted down 2. admiring 3. frequent 4. as usual
5. In this condition 6. worse off 7. wisely

70 The Lion and the Mouse

pp. 82–83

1 Vocabulary Practice: Match.

______	**1**	**set one free**	**A** the foot of some animals such as cats, dogs, and lions
______	**2**	**lose one's temper**	**B** to pay back; to reward someone who has been kind to you
______	**3**	**paw**	**C** to bite something hard repeatedly
______	**4**	**gnaw**	**D** ≠ fail to
______	**5**	**repay**	**E** a loud noise made by an animal, machine, or person
______	**6**	**roar**	**F** to suddenly get angry
______	**7**	**kindness**	**G** the act of being kind
______	**8**	**succeed in**	**H** to let one go free; to release one

Answers

1

1. H 2. F 3. A 4. C
5. B 6. E 7. G 8. D

❷ Listen and fill in the blanks with the correct words. Remember to change the form of verbs or nouns if necessary.

70

The Lion and the Mouse

A lion asleep in his lair was woken up by a mouse running over his face. 1.________________________, he seized it with his paw and was about to kill it.

The mouse, terrified, begged him to 2.________________ its life. "Please let me go," it cried, "and one day I will repay you for your kindness."

The idea of so small a creature ever being able to do anything for him amused the lion so much that he laughed aloud, and happily let it go.

But the mouse's chance came after all. One day the lion got caught in a net which had been spread by some hunters, and the mouse heard and 3.________________ his roars of anger and ran to the spot. Immediately it set to work 4.________________ the ropes with its teeth, and before long succeeded in setting the lion free.

"There!" said the mouse. "You laughed at me when I 5.________________ I would repay you, but now you see that even a mouse can help a lion."

Kindness is never 6.________________.

Answers ❷
1. Losing his temper 2. spare 3. recognized
4. gnawing 5. promised 6. wasted

71 The Milkmaid and Her Pail pp. 84–85

❶ Vocabulary Practice: Match.

______	1	**poultry**	A to turn one's head quickly up and to the side
______	2	**dairy**	B a long dress
______	3	**vanish**	C a place on a farm where milk is kept or cheese is made
______	4	**toss**	D birds such as chickens that are used for meat or eggs
______	5	**hatch**	E (eggs) to break open so that a baby bird, fish, etc. can come out
______	6	**gown**	F something one imagines; a daydream
______	7	**make . . . into**	G several
______	8	**pail**	H to turn . . . into
______	9	**fantasy**	I a bucket
______	10	**a number of**	J to disappear

Answers ❶
1. D 2. C 3. J 4. A 5. E
6. B 7. H 8. I 9. F 10. G

2 Listen and fill in the blanks with the correct words. Remember to change the form of verbs or nouns if necessary.

71

The Milkmaid and Her Pail

A farmer's daughter had been out to milk the cows, and was returning to the 1.______________ carrying her pail of milk upon her head.

As she walked along, she started thinking in this way: "The milk in this pail will provide me with cream, which I will 2.______________ butter and take to the market to sell. With the money I will buy a number of eggs, and these, when hatched, will produce chickens, and by and by I shall have quite a large 3.______________ yard. Then I shall sell some of my chickens, and with the money which they bring in I will buy myself a new 4.______________, which I shall wear when I go to the fair. And all the young fellows will admire it, and 5.__________________ with me, but I shall toss my head and have nothing to say to them."

Lost in her thoughts and forgetting all about the pail, she tossed her head. Down went the pail, all the milk was spilled, and all her fine 6.______________ vanished in a moment!

Do not count your chickens before they are 7.______________.

Answers

2
1. dairy **2.** make into **3.** poultry **4.** gown
5. fall in love **6.** fantasies **7.** hatched

72 The Woman and the Farmer pp. 86–87

1 Vocabulary Practice: Match.

______	1	**shed tears**	A	to replace
______	2	**breast**	B	great sadness
______	3	**ease**	C	chest; the part of one's body above the stomach
______	4	**grief**	D	did often or regularly in the past
______	5	**used to**	E	to feel or express great sadness, especially because of someone's death
______	6	**grave**	F	a place where a dead body has been put underground
______	7	**weep**	G	to make things less difficult, unpleasant, or painful
______	8	**mourn**	H	to cry
______	9	**reasonable**	I	to cry; shed tears
______	10	**take the place of**	J	making good sense; easy to agree with
______	11	**theft**	K	the action or crime of stealing

Answers

1 1. H 2. C 3. G 4. B 5. D 6. F 7. I 8. E 9. J 10. A 11. K

❷ Listen and fill in the blanks with the correct words. Remember to change the form of verbs or nouns if necessary.

72

The Woman and the Farmer

A woman, who had recently lost her husband, 1.______________ go every day to his grave and weep over her loss. A farmer, who was plowing not far from the spot, saw the woman and desired to have her for his wife, so he left his plow and came and sat by her side, and began to 2.______________ himself.

She asked him why he wept, and he replied, "I have just lost my wife, who was very dear to me, and tears 3.______________________." "And I," she said, "have just lost my husband." And so for a while they 4.______________ in silence.

Then he said, "Since you and I are in the same situation, why don't we marry and live together? I shall 5.________________________ your dead husband, and you that of my dead wife." The woman agreed to the plan, which indeed seemed 6.______________ enough, and they dried their tears.

Meanwhile, a thief had come and stolen the 7.______________ which the farmer had left with his plow. On discovering the 8.______________, the farmer beat his breast and cried loudly over his loss.

When the woman heard his cries, she came and said, "Oh! Are you weeping still?" to which he replied, "Yes, and I mean it this time."

Answers ❷
1. used to 2. shed tears 3. ease my grief 4. mourned
5. take the place of 6. reasonable 7. oxen 8. theft

73 The Monkey and the Dolphin pp. 88–89

❶ Vocabulary Practice: Match.

______	1 **disgusted**	A	a harbor
______	2 **port**	B	to mean
______	3 **refer to**	C	feeling very angry and upset
______	4 **assume**	D	one in an important position in a government
______	5 **official**	E	to interrupt someone or something very suddenly
______	6 **distinguished**	F	successful and respected by many people
______	7 **dishonesty**	G	≠ honesty
______	8 **burst upon**	H	to think something is true

Answers

❶ 1. C 2. A 3. B 4. H 5. D 6. F 7. G 8. E

2 Listen and fill in the blanks with the correct words. Remember to change the form of verbs or nouns if necessary.

73

The Monkey and the Dolphin

When people go on a 1.______________, they often take with them small dogs or monkeys as pets to while away the time. Thus it happened that a man returning to Athens from the east had a pet monkey on board with him.

As they neared the coast of Attica, a great storm 2.______________ them, and the ship sank. All on board were thrown into the water, and tried to save themselves by swimming, the monkey among them. A dolphin saw him and, 3.______________ him to be a man, took him on his back and began swimming toward the shore.

When they got near the Piraeus, which is the 4.______________ of Athens, the dolphin asked the monkey if he was an Athenian. The monkey replied that he was, and added that he came from a very 5.____________________ family.

"Then of course you know the Piraeus," continued the dolphin. The monkey thought he was referring to some 6.____________________ or other, and replied, "Oh, yes; he's a very old friend of mine."

At that, detecting the monkey's 7.______________, the dolphin was so disgusted that he dove below the surface, and the unfortunate monkey was quickly drowned.

Answers 2

1. voyage **2.** burst upon **3.** assuming **4.** port
5. distinguished **6.** high official **7.** dishonesty

74 The Ass and His Burdens pp. 90–91

❶ Vocabulary Practice: Match.

______	1	**load up**	**A** a soft item which absorbs water, used for cleaning things
______	2	**a quantity of**	**B** an amount of
______	3	**drain away**	**C** to be carried away by water
______	4	**peddler**	**D** a traveling trader who sells small goods
______	5	**sponge**	**E** to take in; to absorb
______	6	**soak up**	**F** to put a load on or in something or someone
______	7	**burden**	**G** something heavy that one has to carry

Answers

❶ 1.F 2.B 3.C 4.D 5.A 6.E 7.G

❷ Listen and fill in the blanks with the correct words. Remember to change the form of verbs or nouns if necessary.

74

The Ass and His Burdens

A peddler who owned an ass one day bought a quantity of salt, and 1.____________ his beast with as much as he could carry. On the way home, the ass slipped as he was crossing a stream and fell into the water. The salt got thoroughly wet and much of it melted and 2.____________________, so that when he got on his legs again, the ass found his load had become much lighter.

His master, however, drove him back to town and bought more salt, which he added to what remained in the baskets, and 3.____________ again. As soon as they had reached the stream, the ass lay down in it and rose, as before, with a much lighter load.

But his master detected the trick and, turning back once more, bought 4.____________________ sponges and piled them on the back of the ass. When they came to the stream the ass again lay down, but this time, as the sponges 5.____________ large quantities of water, the ass found when he got up on his legs that he had a heavier 6.____________ to carry than ever.

You may 7.__________________ once too often.

Answers ❷

1. loaded up **2.** drained away **3.** started out **4.** a large number of

5. soaked up **6.** burden **7.** play a good card

75 The Farmer, His Boy, and the Rooks

1 Vocabulary Practice: Match.

______	1	**rascal**	A	to fly away
______	2	**fly off**	B	to pay close attention to something in order to protect it
______	3	**get the better of**	C	a dishonest person; a troublemaker
______	4	**hand**	D	to beat or defeat
______	5	**out of range**	E	to tell someone about something dangerous so that he or she can avoid it
______	6	**keep a watch over**	F	too far away to be hit or shot
______	7	**warn**	G	to give

Answers

1

1. C 2. A 3. D 4. G

5. F 6. B 7. E

❷ Listen and fill in the blanks with the correct words. Remember to change the form of verbs or nouns if necessary.

75

The Farmer, His Boy, and the Rooks

A farmer had just sown a field of wheat, and was keeping a careful watch over it, for large numbers of rooks and starlings kept 1.______________ on it and eating up the grain. Along with him went his boy, carrying a sling, and whenever the farmer asked for the sling, the starlings understood what he said and 2.______________ the rooks and they all flew off in a moment. So the farmer thought of a trick. "My boy," he said, "we must 3.______________________ these birds somehow. After this, when I want the sling, I won't say 'sling,' but just 'Humph!' and you must then 4.______________ me the sling quickly."

Presently the whole flock came back. "Humph!" said the farmer, but the starlings 5.__________________, and he had time to sling several stones among them, hitting one on the head, another in the legs, and another on the wing, before they got out of 6.______________.

As they quickly flew away they met some cranes, who asked them what the matter was. "Matter?" said one of the rooks. "It's those 7.______________, men, that are the matter. Don't you go near them. They have a way of saying one thing and meaning another which has just been the 8.______________ of several of our poor friends."

Answers ❷

1. setting 2. warned 3. get the better of 4. hand
5. took no notice 6. range 7. rascals 8. death

76 The Owl and the Birds pp. 94–95

1 Vocabulary Practice: Match.

______	1	**foolishness**	A	to happen; to end up; to become
______	2	**wisdom**	B	to think deeply
______	3	**take one's advice**	C	therefore; thus
______	4	**turn out**	D	complete ruin or damage; death
______	5	**ponder**	E	to do as one suggests
______	6	**hence**	F	the state of being foolish
______	7	**destruction**	G	the ability to make good decisions by using one's knowledge and experience
______	8	**deadly**	H	able or likely to kill people or animals

Answers

1
1. F 2. G 3. E 4. A
5. B 6. C 7. D 8. H

2 Listen and fill in the blanks with the correct words. Remember to change the form of verbs or nouns if necessary.

76

The Owl and the Birds

The owl is a very wise bird, and once, long ago, when the first oak appeared in the forest, she called all the other birds together and said to them, "You see this tiny tree? If you 1.____________________, you will destroy it now, while it is small, for when it grows big, mistletoe will appear upon it, from which birdlime will be prepared for your 2._______________."

Again, when the first flax was sown, she said to them, "Go and eat up that seed, for it is the seed of the flax, out of which men will one day make nets to catch you."

Once more, when she saw the first hunter, she warned the birds that he was their 3.___________________, who would wing his arrows with their own feathers and shoot them.

But the birds took no notice of what she said; in fact, they thought she was rather mad and laughed at her. When, however, everything 4._______________ just as she had said, they changed their minds and developed a great respect for her 5._______________. Hence, whenever she appears, the birds pay attention to her in the hope of hearing something that may be 6._______________ to them. She, however, no longer gives them advice, but just sits sadly 7._______________ the foolishness of her kind.

Answers **2**
1. take my advice **2.** destruction **3.** deadly enemy
4. turned out **5.** wisdom **6.** useful **7.** pondering

77 The Dog and the Cook

pp. 96–97

❶ Vocabulary Practice: Match.

______	1 **wag**	A	cost; loss
______	2 **nasty**	B	excellent; wonderful; very rich and grand
______	3 **splendid**	C	serious; bad
______	4 **plenty**	D	to walk with difficulty because one's foot or leg is hurt
______	5 **expense**	E	(dogs) to move the tail quickly from side to side
______	6 **briskly**	F	a large amount of something
______	7 **limp**	G	fast, swiftly
______	8 **last**	H	(animals) to make a long loud sound
______	9 **howl**	I	to continue to be enough for a period of time

Answers ❶

1. E 2. C 3. B 4. F 5. A
6. G 7. D 8. I 9. H

2 Listen and fill in the blanks with the correct words. Remember to change the form of verbs or nouns if necessary.

77

The Dog and the Cook

A rich man once invited a number of his friends and acquaintances to a feast. His dog thought it would be a good 1.______________ to invite another dog, a friend of his, so he went to him and said, "My master is giving a feast. There'll be 2.______________ of fine food, so come and dine with me tonight." The dog thus invited came, and when he saw the preparations being made in the kitchen, he said to himself, "My word, I'm in luck; I'll make sure to eat enough tonight to 3.______________ me two or three days."

At the same time he wagged his tail 4.______________ to show his friend how delighted he was to have been asked. But just then the cook noticed him and, in his anger at seeing a strange dog in the kitchen, grabbed him by his back legs and threw him out the window. The dog had a nasty fall and 5.______________ away as quickly as he could, howling miserably.

Presently some other dogs met him and said, "Well, what sort of a dinner did you get?" to which he replied, "I had a 6.______________ time. The wine was so good, and I drank so much of it, that I really don't remember how I got out of the house!"

Be shy of favors offered at the 7.______________ of others.

Answers **2**

1. opportunity **2.** plenty **3.** last **4.** briskly **5.** limped
6. splendid **7.** expense

78 The Lion, the Wolf, and the Fox

pp. 98–99

❶ Vocabulary Practice: Match.

______	1 **cure**	A	someone or something that is not included in a group
______	2 **prescription**	B	a particular treatment or medicine which a doctor has told one to take
______	3 **illness**	C	treatment
______	4 **displeasure**	D	a feeling of unhappiness
______	5 **absence**	E	the fact of being absent
______	6 **exception**	F	to arouse feelings; to provoke
______	7 **stir up**	G	sickness
______	8 **inquire after**	H	to ask about the health or condition of someone

Answers

❶
1. C 2. B 3. G 4. D
5. E 6. A 7. F 8. H

❷ Listen and fill in the blanks with the correct words. Remember to change the form of verbs or nouns if necessary.

78

The Lion, the Wolf, and the Fox

A lion, ill with age, lay sick in his den, and all the beasts of the forest came to inquire after his health with the **1.**______________ of the fox.

The wolf thought this was a good opportunity for some **2.**______________ against the fox, so he called the lion's attention to his absence and said, "You see, sire, that we have all come to see how you are except the fox, who hasn't come near you, and doesn't care whether you are well or ill."

Just then the fox came in and heard the last words of the wolf. The lion roared at him in deep **3.**______________, but he begged to be allowed to explain his absence and said, "Not one of them cares for you so much as I, sire, for all this time I have been going around to the doctors and trying to find a cure for your **4.**______________."

"And may I ask if you have found one?" said the lion. "I have, sire," said the fox, "and it is this: you must skin a wolf and **5.**______________ yourself in his skin while it is still warm." The lion thus turned to the wolf and struck him dead with one blow of his paw, in order to try the fox's **6.**______________. But the fox laughed and said to himself, "That's what you get for **7.**______________ ill will."

Answers ❷

1. exception **2.** revenge **3.** displeasure **4.** illness
5. wrap **6.** prescription **7.** stirring up

79 The Eagle and the Beetle pp. 100–101

❶ Vocabulary Practice: Match.

______	**1 protection**	A the act of protecting
______	**2 insult**	B finally
______	**3 lap**	C small pieces of soil or mud
______	**4 dirt**	D to watch something or someone closely
______	**5 protector**	E an insect with a smooth hard back
______	**6 robe**	F one who protects others
______	**7 for dear life**	G an action or comment that seriously hurts someone's feelings
______	**8 deposit**	H to put something somewhere
______	**9 beetle**	I with as much effort as possible, usually to avoid danger
______	**10 eventually**	J the upper part of one's legs when one sits down
______	**11 keep an eye on**	K a long loose piece of clothing

Answers ❶
1. A 2. G 3. J 4. C 5. F
6. K 7. I 8. H 9. E 10. B 11. D

❷ Listen and fill in the blanks with the correct words. Remember to change the form of verbs or nouns if necessary.

79

The Eagle and the Beetle

An eagle was chasing a hare, who was running for dear life and didn't know where to turn for help. 1.________________ she saw a beetle, and begged it to aid her. So when the eagle flew up, the beetle warned her not to touch the hare, which was 2.________________________.

But the eagle never noticed the beetle because it was so small, and seized the hare and ate her up. The beetle never forgot this, and 3.____________________ the eagle's nest, and whenever the eagle laid an egg, the beetle climbed up and rolled it out of the nest and broke it.

At last the eagle got so worried over the loss of her eggs that she went up to Jupiter, who is the special protector of eagles, and begged him to give her a safe place to 4.________________. So he let her lay her eggs in his lap. But the beetle noticed this and made a ball of dirt the size of an eagle's egg, then flew up and 5.________________ it in Jupiter's lap.

When Jupiter saw the dirt, he stood up to shake it out of his 6.________________ and forgetting about the eggs, he shook them out too, and so they were broken just as before. Ever since then, they say, eagles never lay their eggs during the season when beetles are about.

The weak will sometimes find ways to avenge an 7.________________, even upon the strong.

Answers ❷

1. Eventually **2.** under its protection **3.** kept an eye on **4.** nest in **5.** deposited **6.** robe **7.** insult

80 The Old Woman and the Doctor

pp. 102–103

❶ Vocabulary Practice: Match.

______	1	**refusal**	A	to make a legal claim against someone in court
______	2	**payment**	B	to treat successfully
______	3	**state**	C	based on
______	4	**witness**	D	an illness
______	5	**according to**	E	(a doctor) to say or write down what medicine or other treatment one should take
______	6	**defense**	F	to ask for advice from someone who has special knowledge about a subject
______	7	**sue**	G	to express something in a formal way
______	8	**pay one a visit**	H	to visit someone
______	9	**cure**	I	the amount of money one has to pay
______	10	**consult**	J	an excuse or reason one gives in court for doing or not doing something
______	11	**disease**	K	one who watches you sign an official document
______	12	**prescribe**	L	the act of refusing to do something

Answers

❶
1. L 2. I 3. G 4. K 5. C 6. J
7. A 8. H 9. B 10. F 11. D 12. E

❷ Listen and fill in the blanks with the correct words. Remember to change the form of verbs or nouns if necessary.

80

The Old Woman and the Doctor

An old woman became almost totally blind from a disease of the eyes and, after 1.______________ a doctor, made an agreement with him in the presence of witnesses that she would pay him a high fee if he cured her, while if he failed, he was to receive nothing.

The doctor therefore 2.______________ a course of treatment, and every time he paid the old woman a visit, he took away with him something from her house until at last, when he visited her for the last time and the cure was complete, there was nothing left.

When the old woman saw that her house was empty, she refused to pay the doctor his fee, and after repeated refusals on her part, he 3.______________ her before the judges for payment of her debt. On being brought into court, she was ready with her 4.______________.

"The doctor," she said, "has stated the facts of our agreement correctly. I agreed to pay him a fee if he cured me, and he, on his part, promised to 5.________________ if he failed. Now he says I am cured, but I say that I am blinder than ever, and I can prove what I say. When my eyes were bad, I could still see well enough to be aware that my house 6.______________ a certain amount of furniture and other things. But now, when according to him I am cured, I am entirely 7.______________ to see anything there at all."

Answers ❷

1. consulting 2. prescribed 3. sued 4. defense
5. charge nothing 6. contained 7. unable

81 The Fox and the Goat

pp. 104–105

❶ Vocabulary Practice: Match.

______	1	**plant**	A to tell one that he or she should do or remember something
______	2	**firmly**	B strongly; with force
______	3	**remind one of**	C opportunity; chance; possibility; expectation
______	4	**make certain**	D to jump
______	5	**sense**	E to press; to put
______	6	**leap**	F good judgment
______	7	**prospect**	G to check that something is correct or true; to make sure

Answers

❶ 1. E 2. B 3. A 4. G 5. F 6. D 7. C

❷ Listen and fill in the blanks with the correct words. Remember to change the form of verbs or nouns if necessary.

81

The Fox and the Goat

A fox fell into a well and was unable to get out again. By and by a 1.______________ goat came by and, seeing the fox in the well, asked him if the water was good.

"Good?" said the fox. "It's the best water I've ever tasted in all my life. Come down and try it yourself." The goat thought of nothing but the 2.______________ of quenching his thirst, and jumped in at once.

When he had had enough to drink, he looked about, like the fox, for some way of getting out, but could find none. Then the fox said, "I have an idea. You stand on your back legs, plant your front legs 3.______________ against the side of the well, and then I'll climb onto your back and, from there, by stepping on your horns, I can get out. And when I'm out, I'll help you out too." The goat did as he was 4.______________, the fox climbed onto the goat's back and so out of the well, and then he 5.______________ walked away.

The goat called loudly after him and 6.________________ his promise to help him out, but the fox merely turned and said, "If you had as much sense in your head as you have hair in your beard, you wouldn't have jumped into the well without 7.____________________ that you could get out again."

Look before you 8.______________.

Answers ❷
1. thirsty **2.** prospect **3.** firmly **4.** requested
5. coolly **6.** reminded him of **7.** making certain **8.** leap

82 The Town Mouse and the Country Mouse pp. 106–107

❶ Vocabulary Practice: Match.

______	1 **fare**	A	a large strong box
______	2 **flavor**	B	having an easy and comfortable life with a lot of valuable things
______	3 **luxury**	C	to go somewhere that could be dangerous
______	4 **surround**	D	but; while
______	5 **to the taste of someone**	E	to be all around someone or something
______	6 **whereas**	F	clearly; very
______	7 **chest**	G	to one's liking
______	8 **distinctly**	H	taste
______	9 **venture**	I	something one enjoys but does not need, especially something expensive or fancy
______	10 **in the lap of luxury**	J	≠ comfortable
______	11 **uncomfortable**	K	food that is available; to do well or badly in a situation

Answers ❶
1.K 2.H 3.I 4.E 5.G
6.D 7.A 8.F 9.C 10.B 11.J

❷ Listen and fill in the blanks with the correct words. Remember to change the form of verbs or nouns if necessary.

82

The Town Mouse and the Country Mouse

A town mouse and a country mouse were acquaintances, and the country mouse one day invited his friend to come and see him at his home in the fields.

The town mouse came, and they sat down to a dinner of barleycorns and roots, the latter of which had a 1.______________ earthy flavor. The fare was not much to the taste of the guest, and after a while he said, "My poor dear friend, you live here 2.__________________ the ants. Now, you should just see how I fare! My larder is a regular 3.__________________. You must come and stay with me, and I promise you you shall live off the fat of the land."

So when he returned to town, he took the country mouse with him, and showed him into a larder containing flour and 4.______________ and figs and honey and dates. The country mouse had never seen anything like it, and sat down to enjoy the luxuries his friend provided. But before they had well begun, the door of the larder opened and someone came in. The two mice ran off and hid themselves in a narrow and 5.______________ uncomfortable hole. A short time later, when all was quiet, they 6.______________ again, but someone else came in, and off they hurried again. This was too much for the visitor.

"Goodbye," he said, "I'm off. You live in the lap of luxury, I can see, but you are 7.______________ by dangers, whereas at home I can enjoy my simple dinner of roots and corn in peace."

Better a simple meal in peace than a 8.______________ meal in fear.

Answers ❷
1. distinctly 2. no better than 3. treasure chest 4. oatmeal
5. extremely 6. ventured out 7. surrounded 8. fancy

83 The Eagle and the Fox pp. 108–109

❶ Vocabulary Practice: Match.

______	**1 curse**	A	not far away
______	**2 divine**	B	to say bad things about someone so that he or she will have bad luck
______	**3 flesh**	C	meat
______	**4 grove**	D	to take revenge on; to get even with
______	**5 get at**	E	a small wood or group of trees
______	**6 nearby**	F	cooked by fire
______	**7 pay back**	G	loyalty; friendship; belief
______	**8 roasted**	H	to reach or touch someone or something
______	**9 chick**	I	relating to or coming from a god or gods
______	**10 faith**	J	a baby bird

Answers
❶
1. B 2. I 3. C 4. E 5. H
6. A 7. D 8. F 9. J 10. G

❷ **Listen and fill in the blanks with the correct words. Remember to change the form of verbs or nouns if necessary.**

83

The Eagle and the Fox

An eagle and a fox became great friends and decided to live near one another. They thought that the more they saw of each other, the better friends they would be. So the eagle built a nest at the top of a tall tree, while the fox settled in a grove at the foot of it and 1.______________ a litter of cubs.

One day the fox went out searching for food, and the eagle, who also wanted food for her young, flew down into the grove, took the fox's cubs, and carried them up into the tree as a 2.______________ for herself and her family.

When the fox came back and found out what had happened, she was not so much sorry for the loss of her cubs as furious because she couldn't get at the eagle and 3.______________ for her treachery. So she sat down nearby and cursed the eagle. But it wasn't long before she had her 4.______________.

Some villagers happened to be sacrificing a goat on a neighboring altar, and the eagle flew down and carried off a piece of the 5.____________________ to her nest. There was a strong wind blowing and the nest caught fire, with the result that her chicks fell 6.______________ to the ground. Then the fox ran to the spot and ate them all in full sight of the eagle.

False faith may escape human punishment, but cannot escape 7.______________.

Answers ❷

1. produced **2.** meal **3.** pay her back **4.** revenge
5. burning flesh **6.** half-roasted **7.** the divine

84 Mercury and the Woodcutter

pp. 110–111

1 Vocabulary Practice: Match.

_____	1 **despair**	A	to refuse
_____	2 **glance off**	B	an event
_____	3 **decline**	C	showing a strong desire or will; excitedly
_____	4 **occasion**	D	to cut down (a tree)
_____	5 **property**	E	to pull one's body or a part of one's body to full length
_____	6 **previous**	F	last; the time, thing or person right before the present one
_____	7 **try one's luck**	G	to feel that there is no hope at all
_____	8 **chop down**	H	something that one owns
_____	9 **stretch**	I	to take a chance and hope to succeed
_____	10 **eagerly**	J	to hit something lightly and then move quickly in another direction

Answers

1
1.G 2.J 3.A 4.B 5.H
6.F 7.I 8.D 9.E 10.C

❷ Listen and fill in the blanks with the correct words. Remember to change the form of verbs or nouns if necessary.

84

Mercury and the Woodcutter

A woodcutter was chopping down a tree on the bank of a river when his axe, 1.______________ the trunk, flew out of his hands and fell into the water.

As he stood by the water's edge despairing over his loss, Mercury appeared and asked him the reason for his grief. On learning what had happened, 2.______________ for the man he dove into the river and, bringing up a golden axe, asked him if that was the one he had lost. The woodcutter replied that it was not, so Mercury then dove a second time and, bringing up a silver axe, asked if that was his.

"No, that is not mine either," said the woodcutter.

Once more Mercury dove into the river, and brought up the missing axe. The woodcutter was overjoyed at recovering his 3.______________, and thanked Mercury warmly. And the latter was so pleased with the man's honesty that he made the woodcutter a present of the other two axes.

When the woodcutter told this story to his companions, one of them was filled with envy of his good fortune, and decided to 4.__________________________. So he went and began to chop down a tree at the edge of the river, and soon let his axe drop into the water.

Mercury appeared as before and, on learning that the fellow's axe had fallen in, he dove and brought up a golden axe, just as he had done on the 5.______________ occasion. Without waiting to be asked whether it was his or not, the fellow cried, "That's mine! That's mine!" and stretched out his hands 6.______________ for the prize. But Mercury was so disgusted at his dishonesty that he not only 7.__________________ give him the golden axe, but also refused to recover for him the one he had let fall into the stream.

Honesty is the best 8.______________.

Answers ❷

1. glancing off 2. out of pity 3. property 4. try his own luck
5. previous 6. eagerly 7. declined to 8. policy

Translations

1 熊與狐狸

有一頭熊大肆吹噓自己的寬大仁慈，並說和其他動物比起來，自己是多麼地善良。（這指的是熊不吃死人的觀念。）

一隻狐狸聽到熊用那種口吻說話，微笑說道：「我的朋友，等你肚子餓的時候，請把注意力放在死人身上，放過那些活著的人。」

偽君子只能騙自己，騙不了別人。

2 獅子與野驢

獅子與野驢一同外出狩獵，野驢憑藉自己優越的速度迅速追逐獵物，獅子接著便上來將獵物撲殺，他們以此方式成功捕獲獵物，當他們要分享戰利品時，獅子把獵物平分成三等份。

「我要拿第一份，」獅子說：「因為我是萬獸之王，第二份也該我拿，因為我和你是伙伴，我應得剩下的一半，至於第三份呢，除非你放棄拿第三份，把它送給我，或是拿著它馬上跑走，否則相信我，你會非常後悔拿走了第三份！」

力量大就有道理。

3 肉販與客人

兩個人到市場裡的一家肉攤去買肉，他們趁肉販轉身的一瞬間，一人拿起一大塊肉，迅速塞到另一人的大衣裡，這樣別人就看不到了。

當肉販回過頭，立刻發現肉不見了，指控這兩個人偷了他的肉。但是從攤子拿起肉的人說肉不在他那兒，藏有肉的人則說他沒拿肉。

肉販很肯定他們在騙他，但是他只說：「你們或許能說謊騙我，但你們騙不了神明，祂們決不會這麼輕易放過你們。」

隱瞞事實等同於欺騙。

4 母獅與母狐

母獅和母狐在一起談論自己的孩子，就像一般母親談話的內容一樣，他們說到孩子們身體多麼健康，長得多好，毛皮有多細緻以及外表有多像父母親等。

「一看到我那窩孩子們就開心，」母狐說道，接著她又不懷好意地說：「不過我倒是注意到妳一胎只能生一隻啊。」

「是啊！」母獅嚴肅地回答：「不過我生下的可是一頭獅子。」

質重於量。

5 父與子

某人有好幾個兒子，這些兒子老是彼此爭執吵架，他雖然盡量排解，卻沒辦法讓兒子們和睦相處。於是他決定用

下面的方法，讓他們看清自己的謬誤。

他叫兒子去拿一捆木棍來，讓他們輪流壓在膝蓋上折斷，每個兒子試了都沒成功。接著他解開原本捆住的木棍，給兒子一人一根棍子，他們全都毫不費力地將木棍折斷了。

「就是這樣，兒子啊，」他說：「只要團結在一起，你們就能勝過敵人，但如果你們老是爭吵分裂，你們就只能輸給攻擊你們的敵人了。」

團結就是力量。

6 狐狸與葡萄

一隻飢餓的狐狸看見一串串令人垂涎欲滴的葡萄，沿著高牆的葡萄藤垂掛下來，他用盡力氣往上跳，想要摘下葡萄。

但他再怎麼試也是徒勞無功，就是搆不到葡萄，終於他放棄了，昂首闊步、毫不在乎地走了，邊走還邊說著：「本來還以為那些葡萄已經成熟了，不過現在看來根本就是酸的。」

吃不到葡萄說葡萄酸。

7 獨眼雄鹿

一隻瞎了一隻眼的雄鹿在海岸邊吃草，期間他一直用好的那一隻眼睛注視著陸地，以察覺到有獵犬接近，而瞎了的那隻眼就對著大海，從沒想過那頭會有什麼危險威脅到他。

但沒想到的是，航行在海岸線的一些水手發現到他，朝他射了一箭致死。當他倒地將死之際，他對自己說道：「我真是愚蠢！我只想到陸地會帶來的危險，但那裡卻沒有人來傷害我；我不害怕海洋那頭會帶來危險，但它卻毀滅了我。」

不幸常在意想不到之時降臨。

8 狼、狐狸與猩猩

一隻狼指控狐狸偷了他的東西，但是狐狸不承認，於是他們找猩猩幫他們解決爭端。

猩猩聽了兩方的說法後，做出了以下的結論：「我認為，」猩猩說：「狼啊，你根本就沒有如你所說的丟了東西；不過另一方面，我認為狐狸你真偷了東西，即使你否認到底。」

沒有誠信的人即使誠實也得不到信任。

9 三名工匠

某個城市裡的居民聚在一起爭論，在接下來要進行的築城防禦工程，要用什麼建材築牆才能達到防禦城池的最佳效果。

一名木匠站起來建議使用木材，他說木材隨手可得，建築起來也很容易。但是石匠反對使用木材，因為太容易著火，因此建議使用以石頭代替。接著一名製革匠也站起來說道：「我認為沒有什麼材料比皮革更好。」

每個人都以自己的立場說話。

10 男人與獅子

一個男人與一頭獅子結伴上路，在對話時，他們開始對彼此吹噓自己的本事，雙方都說自己的力氣與膽量更勝一籌。他們一路上生氣地爭執著，一直到他們走到一條岔路上，那裡有一座雕像，刻的是一個男人勒斃一頭獅子。

「看那裡！」男人志得意滿地說：「看看那雕像！那不正證明了我們人類比你們強壯嗎？」

「別這麼快下結論，我的朋友，」獅子說：「那是以你們的觀點建的雕像，要是我們獅子會做雕像的話，絕對可以肯定，輸的大多是你們人類。」

任何故事都有兩面說法。

11 農人與鸛

農人在剛播好玉米種子的田裡佈下陷阱，要捕捉會來田裡吃種子的鶴。等他回到田裡察看陷阱時，發現有好幾隻鶴都被捉住了，但其中有一隻鸛，哀求農夫放了他：「你不能殺我，我不是鶴，我是一隻鸛，從我的羽毛就能很容易分辨出來，而且我是最誠實無害的鳥類啊。」

但是農夫回答：「我才不管你是什麼鳥，我看到你和這些破壞我穀物的鶴一起被抓到，你就得和他們一起受苦。」

選擇與壞人為伍，沒有人會相信你是好人。

12 游泳的小男孩

一個小男孩在河裡游泳，不小心跑到水深的地方，就在他快要被淹死的危急時刻，一個行經路邊的男人聽到他呼救，立刻跑到河邊，開始責罵他竟然這麼不小心，跑到水深處，毫無要救他的意思。

「先生，」小男孩吼著：「請你先救我上去之後，再慢慢罵我吧。」

在危急時要給幫助，別給建議。

13 老鷹與公雞

農場裡有兩隻公雞，為了爭誰能做老大而決鬥，當決鬥結束，輸的一方躲在陰暗角落裡，而勝利者飛到馬廄的屋頂上，快樂地咕咕啼。

但這時，一隻老鷹在空中瞧見了這隻公雞，立刻飛下來把他給抓走。而另一隻原本躲在角落的公雞立刻走了出來，他再沒有競爭對手，成為雞舍裡的掌權者。

驕者必敗。

14 跳蚤與人

一隻跳蚤咬了一個人一口，接著又咬了他一口又一口，終於那人再也無法忍受，仔細地找尋跳蚤的蹤跡，最後總算把跳蚤給抓住了。

他用大拇指和食指抓著跳蚤說著——幾乎可以算是用吼的，因他實在太生氣了——「你是誰？你這個可惡的小東西，竟然恣意地咬我。」

跳蚤嚇壞了，小小聲地啜泣回應：「大人！求你讓我走吧，別殺我！我這麼小，對你根本不能造成什麼傷害。」

但那人卻笑著說：「我現在就要掐死你，壞事無論大小就得消滅，無論你造成的傷害多輕微都一樣。」

別把同情心浪費在鬧事者身上。

15 蚊子與公牛

一隻蚊子飛到公牛角上，停留了很長一段時間，等牠休息夠了要飛走時，牠對公牛說：「我現在離開，你介意嗎？」

公牛只掀起眼皮，興致缺缺地說道：「對我來說，這是毫無差別的，你來的時候我根本不知道，你要走，我也不會察覺。」

我們往往把自己看得很重要，別人卻不以為然。

16 蛇與老鷹

一隻老鷹從空中往下飛，用他的爪子抓住一條蛇想要吃了牠。但是蛇的動作太快了，老鷹沒抓到，反遭蛇捲住身體，接著雙方便展開一場攸關生死的打鬥。

一名村夫見到他們的衝突，於是上前幫助老鷹，讓他成功從蛇的纏繞中脫逃。蛇為了報復，在那村夫的水壺裡吐了毒液。

村夫因為剛才使力覺得身上很熱，於是想要從水壺喝口水解解渴，老鷹即時把他手中的水壺給撞翻，而水壺裡的水全都灑到地上了。

一件善行值得另一件善行回報。（善有善報。）

17 冷杉與荊棘

一棵冷杉不屑地對荊棘誇口道：「你這可憐的生物，生來一點用處也沒有。你看看我，我可是對各種事物都很有貢獻，特別是當人類要蓋房子的時候，這時候要是沒有我，那他們可是一點事也做不成。」

但是荊棘回答：「哎，那確實是，不過等到他們拿著斧頭和鋸子來要把你砍下時，你就會希望自己是株荊棘，而不是棵冷杉了。」

寧可無用讓人不屑一顧，也好過用處太多所帶來的義務。

18 烏鴉與渡鴉

烏鴉對於渡鴉能夠預測未來，因而被人們視為神鳥而大受崇敬，感到非常嫉妒。

她非常渴望也能得到同樣的好名聲，某天她見到幾名旅人走近，於是便飛到路邊一棵樹的枝頭上，奮力響亮地發出啼叫。那些旅人聽到這聲音感到些許不安，他們擔心這可能是不祥的預兆，直到其中一人看到這隻烏鴉，對他的同伴說：「別擔心，朋友，我們可以放心往前走，那不過是隻烏鴉，沒什麼大不了的。」

那些將自己佯裝成他人者，只會讓自己變得可笑。(東施笑顰。)

19 旅人與懸鈴木

兩名旅人在酷熱的夏季時分，走在光禿禿、滿是灰塵的路上，見到眼前有一棵懸鈴木，便開心地走過去，在枝葉茂密的樹蔭下躲避炙人的陽光。

當他們坐在那兒休息時，抬頭看著這棵樹，其中一人對同伴說：「這棵樹有什麼用！又沒有結果實，對人一點好處也沒有。」

懸鈴木憤怒地打斷他：「你這不知感激的傢伙！」吼著：「你跑來我這樹下躲避炙熱的陽光，在我的樹陰下享受涼爽，竟還敢亂說我一點用也沒有！」

幫助別人往往得不到感激。

20 綿羊、狼與雄鹿

有一次，一頭雄鹿跑去向綿羊借一些麥，並說他的好朋友狼會為他做擔保。然而綿羊擔心他們故意騙她，於是便託辭說道：「狼常常搶了他要的東西，不付錢就跑掉，而你跑得也比我快多了，那麼等到該還債的時候，我又怎麼追得上你們任何一個呢？」

積非不能成是。

21 烏鴉與水瓶

一隻口渴的烏鴉發現了一個水瓶，瓶子裡還有一些水，但是水只有一點點，她再怎麼努力嘗試，嘴巴也還是碰不到瓶裡的水。看著水就在眼前，但是她卻可能就這麼渴死。

終於，她想到一個聰明的方法；她開始把一顆顆小石子丟進水瓶裡，每當她丟下一顆石子，水瓶裡的水就升高一點，一直到水面接近瓶口，這隻聰穎的烏鴉也解決了自己口渴的問題。

需要為發明之母。

22 獅子、狐狸與驢

獅子、狐狸與驢子一同前往打獵，很快就捕殺了很多動物，於是獅子要驢子為他們分配戰利品。驢子將獵物平分成三份，恭敬地請另外兩位先選他們要的那一份，這時獅子突然爆出怒火，躍到驢子身上把他給撕成碎片。

接著他轉而怒瞪著狐狸，要求他重新分配。狐狸幾乎把所有獵物堆在一起，疊成一大份給獅子，而只留下一小口給自己。

「我親愛的朋友，」獅子說，「你是如何學會分配獵物的技巧？真是做得太好了！」

狐狸回答：「我嗎？喔！我是從驢子那裡學來的教訓。」

聰明人會從別人的不幸中學習教訓。

23 工人與蛇

一名工人的小兒子被蛇咬死了，父親悲痛不已，在怒氣中他拿起斧頭，前往那條蛇的洞口，等待機會要殺了牠。

沒多久蛇出洞了，工人瞄準牠一斧砍下，卻只切下了牠尾端，被蛇溜回洞裡去了。工人想辦法希望讓蛇再次出洞，於是假意要向牠道歉。

但是蛇卻回答他：「我決不可能和你成為好友，因為你砍斷了我的尾巴；而你失去了兒子，也絕對不會成為我的朋友。」

在造成傷害的人面前，永遠無法忘記傷痛。

24 螃蟹與狐狸

有一隻螃蟹，離開了海岸，跑到內陸一片草地上去居住，那片土地看起來很美，綠油油的，似乎是個能餵飽自己的好地方。

但一隻飢餓的狐狸經過，發現螃蟹後把他給抓住了，就在狐狸要吃螃蟹時，螃蟹開口說：「落到這地步真是我活該，我真不該離開海邊的天然棲息地搬到這裡，還當自己是屬於陸地一樣。」

知足常樂。

25 獵犬與野兔

一頭年輕的獵狗追逐一隻野兔，當他抓住野兔時，先用牙齒啃咬她，彷彿要殺了她，然後卻又放開她，與她蹦跳嬉鬧，就像與其他狗玩耍一樣。

最後野兔說道：「我希望你能表現真實的情緒！如果你當我是朋友，為什麼要咬我？如果你當我是敵人，那你又為什麼要和我玩耍？」

態度左右搖擺的不是朋友。

26 貓與公雞

一隻貓撲上一隻公雞，並試著想出了一個吃掉他的藉口，因為貓通常是不吃公雞的，她也明白自己不應該去吃公雞。

終於她說：「你的行為太惹人厭了，天未亮就咕咕叫把人吵醒，所以我來了結你。」

但是公雞為自己辯護，他說自己之所以啼叫，是為了喚醒人們適時著手一天的工作，要是沒有他，人們會不知道該怎麼辦才好。

「或許真是如此，」這隻貓說：「但無論人們需不需要你，我都不能不吃我的晚餐啊。」接著便殺了公雞把他吞下肚了。

壞人總是能找到藉口做惡。

27 盲人與幼獸

從前有位盲眼的人，他的觸覺非常敏銳，任何動物只要經他手摸過，他便能靠觸感得知那是什麼動物。

某天他手中摸到一隻幼狼，人家問他那是什麼動物，他觸摸了一陣子之後回答：「的確，我不確定這是狼還是狐狸的幼兒，不過我很確定的是——絕不能放心把他放進羊欄裡。」

惡性總是在年幼時便展現。

28 老鼠與公牛

一頭公牛追捕在他鼻子上咬了一口的老鼠，但是老鼠跑得太快，一溜煙就鑽進牆下的洞裡去了。公牛極其憤怒，一次又一次猛撞著牆壁，直到精疲力竭，全身無力地倒在地上。

就當一切恢復平靜時，老鼠突然衝出來，又咬了公牛一口，盛怒下公牛又站起來，但這時老鼠已經再次鑽回洞裡去了。公牛無計可施，只能氣得咆哮痛罵。

沒過多久，他聽到牆裡傳來一陣細小尖銳的聲音：「你們那些大塊頭未必總是吃香，你看，有時候我們這些小人物也能佔上風。」

勝利未必總是屬於強的一方。

29 敗家子與燕

有一個揮霍無度的敗家子，把所有財產都花光了，只剩下身上穿的衣服。一個天氣晴朗的早春，他見到一隻燕子，以為夏天就要來臨，心想用不著身上的大衣了，於是便把大衣拿去賣掉，換了一些錢。

然而天氣又發生變化，天氣變得極冷，凍死了那隻不幸的燕子。當這個敗家子見到燕子的屍體時，他哭著說：「真可憐的鳥兒啊！都是因為你，現在我也要被凍死了。」

一燕不足以成夏。

30 狐狸與猴子

一隻狐狸與一隻猴子同行，一路上互相爭論著誰的出身比較高貴。他們各自爭執一番後，直到走到了立滿紀念碑的墓園時，猴子在這兒停下腳步，環顧四周，大大嘆了一口氣。

「你為什麼要嘆氣？」狐狸問。

猴子指著其中眾多墳墓回答：「你在

這裡看到的所有紀念碑，都是在紀念我祖先的榮耀，過去他們可都是聲名顯赫的大人物呢。」

狐狸好一陣子無言以對，但他很快便回過神來，說道：「喔！你就盡量在那兒吹噓騙人吧，老兄，反正你說什麼都安全得很，我相信你的祖先沒有一個會站起來揭穿你的！」

說大話者在無人揭穿時，特別會自吹自擂。

31 牧童與狼

有位牧童在村莊附近照看羊群，他想，如果騙那些村民有狼來攻擊羊群，那一定會很有趣，於是他大喊著：「狼來了！狼來了！」但是當人們急忙跑來時，牧童卻對著他們大笑。

他這麼惡作劇不只一次，而每當村民跑來，就發現自己被騙了，因為根本就沒有狼。最後，狼終於來了，牧童大喊著：「狼來了！狼來了！」他用盡力氣喊叫，但是村民早就習慣聽他這麼吼叫，根本就不理會他的求助。狼於是抓住了所有的羊，輕易地殺了一隻又一隻綿羊。

常說謊話的人，即使說真話也無人相信。

32 烏鴉與天鵝

烏鴉見到天鵝一身潔白無瑕的羽毛，感到非常羨慕，他猜想一定是天鵝經常在水裡洗澡與游泳，羽毛才會如此潔白。

於是他離開靠撿祭祀的肉屑維生的祭壇附近，搬到水池與小溪邊。但即使他每天多次洗澡，清洗自己的羽毛，卻怎麼也沒辦法把羽毛變白，最後還因此死於飢餓。

習慣可以改變，但天性無法改變。

33 狼與馬

一匹狼漫無目的地遊走，來到一片燕麥田，不過因為他不能吃大麥，於是便走開了，繼續前行，路上他遇到一匹馬走過來。

「喂，」這匹狼說道：「這兒有一片很好的燕麥田，我特別為你留下來沒吃，而且我很喜歡聽馬大口咀嚼成熟穀物的聲音。」

但是馬卻回答：「要是狼會吃燕麥的話，我親愛的朋友，你才不會只滿足耳朵的享受，而只會顧著填飽你的肚子了。」

將己所不欲施予他人，並無美德可言。

34 籠中鳥與蝙蝠

掛在窗外的鳥籠裡關著一隻會歌唱的鳥兒，她總在夜裡其他鳥兒入睡後唱歌。有一晚，一隻蝙蝠飛來攀在鳥籠的鐵條邊，詢問鳥兒為何白天安靜，只在夜裡歌唱。

「我會這麼做當然是有很好的理由，」鳥兒說：「這是因為我以前在白天唱歌時，一名獵人被我的歌聲吸引，撒網把我給捉住了，從那時候起我就只在夜裡唱歌了。」

但是蝙蝠卻回答：「你現在已經是籠中鳥，這麼做一點用也沒有了，要是你在被捕到之前就這麼做的話，說不定你至今仍逍遙自在呢。」

事情發生後才開始警覺提防也是徒然。

35 農夫與狐狸

一隻狐狸老是在夜裡潛入農夫的院子，偷走他養的母雞，把農夫惹得很不高興，於是他設下陷阱抓住狐狸，想要報復他。農夫在狐狸尾巴上綁了一捆麥稈，點了火後再放了他。

但是很倒楣的是，狐狸偏偏直接跑向穀粒成熟、正值收成的玉米田裡，很快地田裡著了火，燒光了一切，農夫也失去他所有的收成。

報復是一把雙面刃。

36 獅子與公牛

獅子見到一頭肥美的公牛在牛群中吃草，想辦法要讓他成為自己的囊中物，於是獅子對公牛說他要殺一頭綿羊吃，問自己是否有榮幸與他一同享用，公牛接受了獅子的邀請。但是當他抵達獅子住的洞穴，見到一大排燉鍋與鐵叉，卻毫無綿羊的蹤跡，於是公牛轉身，靜靜地離開。

獅子在他身後以難過的語氣詢問他離開的理由，於是公牛回頭對他說：「我的理由很充分，當我見到你準備好的一切，我馬上就知道這次的主食是牛，不是綿羊。」

當著鳥兒的面撒網是枉費工夫的。

37 龜兔賽跑

一隻野兔某天取笑烏龜腳程慢。

「等一下，」烏龜說：「我和你比賽跑，我保證自己會贏。」

「喔，好啊！」野兔回答，對這個主意感到可笑，「我們就試試看吧。」於是便同意由狐狸為他們訂下路程，並擔任裁判。

時間一到，烏龜與野兔同時出發，野兔的速度迅速，大幅領先，他想還可以休息一下，於是便躺下來睡著了。同時，烏龜踏著步伐慢慢爬行，及時抵達了終點。

終於野兔突然從睡夢中驚醒，用最快的速度衝向終點，但卻發現烏龜早就已經抵達，贏得比賽了。

緩慢穩步前進者終能得勝。

38 牧羊人與山羊

某天，一名牧羊人把他的羊全都趕

回了羊欄裡，但卻有一隻羊離隊，不願與其他羊一起回去，牧羊人花了很長時間叫喚她、對她吹口哨，但卻完全無法得到這隻山羊的注意，於是他拿起一顆石頭丟向她，打破了她的一隻角。

牧羊人因此很害怕，絕望中哀求山羊別把事情告訴他的主人，但是山羊回答：「你這蠢人，就算我閉口不說，我的角也會把事情大聲的說出來啊！」

瞞不了的事要隱瞞也沒用。（紙包不了火。）

39 下金蛋的鵝

有個男人與他太太很好運，因為他們有了一隻每天會下一顆金蛋的鵝。他們雖然幸運地擁有這隻鵝，卻很快地開始覺得財富增加得不夠快，他們以為這隻鵝的肚子裡一定都是金子，於是決定把鵝宰了，確保能立刻拿到所有珍貴的金子。

但是當他們把鵝剖開後，發現他肚裡就跟其他的鵝一模一樣。於是他們不僅沒有如原本所希望的一樣馬上致富，也失去了每天增加一點財富的樂趣。

貪得無厭，便會失去一切。

40 蝙蝠與黃鼠狼

一隻蝙蝠落在地上，被黃鼠狼叼去，就在黃鼠狼要殺了牠吃掉時，牠趕緊求饒。黃鼠狼說他做不到，因為自己生來就是所有鳥類的天敵。

「喔！可是啊，我根本不是鳥。」蝙蝠說：「我是一隻老鼠！」

黃鼠狼說，「讓我仔細瞧瞧，你真的是老鼠呀。」於是便放牠走了。

過了一段時間，這隻蝙蝠又在同樣的情況下，被另一隻黃鼠狼抓住了，而就像上一回一樣，牠用同樣的方法懇求黃鼠狼饒牠一命。

「不行，」這隻黃鼠狼說，「我從不為了任何理由放過任何一隻老鼠。」

「但是我不是老鼠，」蝙蝠說，「我是一隻鳥。」

「啊，你的確是。」黃鼠狼說，於是也放牠走了。

認清形勢，隨機應變。

41 驢子、公雞與獅子

一頭驢子和一隻公雞一同生活在牛欄裡，沒多久，一隻餓了很多天的獅子正要撲上驢子，準備飽餐一頓之時，公雞伸直了身子，猛力拍著翅膀，發出響亮的啼叫。

如果說有什麼事能嚇到獅子，那肯定就是公雞啼了，這獅子聽到公雞叫，立刻逃之夭夭。

驢子見到這情形洋洋得意，心想若是獅子連公雞都怕，那更就別提見到驢子會有什麼反應了。於是他跑出去追捕獅子，但當他們跑到遠處，見不到公雞身影也聽不到雞啼時，獅子赫然轉過身撲上去，將驢子給吃了。

盲目的自信往往導致災禍。

42 吹噓的旅人

有個人到國外旅遊，回來之後，他對大家說他在外國發生的許多有趣的故事，還說了他在羅德島參加了一場跳遠比賽，在比賽時他跳得太好了，根本沒人能打敗他的紀錄。「你們可以去羅德島問問那裡的人，」他說，「每個人都會告訴你這是真的。」

這時其中一個聽到的人說：「如果你真能跳那麼遠，我們也不用去羅德島證明啊，我們就想像這裡就是羅德島，你跳吧！」

行動勝於空談。

43 獅子與三頭公牛

三頭公牛一同在草地上吃草，被獅子看到了，他一直想抓住這幾隻公牛吃了他們，但只要他們三個團結在一起，他就不是他們的對手。

於是獅子開始到處散播惡意不實的謠言，刻意挑起他們之間的嫉妒與不信任，這項計謀非常成功，公牛之間不久就變得冷漠疏遠，最後他們避開彼此，各自前去吃草。

獅子一見到這情況，便分別撲向這三隻公牛，一頭接著一頭吃了。

朋友不合便是敵人的機會。

44 狼與狗

很久很久以前，狼群對狗兒們說：「我們為什麼得一直這麼敵對下去？你們和我們有這麼多相同點，我們之間唯一的差別，只在於你們受人訓練。我們過著自在的生活，你們卻得做人類的奴隸，他們鞭打你們，在你們脖子上套上沈重的項圈，強迫你們為他們看守牛羊群，而獎賞除了骨頭之外，什麼也沒有。別再這麼忍受下去了，把羊群交給我們吧，我們可以過著輕鬆飽食的生活，一起享用大餐。」

狗兒們被這番話說服，同意了狼的做法，便與他們一同回到狼的洞穴裡，而當他們一走進洞裡，狼群就對他們展開猛烈攻擊，把他們全都撕成片片。

叛徒應受最嚴重的懲罰。

45 螞蟻

很久以前，螞蟻本來是人類，靠耕地維生，但是因為對自己工作的成果不滿意，他們老是渴望地看著鄰居種的作物與果實，只要有機會就把這些屬於鄰居的東西偷走，增加自己糧食的存量。最後他們的貪婪讓宙斯發怒，於是把這些人全都變成螞蟻。

但即使他們的外貌改變了，本性卻不變，所以直到今日，他們還是會跑到田地裡，搬走別人辛勤工作的成果，儲存起來自己用。

你可以懲罰小偷，但卻無法改變他的習性。

46 北風與太陽

北風與太陽之間起了爭執，雙方都聲稱自己比對方強大，最後他們同意在一位旅人的身上試試自己的力量，看誰能最快讓路人脫下身上的斗篷。

北風先試，他聚集起所有的力量攻擊，在旅人的身上颳起劇烈強風，拖住他的斗篷彷彿要一股作氣扯下他身上的斗篷，但是他吹得越猛，旅人就把斗篷裹得越緊。接著輪到太陽了，一開始他溫和地照耀著旅人，很快地旅人便把扣子解開，讓斗篷寬鬆地掛在肩膀上行走。接著太陽使盡全力照耀出光芒，而旅人沒走幾步，就開心地把斗篷脫下，衣著輕鬆地走完他的旅程。

勸說往往比強迫更有效。

47 雄鹿與葡萄藤

一隻雄鹿為了躲避獵人們的追捕，躲藏在濃密的葡萄藤後，獵人們沒見到他的蹤跡，就這麼經過他的藏身處，絲毫沒發現雄鹿就在附近。

雄鹿以為危險已經過去了，便開始吃起葡萄藤上的葉子，這個舉動卻引起折返回來的獵人注意，其中一人以為有什麼動物躲藏在那裡，於是往枝葉茂密處射了一隻箭。不幸的雄鹿被箭射穿心臟，就在他即將斷氣之時，說道：「這是我應得的報應，因為我竟恩將仇報，去吃保護我的葡萄藤。」

忘恩負義者自會受到懲罰。

48 淘氣的狗

以前有隻狗，老是無理由地咬人，惹得每個到他主人家拜訪的人都很厭惡，於是他的主人在他脖子上掛了個鈴鐺，警告接近狗的人。狗兒對掛上這個鈴鐺感到很神氣，昂首闊步地走著弄響鈴鐺，從中獲得極大的滿足。

但是一隻老狗跑到他面前對他說：「你的態度別那麼得意才好啊，我的朋友。你不會以為這個鈴鐺是你做好事的獎賞吧？剛好相反，這可是不光彩的象徵啊。」

惡名常被誤以為好名聲。

49 農夫與命運女神

一名農夫某天在他的田地耕田時，用犁翻出了一大罐金幣，開心得不得了，從那天起便每日到神廟祭祀大地女神。

命運女神對此很不高興，來到農夫面前對他說：「喂，小子，那些金子是我送給你的禮物，你怎麼會以為是大地女神的恩惠呢？你從來沒想過要感謝我賜給你好運，但要是你不走運，弄丟了那些金幣，到時你就會怪我這命運女神沒帶給你好運。」

在該感恩處就該感恩。

50 養蜂人

一個小偷趁著養蜂人出門時進入養蜂場，把所有的蜂蜜都偷走了，當養蜂人回家發現蜂巢裡的蜂蜜都被搬空了，氣得不得了，站在那兒瞪了好久。

不久後蜜蜂採蜜回來，發現蜂巢都被打翻，而養蜂人就站在一旁，他們便用螫針刺他。

養蜂人勃然大怒道：「你們這群不知感恩的壞蛋！讓偷走蜂蜜的小偷脫逃，卻叮我這個一直照顧你們的人！」

找人報復之前，先確定自己找對了對象。

51 男孩與榛果

一個小男孩把手伸進裝滿榛果的罐子裡，想盡量一次抓一大把。當他想要把手伸出來時，手卻拔不出來，因為瓶口太小，而他的手抓了太多東西，沒辦法通過。

男孩不想放棄手抓裡的榛果，卻又沒辦法把手伸出來，於是便大哭了起來。旁邊的人看到問題所在，對他說：「好孩子，別那麼貪心了，知足一點，拿一半就好，那樣你就能毫不費力地把手伸出來啦。」

不要一次貪多。

52 牧羊人與狼

一位牧羊人在牧草地上發現了一頭迷路的幼狼，於是把他帶回家與自己的狗兒們養在一起。當小狼成長後，如果有狼想要從羊群中偷走綿羊，他會加入狗兒的行列，去追捕那匹狼。

有時候狗兒未必能抓住偷羊的狼，這時他們會放棄追逐返回家中，小狼在這種情況下會獨自繼續追捕小偷，等到他追到那個罪魁禍首，便會停下來，和小偷一起享用羊肉大餐，飽餐後再回到牧羊人家裡。

但是如果有一段時間都沒有狼來把綿羊抓走，小狼就會自己偷一隻，和狗兒一起享用他偷走的羊。後來牧羊人漸起了疑心，而某天就正好讓他抓到小狼正在偷羊，於是牧羊人拿出繩子繞在狼的脖子上，將他吊死在最近的一棵樹上。

骨子裡的本性，最後必會表現於外在行為。

53 池邊的雄鹿

一隻口渴的雄鹿走到池邊喝水，當他彎下腰接近水面時，見到自己在水中的倒影，突然對自己頭上生長的細緻鹿角感到自豪，但同時卻對自己瘦弱的腿感到嫌棄。

正當他在池邊欣賞自己的外貌時，一頭獅子發現了他，對他展開攻擊，接著便是一陣追逐，雄鹿很快地就跑在獅子前面。只要在沒有樹木的空曠土地上，雄鹿都一直跑在前面。但沒多久他跑進一片森林，鹿角被樹枝卡住，使他成為敵人口爪下的犧牲品。

「唉！我實在愚蠢！」臨死之前雄鹿喊道：「我瞧不起自己的腿，但我的腿卻能救我一命，我為頭上的角沾沾自喜，但我的角卻害死我。」

最有價值的東西往往最不被重視。

54 蜜蜂與宙斯

一隻女王蜂從伊米托斯山飛到奧林帕斯山，帶了蜂巢裡的新鮮蜂蜜給宙斯當作禮物，宙斯對這禮物感到很滿意，於是承諾答應她的所有要求。她說，如果宙斯能賜螫針給蜜蜂，當人類搶奪牠們的蜂蜜時，牠們便能用螫針殺死人，那她便會感到十分感激。

宙斯對這個請求非常不悅，因為他很喜愛人類，但是他之前已經承諾過了，所以他說蜜蜂將能獲得螫針，但是他雖然賜螫針給牠們，但是只要蜜蜂用螫針叮人，那螫針就會斷掉留在人的傷口上，而蜜蜂自己也會死去。

懷抱惡意總會自食其果。

55 大力士海克力斯與馬車夫

一名馬車夫駕著後面滿載貨物的馬車，行駛在泥濘的小路上，當馬車的車輪深陷泥濘，他的馬匹用盡力氣也拉不出來。

馬車夫無助地站在那兒，時而大聲地呼喊，請求大力士海克力斯的幫助，這時海克力斯出現了，對他說：「小子，用你的肩膀去頂車輪，鞭策你的馬匹用力拉，等這些事你都做到了以後，再呼喚海克力斯來幫你。如果你連一根手指都不動，那也別期望海克力斯或任何其他人會幫你的忙。」

天助自助者。

56 驢子與買主

有個人想要買一頭驢子，於是前往市場，他看到一頭頗為合適的驢子，於是便和主人商量，帶他回去試用，看看他到底適不適合。

一到家，他便把驢子牽進馬廄，和其他驢子關在一起。這新到的驢子往四周瞧了瞧，立刻就走到畜欄裡最懶惰、最貪婪的驢子身邊待著，這人一看到這情形，立刻為他套上轡繩，帶他回去交給原來的主人。

原主人見到驢子這麼快就回來，大吃一驚，問道：「你已經測試出他了嗎？」那人回答：「我不用再測試了，從他自己選擇的同伴，我就能看出他是哪一種動物。」

物以類聚，人以群分。

57 熊與旅人

兩個人一同上路旅遊，一隻熊突然出現在途中，當熊看著這兩人時，其中一人已經跑到路邊的樹木旁，爬到樹枝上躲了起來。

另一個人的動作沒有同伴那麼靈活，他因為逃不了，便索性讓自己倒在地上裝死。那隻熊走近他，在他身邊到處嗅了嗅，而他依然動也不動，屏住呼吸，因為聽人說熊是不吃死人的。那隻熊以為他是屍體，於是便走開了。

當危險過去，躲在樹上的人爬下來，問另一人剛才那隻熊把嘴湊到他耳邊說了些什麼，那人回答：「他告訴我，絕對不要和一有危險就拋棄你的朋友一起旅行。」

患難見真情。

58 家驢和野驢

一天，一頭在各處閒晃的野驢遇見一隻馱貨驢伸展著四肢，躺在陽光照耀處，享受得很，於是野驢走上前對他說：「你還真是個幸運的傢伙！光滑的毛皮顯示你的生活優渥舒適，我實在很羨慕你！」

但沒過多久，野驢再次見到這位朋友，這次他卻馱著重重的貨物，車夫則跟在後面用粗棍子鞭打他。

「啊！我的朋友！」野驢對他說：「我再也不羨慕你了，因為現在我看見你為舒適享受的生活所付出的代價。」

要付出大代價才得到的利益不見得是福氣。

59 青蛙和井

兩隻青蛙共同住在一個池塘，但某個炎熱的夏季，池塘乾枯了，於是他們離開此處去尋找其他地方居住，因為青蛙總是喜歡居住在潮濕的地區。

不久他們來到一座深井邊，其中一隻青蛙往裡面瞧了瞧，對另一隻說道：「這個地方看起來很不錯，我們就跳下去在這裡定居吧。」

但另一隻較有智慧的青蛙回答：「先別急，朋友。萬一這座井就像先前那個池塘一樣乾枯了，那我們要怎麼出來呢？」

三思而後行。

60 狗與狼

一條狗躺在農家庭院的大門口前曬太陽，一隻狼突然撲向他，正準備張開口把他吃下肚時，狗開口為自己的性命求饒：「你看我這麼瘦，你吃起來會是多不盡興的一餐啊！但是你只要等幾天，過幾天我主人要辦一場筵席，那些豐盛的殘羹剩餚最後都會進我肚子裡，到時我會變得又肥又胖，到時候你再來吃我也不遲啊。」

狼對這個計畫感到很滿意，於是就先離開了，過了一段時間他又回到這農家，卻發現狗兒躺在他搆不著的馬廄屋頂上。

「下來吧！」他大叫，「下來讓我吃吧，還記得我們的約定吧？」

但這時狗卻冷淡地說：「這位朋友，要是下次你又在大門口抓住我，可千萬別再等什麼筵席了。」

一朝被蛇咬，十年怕草繩。

61 農人與蘋果樹

一位農夫的花園裡長了一顆蘋果樹，但是樹上卻長不出蘋果，只能提供麻雀和蚱蜢一個遮蔭避熱的地方，他們會棲在樹枝上唱歌。農夫對果樹不能結出果實非常失望，決定砍了這棵樹，於是回去拿了斧頭過來。

但是當麻雀和蚱蜢看到農夫要這麼做時，他們懇求他別砍這棵樹，還對農夫說：「如果你砍了這棵樹，我們就得到別處找棲身之所，而你工作時，花園裡就不會有活潑愉快的鳴叫聲陪伴你了。」

但農夫不願聽他們的，下定決心開始往樹幹上砍，他砍了幾下之後，發現樹幹裡是空的，裡面住了一群蜜蜂，還存放了一大堆蜂蜜。農夫對這項發現感到愉悅，丟了斧頭說：「這老樹總算是值得保留的。」

實用性是大多數人衡量價值的標準。

62 蝙蝠、荊棘與海鷗

蝙蝠、荊棘與海鷗合夥做生意，決定要一起航行經商。蝙蝠為了這趟投資借了一筆錢，荊棘搜集了各式各樣的衣物，海鷗則是帶著大量的鉛，就這樣他們出發了。

但沒多久他們便遇上一場暴風雨，整艘船連同所有貨物都翻覆沈到海底，而他們則想辦法回到陸地上。

此後，海鷗就不斷在海上來回飛行，時不時潛下海面，尋找他遺失的鉛；蝙蝠則是害怕遇到債主，於是白天躲起來，晚上才敢出門覓食；荊棘會抓住路人的衣服，希望有天能認出並找回自己丟掉的衣物。

人們總是想找回他們失去的，卻不去尋找自己所缺少的。

63 老鼠與黃鼠狼

老鼠與黃鼠狼間起了戰爭，老鼠每回都屈居下風，被黃鼠狼吃了許多同伴，於是他們開了一場作戰會議，一隻年長的老鼠站起來發言：「難怪我們老是吃敗仗，因為我們沒有將領為我們規畫戰役，指揮我們在戰場上的行動。」

聽從他的建議後，大家選出幾隻最大的老鼠當作指揮官，而這幾隻老鼠為了區分自己與其他普通士兵的不同，便戴上了有稻草裝飾的大頭盔。

接著他們帶領老鼠們前往戰鬥，自信滿滿會贏得勝利。然而他們卻還是像過去一樣吃了敗仗，個個都飛快地跑回他們的洞裡，大多數老鼠們都能安全無虞地跑回洞裡，除了那些將領，他們被自己頭上階級的象徵阻礙了行動，沒辦法回到洞裡去，全都輕易落入敵人的手中。

偉大自有其痛苦的代價。

64 驢、狐狸與獅子

一頭驢子與一隻狐狸結伴前去覓食，但走沒多久，便見到一頭獅子朝他們過來，他們倆都害怕得不得了。

這時，狐狸想到一個可以自救的辦法，於是大膽地跑到獅子面前，在他耳邊小聲說道：「如果你答應放我走，我可以幫你抓住驢子，你不必費事地追著他就能逮住他。」

獅子同意了。於是狐狸回到同伴身邊，很快把驢子帶到一個隱藏的坑洞邊，那是獵人挖來捕捉動物的陷阱，結果驢子就這麼掉進陷阱裡了。

當獅子見到驢子已經被捉住，再也跑不掉，反而先把注意力轉向狐狸，他很快地先把狐狸解決，接著再從容地享用驢子大餐。

出賣朋友，自己往往也沒有好下場！

65 騙子

有個人生了病，病況非常嚴重，於是他對神明許下誓言，如果能讓他恢復健康，那麼他願意拿一百頭牛奉獻給神明。神明想看看這人能不能遵守諾言，於是讓他在短時間內恢復了健康。

不過他連一頭牛都沒有，於是他用蠟做成一百頭小牛，把這些小牛放在祭壇上，同時說道：「諸位神明，我請你們見證我已履行了誓言。」

神明為了報復他，於是讓他做了一個夢，在夢中祂們命他前往海邊，去拿一百個金幣，他興奮不已，急忙來到海邊，卻落入一群強盜手中，他們抓住這人把他賣了做奴隸，賣出的價錢正好是一百個金幣。

自己做不到的事別任意承諾。

66 貓與鼠

從前有一戶人家家裡鼠滿為患，一隻貓聽到了這事，對自己說道：「那地方太適合我了。」於是她立刻出發，到那戶人家裡住下，一隻又一隻地捉住老鼠，把牠們都吞下了肚。

終於那些老鼠受不了了，下定決心要一直待在洞裡不出去。

「這可不好對付，」這隻貓心想，「唯一的方法，就是想個計謀把牠們給騙出來。」

於是她思忖了一會兒，接著爬到牆上，用兩隻後腳鉤住釘子，身體往下吊著，假裝自己已經死了。過了一會兒，一隻老鼠往外偷看，見到貓吊在那兒。

「哈！」老鼠大喊：「這位女士，不可否認妳是很聰明，不過哪怕妳把自己變成一袋麵粉掛在那裡，也沒辦法把我們騙去妳旁邊讓妳抓。」

一旦一朝為患，聰明人便會時時警戒。

67 老鷹、寒鴉與牧羊人

某天，寒鴉見到一隻老鷹突然俯衝向一隻羔羊，用爪子把牠抓走。

「哇！」寒鴉見狀說道：「我也要這麼做。」

於是牠高高飛至空中，翅膀大力揮動咻地一聲，往下衝向一隻公羊背上，但牠一落在羊背上，爪子就被羊毛給纏住了，而牠用盡辦法也拔不出來，只能卡在那兒拍打著翅膀，但這徒讓情況變得更糟。

過了不久牧羊人來了，「唉呀！」他說：「你就一直在做這事啊？」接著他修剪寒鴉的翅膀，把牠帶回家給孩子們，牠現在外表看起來怪得很，孩子們搞不清牠是什麼動物。

「牠算是哪一種鳥類啊，父親？」孩子們問。

「這是一隻寒鴉，」他回答，「他就只是一隻寒鴉，但卻希望別人以為牠是一隻老鷹。」

自不量力只會讓努力白費，不僅自找麻煩也招來訕笑。

68 雲雀與農夫

一隻雲雀在一片田裡築巢，並把一窩小鳥帶在逐漸成熟的穀粒下養大。在小鳥兒們羽翼未豐的某一天，農夫前來察看自己的收成，發現穀物成長得很快，於是說：「我得傳話給鄰居，請他們來幫忙收割。」

一隻小雲雀無意中聽到農夫說的話，非常害怕，跑去跟媽媽說要立刻搬家。

「不必急，」媽媽回答：「一個人會找朋友幫忙，就表示事情還不急。」過了幾天農夫又來了，見到作物已經過熟，穀穗都已經落到地上了。

「這下我可不能再拖延了，」他說：「這段時間我得立刻雇幾個人並叫他們立刻上工。」雲雀聽到農夫的話後，對孩子們說：「來吧，孩子們，我們得走了。現在他不再提要請朋友幫忙，而是要親自採取行動了。」

自助是最好的幫助。

69 守財奴

一個守財奴賣掉了自己所有的物品，並將存下的黃金熔成一塊金塊，偷偷埋藏在地裡。每天他都去看那金塊，有時會看著這金塊許久，沾沾自喜於他的財寶。

守財奴的一名工人注意到他經常到這個地方，於是一天，這工人偷看著守財奴的一舉一動，發現了他的秘密。工人等待著時機，某天夜裡，到那裡去把金塊挖了出來，偷走了。

第二天，守財奴像往常一樣到埋金塊的地方，發現他的財寶被偷了，開始拉扯自己的頭髮，呻吟哀怨自己的損失。

此時，一位鄰居看到了守財奴的情況，問他怎麼回事。守財奴訴說了自己的不幸，但是另外一個鄰居卻說：「不要哭得這麼傷心，我的朋友；把一塊磚放進洞，然後每天看看它，相信我，你不會再更糟了，因為即使當你擁有金塊時，你也沒有好好使用它啊。」

貨幣真正的價值不在於擁有它，而是明智地使用它。

70 獅子與老鼠

在巢穴裡睡著的獅子，被一隻跑過他臉上的老鼠給吵醒了，盛怒下，他舉起爪子抓起老鼠，準備一口吃掉。老鼠十分害怕，求獅子饒牠一命，大喊著說：「這一次就放過我吧！說不定哪天，我可以報答您的慈悲。」

聽到老鼠這麼一個弱小動物居然說他能幫助自己，獅子覺得很好笑，哈哈大笑後開心地把爪子鬆開，放走了老鼠。

但老鼠報恩的機會來了。一天，獅子被獵人撒下的網給抓住了，這時候，老鼠聽見並認出了獅子憤怒的吼聲，趕忙前去，立刻用牙齒咬斷繩子，不久就成功救出獅子。

老鼠說：「你看，之前你笑我如何能報答你，但現在你知道了，即使是一隻小老鼠也能救出大獅子。」

幫助別人永遠不會徒勞無功

71 擠牛奶的姑娘

一個農夫的女兒出門擠牛奶，擠完後，她把裝著牛奶的桶子頂在頭上，返回製乳場。

她一邊走著，一邊思忖著：「這桶子裡的牛奶，可以做成乳脂，我再把它做成奶油，拿到市場去賣，這些奶油賣出的錢，可以買好幾個雞蛋；等到雞蛋孵化，就會生出小雞，這麼不斷生下去，不久我就可以開個很大的養雞場；到時候我再拿些小雞去賣，賣出的錢，就可以為自己買一件新長裙。我要穿著裙子去慶典，到時候所有的青年都會欣賞我穿的新裙子而愛上我，但是這時我要撇開頭，不跟他們說話。」

她想得太入迷，竟忘了頭上還有個桶子，就把頭甩開，於是桶子掉了下來，牛奶灑滿了一地，而她所有的夢想，也都在那剎那幻滅了！

雞還沒孵出來之前，先別急著數數。

72 女人與農人

一位近日喪偶的女子，日日前往亡夫墳前哭泣。此時，在不遠處犁田的農夫看見了這名女子，想娶她為妻，於是他拋下犁、跑到她身旁坐下來，也開始掉淚。

女子問農夫為何哭泣，他答道：「我摯愛的妻子最近也去世，眼淚能減輕我的悲傷。」女子說：「我也剛剛失去了丈夫。」兩人默哀了一陣子。

農夫提議：「既然我們同病相憐，何不結為夫妻作伴呢？我可以代替妳死去的丈夫，而妳可以代替我死去的妻子。」女子同意了這聽起來頗合理的主意，於是兩人擦乾眼淚。

此時，一名竊賊偷走了農夫的幾頭牛，只剩下犁。發現牛被偷了，農夫為損失搥胸放聲大哭。當女子聽到農夫的哭聲時，她走近問：「喔！為何你還在哭呢？」農夫回答：「這次，我是真的哭了。」

73 猴子與海豚

從前，人們航行時，時常隨身帶著寵物小狗或猴子作為旅伴娛樂，故一名從東方返回雅典城的男子也帶著一隻小猴子上了船。

就當他們接近阿提卡區的沿岸時，突然襲來一陣暴風雨，船沉了，所有船上的人都翻覆至海中，拚著游泳保命，猴子也一樣。一隻海豚看到這猴子，以為他是人類就將他放在背上，載他游往岸邊。

當他們接近雅典城的港口——比雷埃夫斯，海豚問猴子是不是雅典人，猴子回答他正是，並說自己出身於一個非常顯赫的家族。

「那你一定知道比雷埃夫斯囉，」海豚說道。猴子以為海豚指的是一名高官或其他人，便回說：「當然，他是我的老朋友了。」

察覺猴子的謊言，海豚十分厭惡便逕自潛入海中，拋下了猴子，這隻不幸的猴子也很快地溺死了。

74 驢子與馱貨

有個小販養了一隻驢子，一天他買了大量的鹽，盡可能把這些鹽堆在驢子身上讓他揹。在回家的路上，驢子渡溪時不小心摔了一跤，跌倒在水裡，結果鹽被浸濕，大部分的鹽溶解並被水沖走了，因此當驢子再站起來，發現他身上背的貨物輕多了。

但是小販卻騎著他回到城裡買了更多鹽，放進原本就裝鹽的馱籃中，再讓驢子揹著往前走。等他們一走到溪邊，驢子便在溪裡躺下又站起來，就像上回一樣，身上背的貨物輕多了。

不過這時主人發現了驢子的把戲，再次回到城裡，買了大量的海綿，堆放在驢子的背上，當他們再度走到溪邊，驢子又躺下了，但這次海綿吸收了大量的溪水，當驢子站起來，發現他背負的貨物比之前重太多了。

好牌只能久久出一次。

75 農夫、農子與禿鼻烏鴉

一位農夫剛播種一片麥田，並小心翼翼地看顧這片作物，因為很多禿鼻烏鴉與椋鳥老是棲息在田上，吃光他的穀物。在農夫旁的兒子手裡拿著彈弓，每當農夫要取彈弓時，椋鳥因為聽得懂農夫説的話，就示警禿鼻烏鴉，一下子全部鳥兒都飛走了。於是農夫想了一招妙計，説道：「兒啊，我們總要趕走這些壞鳥，以後，當我要彈弓時，我不説『彈弓』，而是説『哼』，你就要馬上把它給我。」

不久這群鳥又來了。「哼！」農夫説著，但椋鳥無法察覺，所以農夫好整以暇地拿著彈弓對這群鳥發射多發石頭，一隻被射中頭，另一隻射中腿，另一個則是翅膀，直到他們倉皇逃離射程。

當禿鼻烏鴉與椋鳥逃走時遇見了幾隻鶴，鶴問他們出了什麼問題？「你説問題嗎？」其中的一隻禿鼻烏鴉回答，「那些壞蛋人類就是問題！千萬不要靠近他們，他們那表面説一套卻暗懷詭計，害死了我們許多可憐的朋友。」

76 貓頭鷹與鳥

貓頭鷹是很有智慧的鳥，而在很久以前，當森林出現了第一棵橡樹時，她召集所有的鳥並跟他們説：「看到了這棵小樹沒？如果你們聽從我的建議，趁它還是株小樹時，現在就毀了它，等到它長成大樹，槲寄生（一種寄生在樹木的植物）便會長在樹上，而黏鳥膠塗在槲寄生上時，你們的死期就不遠了。」

同樣地，當第一棵亞麻樹種下時，貓頭鷹對鳥兒説：「快去將亞麻結出的種子吃掉，因為那是亞麻子，總有一天，人類將用亞麻做成網子捕捉你們。」

又一次，當貓頭鷹看見森林裡出現了第一名獵人，她諄諄警告鳥群，告誡他們獵人是致命的敵人，會用同是鳥類的羽毛做的箭來射他們。

但其他鳥兒根本不將貓頭鷹的話放在心上，反而覺得她瘋了，甚至取笑她。然而，每件事就如同貓頭鷹所說的發生了，於是其他鳥兒對貓頭鷹改觀，並漸漸地敬佩她的智慧。因此，她所到之處，鳥兒總是關注、殷殷期待能從貓頭鷹口中聽到有用的警語。但貓頭鷹再也不給任何建議了，就只是哀傷地佇立著、沉思同類的愚昧。

77 狗與廚師

一名富人邀請了許多親朋好友參加一場豐盛的宴席，他養的狗心想，正好趁這個機會邀請他的狗好友來參加，於是他跑去對朋友說：「我的主人要辦一場筵席，到時會有大餐可吃，今晚你就來與我一起享用吧！」於是那隻被邀請的狗便赴約了。當他看到廚房裡準備的豐盛食物時，心想：「我的天啊！這下我可走運了，我要吃得飽飽的，接下來的兩三天就都可以不用吃飯了。」

這時他輕快地搖著尾巴，讓他朋友知道被邀請來有多麼開心，但就在這時候廚師看到他了，看到一隻陌生的狗待在廚房裡，廚師惱火地抓住他兩隻後腳，把他從窗戶扔了出去。他摔得很慘，跛著腳，快速地逃跑了，沿途還發出悲慘的哀嚎。

不久之後其他狗遇到他，便問他：「你的晚餐吃了些什麼啊？」而他回答：「我玩得可開心了，酒很醇，所以我喝了很多，醉到我連後來怎麼走出大門都不記得了。」

提防他人借花獻佛之舉。

78 獅子、狼與狐狸

一隻年老而生病的獅子病懨懨地待在他的洞穴，所有森林裡的動物都前來探視問候，唯獨狐狸例外。

和狐狸結怨的狼心想，這可是一個報仇狐狸的好機會，便有意對獅子提起狐狸未前來：「陛下您看，我們全都來探望您了，只有狐狸至今未來，對您健康或生病根本毫不在意。」

就在此時，狐狸來了並聽到狼說的最後一句話。獅子十分不悦地對狐狸低吼，而狐狸哀求，請求森林之王給予機會解釋自己沒來的原因，並說：「陛下，沒有人像我如此關心您的健康了，這些時日以來我四處走訪醫生，試著為您的病找尋解藥。」

「那請問你找到了嗎？」獅子問。「有的，陛下，」狐狸回答並說：「解藥就是：您必須剝了狼皮，並將餘溫尚存的狼皮披在身上，病才會好。」獅子於是轉向狼，用他的爪子一拳打死狼，嘗試了狐狸的良方。一旁的狐狸笑著喃喃自語道：「這就是你挑起惡意的下場。」

79 老鷹與甲蟲

一隻野兔被老鷹追逐，使勁逃跑以求活命，實在想不出要去哪裡尋求幫助，最後她見到一隻甲蟲，於是便懇求甲蟲幫助她。於是當老鷹飛下來，甲蟲警告她別靠近野兔，因為野兔是受牠保護的。

但是甲蟲實在太小了，老鷹根本沒注意到牠，於是抓走野兔把她給吃了。甲蟲一直無法忘懷這件事，便一直將雙眼盯著老鷹巢，只要老鷹一下蛋，牠就爬上去把蛋滾出鷹巢摔破。

最後老鷹很煩惱自己一直失去蛋，於是便跑去找老鷹的守護者宙斯，請求祂讓自己在一個安全的地方築巢下蛋，於是宙斯就讓老鷹在自己的腿上下蛋。甲蟲發現了這件事，就用泥巴做出一個和老鷹蛋差不多大小的泥球，飛上去放在宙斯的腿上。

當宙斯見到這團泥，立刻站起來要把它從袍子上抖落，完全忘了腿上還有蛋，於是蛋也一起被抖下腿了，就像之前一樣又摔破了。從此以後人們就說，老鷹決不會在甲蟲出沒的季節下蛋。

弱勢者也會找到自己的方法去報復強者的冒犯。

80 老婦與醫生

老婦因患眼疾而幾乎完全失明，諮詢醫生後，在見證人面前，老婦與醫生約定：若醫生成功治癒老婦的雙眼，她將付醫生高額的診療費，但若醫生治不好她，醫生半毛錢也收不到。

醫生於是開了療程的處方到老婦家中治病，但每一次醫生到訪，他就從老婦房子裡偷走物品，直到療程結束、最後一次到老婦家時，老婦家中的東西都被搬光了。

當老婦看到家裡空無一物，便拒絕付醫生診療費。多次拒絕付費後，醫生於是在法官面前控告老婦欠他診療費。上了法庭，老婦已準備好替自己辯護。

老婦說：「醫生正確地陳述了我們當時的約定：若他成功治癒我的雙眼，我同意付他高額費用，但他也承諾，若治療失敗，分文不取。如今他說我已痊癒，但我卻覺得自己的雙眼比先前更糟，這我可證明，因為治療前我還可以看到家裡一些家具與其他物品，但現在醫生說我好了，而我卻連一件物品也看不到了。」

81 狐狸與山羊

一隻狐狸失足掉進了井裡，找不到方法出來，過了一會兒，一隻口渴的山羊經過，看到井裡的狐狸，便問他井裡的水好不好喝。

「好喝？」狐狸回答：「這是我這輩子喝過最棒的水了，快下來嚐嚐吧！」山羊只想著趕緊為自己解渴，於是想也沒想就立刻跳了下去。

當山羊喝夠了水，他看看四周，就像狐狸之前一樣尋找出去的路，卻找不著。過了一會兒，狐狸開口了：「我想到了一個辦法，你用兩隻後腳站立，再把兩隻前腳抬起使力放在牆上，然後我順著你的後背爬到你的角上，這樣我就能出去了。等我出了井，我再幫忙你出來。」山羊照著狐狸的要求做了，於是狐狸便從他的背上爬出井裡，自顧自的走了。

山羊在後面大喊問他，提醒狐狸答應過要幫他出井，但是狐狸只回頭說著：「要是你腦袋裡的判斷能力和你的鬍子一樣多，你就不會在沒確定是否能出井前就跳下井了。」

三思而後行。

82 城市老鼠與鄉下老鼠

城市老鼠與鄉下老鼠是朋友，某天鄉下老鼠邀城市老鼠到他田野的家中一聚。

城市老鼠來時，鄉下老鼠準備了大麥與植物根部當晚餐，但根部吃起來就有強烈的泥巴味，這頓飯不太合城市老鼠的胃口，過一會兒他說：「我可憐的朋友啊，你過得跟螞蟻一樣糟，你應該來看看我平時吃什麼！我家中的食物儲藏室就像一個藏寶箱，你一定要來看看，我保證你日子過得很優渥。」

於是城市老鼠帶著鄉下老鼠回到城市，讓他看看滿是麵粉、燕麥粉、無花果、蜂蜜與棗子的儲藏室。鄉下老鼠從未見過此等山珍海味，便坐下好享用朋友提供的大餐。但開動前，儲藏室的門突然開了，有人走進，老鼠們只好逃跑躲入一個狹小不堪的洞裡。不久，一切都沉靜後，兩鼠再度冒險外出，但又有人進出，他們只得再次倉皇逃走。鄉下老鼠再也無法忍受這一切躲躲藏藏。

「再見，我要離開了，」鄉下老鼠說：「我看得出你生活優渥，但四周卻充斥著危險，然而在我那田裡，我卻能安然享用一頓粗茶淡飯。」

在平靜中吃著簡單的一餐，勝過在恐懼中吞下美食。

83 老鷹與狐狸

一隻老鷹與一隻狐狸結為好友，決定彼此住得近一點，他們想只要彼此多見面，感情就會越來越好。於是老鷹在一棵大樹頂築了個巢，而狐狸就在大樹

旁的樹叢裡定居，還生了一窩幼狐。

一天狐狸出門去獵捕食物，而老鷹也想為自己的孩子找些食物，於是她往下飛到樹叢裡，抓起了狐狸寶寶，飛回樹上餵飽自己和家人。

當狐狸回來，知道了所發生的事，為失去孩子感到傷心，更氣自己沒辦法抓住老鷹，對她的背信忘義報仇，她只能坐在不遠處咒罵老鷹，但沒多久她就找到報仇的機會。

一些村民正好在附近的祭壇以一隻山羊獻祭，老鷹飛下來叼了一小塊炙燒的山羊肉回到巢裡，當時的風很大，於是鷹巢起火了，結果雛鷹都被烤得半熟，掉落地，接著狐狸跑到現場，在老鷹的注視下迅速地把這些雛鷹給吃了。

背信棄義者即使能逃過人的懲罰，卻無法逃過天譴。

84 水神與樵夫

有個樵夫在河邊砍柴，當他用斧頭砍向樹幹時，斧頭擦過樹幹從他手中飛出去，掉到了河裡。

他站在岸邊哀悼自己的損失，這時水神出現，問他為何這麼難過。當祂知道樵夫的遭遇後，對他的遭遇感到十分同情，於是祂潛入河裡，拿了一把金斧頭出來，詢問樵夫這是不是他弄丟的那把斧頭。樵夫回答不是，水神便再次潛入水裡，拿了一把銀斧頭出來，又問樵夫這是不是他丟掉的那一把。

「不是，這一把也不是我的。」樵夫回答。

於是水神再度潛入河中，帶回了樵夫弄丟的斧頭，看到失而復得的斧頭，樵夫大喜過望，誠心地感謝他的恩人。而水神則對他誠實的態度感到滿意，把另外兩把斧頭也送給了他。

樵夫回去把這件事告訴朋友們，其中一位對樵夫的好運滿心嫉妒，決定也要去碰碰運氣。於是他出發前往河邊砍樹，沒砍多久，便刻意讓他的斧頭落進水裡。

水神就像先前一樣也出現了，而在得知他的斧頭掉進水裡後，祂也潛下去拿了一把金斧頭出來，就像上一回的情況一樣。還沒等水神問樵夫這把金斧頭是不是他的，他便大喊：「那是我的，那就是我的。」他急忙伸出手，迫切地想要拿到這個獎賞。然而，水神對他不誠實的態度十分厭惡，不僅沒把金斧頭給他，連他原本掉進河裡的斧頭也不還給他了。

誠實為上策。

Answers

(Answers will vary for open-ended questions.
開放性問題，答案僅供參考。)

pp. 2–3 Fables 1–2

Stop & Think

- According to the fable, will a bear eat a dead body?
  ➡ No, it won't.
- What did the wild ass get to eat after he went out hunting with the lion?
  ➡ He got nothing.

Check Up

1. F 2. T 3. F

pp. 4–5 Fables 3–4

Stop & Think

- Where did the man put the joint after he stole it?
  ➡ He put it inside his friend's coat.
- What do "quality" and "quantity" refer to in this fable?
  ➡ "Quality" refers to the lioness's cub, and "quantity" refers to the vixen's litter of cubs.

Check Up

1. accused 2. cubs 3. grimly

pp. 6–7 Fables 5–6

Stop & Think

- What does this fable teach people?
  ➡ It teaches people that it's important to work together.
- Why did the fox say the grapes were sour?
  ➡ Because he couldn't reach them.

Check Up

1. c 2. a 3. b

pp. 8–9 Fables 7–8

Stop & Think

- Where did the stag keep his good eye turned?
  ➡ He kept it turned towards the land.
- Did the ape believe the fox's denials?
  ➡ No, he didn't.

Check Up

1. suspected 2. charged 3. evidence
4. denials

pp. 10–11 Fables 9–10

Stop & Think

- Why did the stonemason object to wood?
  ➡ Because it could burn so easily.
- Did the lion believe that men were superior to lions?
  ➡ No, he didn't. / No, he thought lions were superior to men.

Check Up

1. c 2. b

pp. 12–13 Fables 11–12

Stop & Think

- What does this fable teach people?
  ➡ It teaches people to choose good companions.
- What did the man do when he saw the boy in danger?
  ➡ He scolded him for being so careless.

Check Up

1. T 2. T 3. F

pp. 14–15 Fables 13–14

Stop & Think

- What happened to the proud cock?
  ➡ An eagle flew down and carried him off.
- According to this fable, what should we do when we find a small problem?
  ➡ We should try to solve or get rid of it.

Check Up

1. c 2. a 3. b

pp. 16–17 Fables 15–16

Stop & Think

- Did the bull care what the gnat did? Why?
  ➡ No, he didn't, because he didn't even notice the gnat.
- What did the eagle do to thank the countryman for helping him?
  ➡ He knocked the drinking horn out of the man's hand and spilled its contents upon the ground.

Check Up

1. remained 2. witnessed 3. spat

pp. 18–19 Fables 17–18

Stop & Think

- Did the bramble think of itself as a poor creature? Why?
  ➡ No, it didn't, because it knew it wouldn't be cut down for men to build houses.
- Why was the crow jealous of the raven?
  ➡ Because people believed the raven could tell the future.

Check Up

1. no use 2. latter 3. reputation
4. upset

pp. 20–21 Fables 19–20

Stop & Think

- What does this fable teach people?
  ➡ It teaches people to be grateful for what others have done for them.
- What was the wolf's bad habit?
  ➡ He seized whatever he wanted and ran off with it without paying.

Check Up

1. c 2. a

pp. 22–23 Fables 21–22

Stop & Think

- How did the crow solve her problem?
  ➡ She dropped pebbles into the pitcher, so the water rose higher and higher until it reached the top.
- What did the lion do after the ass divided the food into three equal parts?
  ➡ He furiously sprang upon the ass and tore him to pieces.

Check Up

1. T 2. F 3. T

pp. 24–25 Fables 23–24

Stop & Think

- Did the laborer really want to apologize to the snake?
  ➡ No, he didn't. /
  No, he wanted to kill the snake.

- Why did the crab regret moving inland?
  ➡ Because he was caught by a hungry fox. / Because he didn't cherish his natural home.

Check Up

1. c 2. a 3. b

pp. 26–27 Fables 25–26

Stop & Think

- How did the hare feel about the hound?
  ➡ She felt confused by what he did to her.
- What was the cat's excuse for eating the cock?
  ➡ She said the cock made a great nuisance of himself at night by crowing and keeping people awake.

Check Up

1. snapped at 2. ought 3. nuisance
4. defended

pp. 28–29 Fables 27–28

Stop & Think

- How did the blind man know what was in his hands?
  ➡ He knew what it was merely by the feel of it.
- What does this fable teach people?
  ➡ The strong do not always beat the weak.

Check Up

1. merely 2. roar 3. battle

pp. 30–31 Fables 29–30

Stop & Think

- What did the spendthrift think when he first saw the swallow?
  ➡ He thought that summer had come, so he sold his coat.
- Look at "They kept it up for some time." What does "it" refer to?
  ➡ It refers to the dispute.

Check Up

1. b 2. c

pp. 32–33 Fables 31–32

Stop & Think

- Why did the villagers ignore the boy's cries for help?
  ➡ Because they thought he was fooling them again.
- What did the crow do to make himself look like a swan?
  ➡ He bathed and washed his feathers many times a day.

Check Up

1. F 2. T 3. F

pp. 34–35 Fables 33–34

Stop & Think

- Why did the wolf leave the field of oats untouched?
  ➡ Because he wasn't able to eat them.
- Did the bat think the caged bird's reason for singing at night sounded reasonable?
  ➡ No, he didn't. /
  No, he thought it was no use for the bird to sing at night anymore.

Check Up

1. b 2. c 3. a

pp. 36–37 Fables 35–36

Stop & Think

- What does this fable teach people?
  ➡ Think twice before taking revenge. / When we take revenge, we might also hurt ourselves.
- Why did the lion make so many preparations?
  ➡ Because he wanted to kill and eat the bull.

Check Up

1. caught fire 2. harvest
3. arrangement

pp. 38–39 Fables 37–38

Stop & Think

- Why did the hare lose the race?
  ➡ Because he fell asleep in the middle of the race. /
  Because he looked down on the tortoise.
- How did the goatherd break the horn of the goat?
  ➡ He threw a stone at it.

Check Up

1. amused 2. dashed 3. whistling
4. notice

pp. 40–41 Fables 39–40

Stop & Think

- What does this fable teach people?
  ➡ It teaches people to be content with what they have.
- Look at "it begged to be let go." What does "it" refer to?
  ➡ It refers to the bat.

Check Up

1. a 2. b

pp. 42–43 Fables 41–42

Stop & Think

- What was the lion afraid of?
  ➡ He was afraid of the cock's crowing.
- What did the man claim to have taken part in at Rhodes?
  ➡ He claimed to have taken part in a jumping match.

Check Up

1. F 2. T 3. F

pp. 44–45 Fables 43–44

Stop & Think

- When did the lion succeed in killing the three bulls?
  ➡ He succeeded in killing them when they avoided each other and ate separately.
- What was the fate of the traitors in this story?
  ➡ They were torn to pieces.

Check Up

1. distrust 2. collars 3. accompanied

pp. 46–47 Fables 45–46

Stop & Think

- What was the nature of the ants when they were men?
  ➡ They were greedy and stole their neighbors' crops and fruits.

- Who used a gentler method to win in this story?
  ➡ The sun used a gentler method to win.

Check Up

1. b 2. c 3. a

pp. 48–49 Fables 47–48

Stop & Think

- Where did the stag hide from the hunters?
  ➡ He hid behind a thick vine.
- What does the bell really mean in the story?
  ➡ It means that the dog behaves very badly in the story.

Check Up

1. concealed 2. pierced 3. nuisance
4. reward

pp. 50–51 Fables 49–50

Stop & Think

- What did the farmer find when he was plowing on his farm?
  ➡ He found a pot of golden coins.
- Look at the title "The Beekeeper." Is a "beekeeper" a place, person, or thing?
  ➡ The word "keeper" means someone who takes care of something, so a beekeeper is a person who takes care of bees.

Check Up

1. c 2. a

pp. 52–53 Fables 51–52

Stop & Think

- What was the boy's problem?
  ➡ He wanted too many nuts at one time. / He was too greedy.
- What would the wolf do if the dogs failed to catch a thief?
  ➡ He would overtake the thief, stop him, and share the sheep with him.

Check Up

1. F 2. T 3. T

pp. 54–55 Fables 53–54

Stop & Think

- What caused the stag to get stuck in the branches?
  ➡ His antlers caused him to get stuck in the branches.
- Why was Jupiter greatly displeased with the queen bee's request?
  ➡ Because he loved mankind.

Check Up

1. disgust 2. gloried 3. robbed

pp. 56–57 Fables 55–56

Stop & Think

- What does this fable teach people?
  ➡ It teaches people that when they face problems, they should first try to solve them themselves.

Check Up

1. c 2. a 3. b

pp. 58–59 Fables 57–58

Stop & Think

- What did the second traveler do when he could not run away?
  ➡ He pretended to be dead.

- Did the wild ass envy the pack ass when he saw him again? Why?
  ➡ No, he didn't, because the pack ass was carrying a heavy load and being beaten by his driver.

Check Up

1. observed 2. escape 3. idly
4. comforts

pp. 60–61 Fables 59–60

Stop & Think

- What does this fable teach people?
  ➡ It teaches people to think carefully before they do anything.
- Why didn't the wolf eat the dog the first time he caught him?
  ➡ Because he wanted to wait until the dog got nice and fat.

Check Up

1. a 2. c

pp. 64–65 Fable 61

Stop & Think

- Where was the sparrows' and grasshoppers' shelter?
  ➡ In the branches of the apple tree.
- What was inside the apple tree's trunk?
  ➡ A swarm of bees and a large store of honey.

Check Up

1. T 2. F 3. T

pp. 66–67 Fable 62

Stop & Think

- What happened during the trading voyage?
  ➡ A great storm came and sank the boat.
- Why does the bat only come out at night to feed?
  ➡ Because he is so afraid of meeting his creditors.

Check Up

1. voyage 2. venture 3. cargo

pp. 68–69 Fable 63

Stop & Think

- What did the mice decide to do after the council?
  ➡ They decided to choose the biggest mice to be their leaders.
- What happened to the leaders of the mice?
  ➡ They were caught by the weasels.

Check Up

1. c 2. a 3. b

pp. 70–71 Fable 64

Stop & Think

- How did the fox try to save himself?
  ➡ He told the lion that he would help him catch the ass.
- What does this fable teach people?
  ➡ It teaches people that they should not betray their friends.

Check Up

1. dreadfully 2. boldly 3. pit
4. proceeded

pp. 72–73 Fable 65

Stop & Think

- What did the man do to keep his promise?
  ➡ He made a hundred little oxen out of wax and offered them up on an altar.
- Were the gods satisfied with the man's wax oxen? How do you know?
  ➡ No, they weren't, because they sent him a harmful dream.

Check Up

1. c 2. b

pp. 74–75 Fable 66

Stop & Think

- What was the cat's trick?
  ➡ She pretended to be dead to lure the mice out.
- Did the cat succeed in deceiving the mice?
  ➡ No, she didn't.

Check Up

1. F 2. T 3. F

pp. 76–77 Fable 67

Stop & Think

- What was the jackdaw's problem?
  ➡ It got caught in the ram's wool.
- What does this fable teach people?
  ➡ It teaches people not to attempt things that are beyond their abilities.

Check Up

1. b 2. c 3. a

pp. 78–79 Fable 68

Stop & Think

- Where did the lark raise her young?
  ➡ She raised them in a field of corn.
- Why did the lark decide to move after the farmer came back?
  ➡ Because the farmer had decided to harvest the field at once.

Check Up

1. look to 2. overripe 3. no longer
4. in hand

pp. 80–81 Fable 69

Stop & Think

- How did the miser lose his lump of gold?
  ➡ One of his workers dug up the gold and stole it.
- What was the neighbor's advice?
  ➡ He told the miser not to take his loss so badly.

Check Up

1. b 2. a

pp. 82–83 Fable 70

Stop & Think

- Why did the lion lose his temper?
  ➡ Because a mouse was running over his face.
- What does this fable teach people?
  ➡ It teaches people that they should be kind to others.

Check Up

2 4 3 1

pp. 84–85 Fable 71

Stop & Think

- Where did the milkmaid put her pail of milk?
  ➡ She put it upon her head.
- Did the milkmaid's dream come true?
  ➡ No, it didn't.

Check Up

1. T 2. F 3. T

pp. 86–87 Fable 72

Stop & Think

- Do you think that the farmer had really lost his wife? Why?
  ➡ No, I don't think so, because he wanted to marry the woman he saw.
- What does this fable teach people?
  ➡ It teaches people that they should not always believe that tears are real.

Check Up

1. c 2. a 3. b

pp. 88–89 Fable 73

Stop & Think

- What happened when the ship was near the coast of Attica?
  ➡ A great storm came and sank it.
- Why did the dolphin dive down into the sea?
  ➡ Because he was so disgusted by the monkey's dishonesty.

Check Up

1. assumed 2. referring to
3. distinguished

pp. 90–91 Fable 74

Stop & Think

- What did the peddler load the ass up with at first?
  ➡ He loaded him up with salt at first.
- Was the peddler nice to the ass?
  ➡ No, he wasn't.

Check Up

1. peddler 2. drained 3. soaked
4. burden

pp. 92–93 Fable 75

Stop & Think

- Why did the farmer keep a careful watch over his wheat?
  ➡ Because rooks and starlings kept eating it up.
- What was the farmer's new way of asking for his sling?
  ➡ His new way was to say "Humph!"

Check Up

1. c 2. b

pp. 94–95 Fable 76

Stop & Think

- How did the other birds react to the owl's advice?
  ➡ They thought she was mad and laughed at her.
- What does this fable teach people?
  ➡ It teaches people to be aware of danger even when they live in peace.

Check Up

1. F 2. F 3. T

pp. 96–97 Fable 77

Stop & Think

- What did the cook do to the dog that had been invited to the feast?
  - ➡ He grabbed him by his back legs and threw him out the window.
- Why did the poor dog lie to the other dogs about what had happened at the feast?
  - ➡ Because he felt embarrassed about it. / Because he wanted them to envy him.

Check Up

1. b 2. c 3. a

pp. 98–99 Fable 78

Stop & Think

- Which animal was the last to visit the ill lion?
  - ➡ The fox was the last one.
- Was there really a doctor's prescription for the lion?
  - ➡ No, there wasn't. / No, it was just the fox's way of taking revenge on the wolf.

Check Up

1. inquire after 2. displeasure
3. illness

pp. 100–101 Fable 79

Stop & Think

- Who did the hare turn to for help?
  - ➡ She turned to a beetle for help.
- How did Jupiter accidentally break the eagle's eggs?
  - ➡ He shook the dirt out of his robe, and at the same time shook the eggs out as well.

Check Up

1. protection 2. protector 3. dirt
4. lap

pp. 102–103 Fable 80

Stop & Think

- What did the doctor do whenever he visited the old woman?
  - ➡ He stole something from her house.
- What was the real reason why the old woman refused to pay for the treatment?
  - ➡ She refused to pay because she knew the doctor had stolen everything from her house.

Check Up

4 3 1 2

pp. 104–105 Fable 81

Stop & Think

- Do you think that the fox will help the goat get out of the well? Why?
  - ➡ No, I don't think so, because the fox did not help the goat after he got out, but only made fun of him.
- What does this fable teach people?
  - ➡ It teaches people that they should think thoroughly before they take action.

Check Up

1. b 2. b

pp. 106–107 Fable 82

Stop & Think

- Did the town mouse like the dinner that the country mouse offered him?
  ➡ No, he didn't.
- Why did the country mouse decide to leave his friend's home?
  ➡ Because even though the town mouse lived in luxury and had fine food, he was surrounded by dangers.

Check Up

1. F 2. T 3. F

pp. 108–109 Fable 83

Stop & Think

- What terrible thing did the eagle do to the fox?
  ➡ She took the fox's cubs as food for herself and her family.
- What does this fable teach people?
  ➡ It teaches people that if they betray their friends, the gods may take revenge on them.

Check Up

1. grove 2. get at 3. chicks
4. faith

pp. 110–111 Fable 84

Stop & Think

- How many times did Mercury dive into the river for the poor woodcutter?
  ➡ He dove into the river three times.
- What does this fable teach people?
  ➡ It teaches people that they should always tell the truth.

Check Up

1 4 2 3